John Douglas S. Argyll

Memories of Canada and Scotland

Speeches and Verses

John Douglas S. Argyll

Memories of Canada and Scotland
Speeches and Verses

ISBN/EAN: 9783337192754

Printed in Europe, USA, Canada, Australia, Japan

Cover: Foto ©Andreas Hilbeck / pixelio.de

More available books at **www.hansebooks.com**

MEMORIES

OF

CANADA AND SCOTLAND

SPEECHES AND VERSES

BY THE

RIGHT HON. THE MARQUIS OF LORNE

K.T., G.C.M.G., &c.

MONTREAL
DAWSON BROTHERS, PUBLISHERS
1884

Entered by Dawson Brothers, according to Act of Parliament of
Canada, in the year 1883, in the office of the Minister of Agriculture.

Dedicated

WITH RESPECT AND AFFECTION

TO

THE MEMBERS

OF

THE ROYAL SOCIETY OF CANADA

CONTENTS.

———o———

VERSES CHIEFLY FROM HIGHLAND STORIES.

APPENDIX.

VERSES

ON

CANADIAN SUBJECTS.

A

CANADA, 1882.

"ARE hearts here strong enough to found
    A glorious people's sway?"
Ask of our rivers as they bound
From hill to plain, or ocean-sound,
    If they are strong to-day?
If weakness in their floods be found,
    Then may ye answer "Nay!"

"Is union yours? may foeman's might
    Your love ne'er break or chain?"
Go see if o'er our land the flight
Of Spring be stayed by blast or blight;
    If Fall bring never grain;
If Summer suns deny their light,
    Then may our hope be vain!

"Yet far too cramped the narrow space
    Your country's rule can own?"
Ah! travel all its bounds and trace
Each Alp unto its fertile base,
    Our realm of forests lone,
Our world of prairie, like the face
    Of ocean, hardly known!

"Yet for the arts to find a shrine,
    Too rough, I ween, and rude?"
Yea, if you find no flower divine
With prairie grass or hardy pine,
    No lilies with the wood,
Or on the water-meadows' line
    No purple Iris' flood !

"You deem a nation here shall stand,
    United, great, and free?"
Yes, see how Liberty's own hand
With ours the continent hath spanned,
    Strong-arched, from sea to sea :
Our Canada's her chosen land,
    Her roof and crown to be !

QUEBEC.

O FORTRESS city, bathed by streams
   Majestic as thy memories great,
   Where mountains, floods, and forests mate
The grandeur of the glorious dreams,
   Born of the hero hearts who died
   In founding here an Empire's pride;
Prosperity attend thy fate,
   And happiness in thee abide,
Fair Canada's strong tower and gate !

May Envy, that against thy might
   Dashed hostile hosts to surge and break,
   Bring Commerce, emulous to make
Thy people share her fruitful fight,
   In filling argosies with store
   Of grain and timber, and each ore,
And all a continent can shake
   Into thy lap, till more and more
Thy praise in distant worlds awake.

Who hath not known delight whose feet
   Have paced thy streets or terrace way;
   From rampart sod or bastion grey
Hath marked thy sea-like river greet

The bright and peopled banks which shine
 In front of the far mountain's line ;
Thy glittering roofs below, the play
 Of currents where the ships entwine
Their spars, or laden pass away ?

As we who joyously once rode
 Past guarded gates to trumpet sound,
 Along the devious ways that wound
O'er drawbridges, through moats, and showed
 The vast St. Lawrence flowing, belt
 The Orleans Isle, and sea-ward melt ;
Then by old walls with cannon crowned,
 Down stair-like streets, to where we felt
The salt winds blown o'er meadow ground.

Where flows the Charles past wharf and dock.
 And Learning from Laval looks down,
 And quiet convents grace the town.
There swift to meet the battle shock
 Montcalm rushed on ; and eddying back,
 Red slaughter marked the bridge's track :
See now the shores with lumber brown,
 And girt with happy lands which lack
No loveliness of Summer's crown.

Quaint hamlet-alleys, border-filled
 With purple lilacs, poplars tall,
 Where flits the yellow bird, and fall
The deep eave shadows.   There when tilled

The peasant's field or garden bed,
  He rests content if o'er his head
From silver spires the church-bells call
  To gorgeous shrines, and prayers that gild
The simple hopes and lives of all.

Winter is mocked by garbs of green,
  Worn by the copses flaked with snow,—
  White spikes and balls of bloom, that blow
In hedgerows deep ; and cattle seen
  In meadows spangled thick with gold,
  And globes where lovers' fates are told
Around the red-doored houses low ;
  While rising o'er them, fold on fold,
The distant hills in azure glow.

Oft in the woods we long delayed,
  When hours were minutes all too brief,
  For Nature knew no sound of grief ;
But overhead the breezes played,
  And in the dank grass at our knee,
  Shone pearls of our green forest sea,
The star-white flowers of triple leaf
  Which love around the brooks to be,
Within the birch and maple shade.

At times we passed some fairy mere
  Embosomed in the leafy screen,
  And streaked with tints of heaven's sheen,
Where'er the water's surface clear

Bore not the hues of verdant light
  From myriad boughs on mountain height,
Or near the shadowed banks were seen
  The sparkles that in circlets bright
Told where the fishes' feast had been.

And when afar the forests flushed
  In falling swathes of fire, there soared
  Dark clouds where muttering thunder roared,
And mounting vapours lurid rushed,
  While a metallic lustre flew
  Upon the vivid verdure's hue,
Before the blasts and rain forth poured,
  And slow o'er mighty landscapes drew
The grandest pageant of the Lord:

The threatening march of flashing cloud,
  With tumults of embattled air,
  Blest conflicts for the good they bear!
A century has God allowed
  None other, since the days He gave
  Unequal fortune to the brave.
Comrades in death! you live to share
  An equal honour, for your grave
Bade Enmity take Love as heir!

We watched, when gone day's quivering haze,
  The loops of plunging foam that beat
  The rocks at Montmorenci's feet
Stab the deep gloom with moonlit rays;

Or from the fortress saw the streams
    Sweep swiftly o'er the pillared beams ;
White shone the roofs, and anchored fleet,
    And grassy slopes where nod in dreams
Pale hosts of sleeping Marguerite.

Or when the dazzling Frost King mailed
    Would clasp the wilful waterfall,
    Fast leaping to her snowy hall
She fled ; and where her rainbows hailed
    Her freedom, painting all her home,
    We climbed her spray-built palace dome,
Shot down the radiant glassy wall
    Until we reached the snowdrift foam,
As shoots to waves some meteor ball.

Then homeward, hearing song or tale,
    With chime of harness bells we sped
    Above the frozen river bed.
The city, through a misty veil,
    Gleamed from her cape, where sunset fire
    Touched louvre and cathedral spire,
Bathed ice and snow a rosy red,
    So beautiful that men's desire
For May-time's rival wonders fled :

What glories hath this gracious land,
    Fit home for many a hardy race ;
    Where liberty has broadest base,
And labour honours every hand !

Throughout her triply thousand miles
The sun upon each season smiles,
And every man has scope and space,
  And kindliness, from strand to strand,
Alone is born to right of place !

Such were our memories.   May they yet
  Be shared by others, sent to be
  Signs of the union of the free
And kindred peoples God hath set
  O'er famous isles, and fertile zones
  Of continents !   Or if new thrones
And mighty States arise, may He
  Whose potent hand yon river owns
Smooth their great future's shrouded Sea !

PROLOGUE.

GOVERNMENT HOUSE, *March* 1879.

A MOMENT'S pause before we play our parts,
To speak the thought that reigns within your hearts.—
Now from the Future's hours, and unknown days,
Affection turns, and with the Past delays;
For countless voices in our mighty land
Speak the fond praises of a vanished hand;
And shall, to mightier ages yet, proclaim
The happy memories linked with Dufferin's name.

Missed here is he, to whom each class and creed,
Among our people lately bade "God speed;"
Missed, when each Winter sees the skater wheel
In ringing circle on the flashing steel;
Missed in the Spring, the Summer and the Fall,
In many a hut, as in the Council Hall;
Where'er his wanderings on Duty's hest
Evoked his glowing speech, his genial jest.
We mourn his absence, though we joy that now
Old England's honours cluster round his brow,
And that he left us but to serve again
Our Queen and Empire on the Neva's plain!

Amidst the honoured roll of those whose fate
It was to crown our fair Canadian State,
And bind in one bright diadem alone,
Each glorious Province, each resplendent stone,
His name shall last, and his example give
To all her sons a lesson how to live :
How every task, if met with heart as bold,
Proves the hard rock is seamed with precious gold,
And Labour, when with Mirth and Love allied,
Finds friends far stronger than in Force and Pride,
And Sympathy and Kindness can be made
The potent weapons by which men are swayed.
He proved a nation's trust can well be won
By loyal work and constant duty done ;
The wit that winged the wisdom of his word
Set forth our glories, till all Europe heard
How wide the room our Western World can spare
For all who nobly toil and bravely dare.

And while the statesman we revere, we know
In him the friend is gone, to whom we owe
So much of gaiety, so much which made
Life's duller round to seem in joy repaid.
These little festivals by him made bright,
With grateful thoughts of him renewed to-night,
Remind no less of her who deigned to grace
This mimic world, and fill therein her place
With the sweet dignity and gracious mien
The race of Hamilton has often seen ;

But never shown upon the wider stage
Where the great " cast " is writ on History's page,
More purely, nobly, than by her, whose voice
Here moved to tears, or made the heart rejoice,
And who in act and word, at home, or far,
Shone with calm beauty like the Northern Star!

Green as the Shamrock of their native Isle
Their memory lives, and babes unborn shall smile
And share in happiness the pride that blends
Our country's name with her beloved friends!

A NATIONAL HYMN.

GOVERNMENT HOUSE, *March* 1880.

FROM our Dominion never
  Take Thy protecting hand,
United, Lord, for ever
  Keep Thou our fathers' land!
From where Atlantic terrors
  Our hardy seamen train,
To where the salt sea mirrors
  The vast Pacific chain.
    Aye one with her whose thunder
      Keeps world-watch with the hours,
    Guard Freedom's home and wonder,
    "This Canada of ours."

Fair days of fortune send her,
  Be Thou her Shield and Sun!
Our land, our flag's Defender,
  Unite our hearts as one!
One flag, one land, upon her
  May every blessing rest!
For loyal faith and honour
  Her children's deeds attest.
    Aye one with her, &c.

No stranger's foot, insulting,
  Shall tread our country's soil ;
While stand her sons exulting
  For her to live and toil.
She hath the victor's guerdon,
  Her's are the conquering hours,
No foeman's yoke shall burden
  " This Canada of ours."
      Aye one with her, &c.

Our sires, when times were sorest,
  Asked none but aid Divine,
And cleared the tangled forest,
  And wrought the buried mine.
They tracked the floods and fountains,
  And won, with master-hand,
Far more than gold in mountains,
  The glorious Prairie-land.
      Aye one with her, &c.

O Giver of earth's treasure,
  Make Thou our nation strong ;
Pour forth Thine hot displeasure
  On all who work our wrong !
To our remotest border
  Let plenty still increase,
Let Liberty and Order,
  Bid ancient feuds to cease.
      Aye one with her, &c.

May Canada's fair daughters
   Keep house for hearts as bold
As theirs who o'er the waters
   Came hither first of old.
The pioneers of nations !
   They showed the world the way ;
'Tis ours to keep their stations,
   And lead the van to-day.
      Aye one with her, &c.

Inheritors of glory,
   O countrymen ! we swear
To guard the flag whose story
   Shall onward victory bear.
Where'er through earth's far regions
   Its triple crosses fly,
For God, for home, our legions
   Shall win, or fighting die !
      Aye one with her, &c.

RIVER RHYMES.

1. We have poled our staunch canoe
   Many a boiling torrent through ;
   Paddling where the eddies drew,
   Athwart the roaring flood we flew.

Chorus—

    Dip your paddles ! make them leap,
    Where the clear cold waters sweep.
    Dip your paddles ! steady keep,
    Where breaks the rapid down the steep.

2. Where the wind, like censer, flings
   Smoke-spray wider as it swings,
   Hark ! the aisle of rainbow rings
   To falls that hymn the King of kings.

3. Lifting there our vessel tight,
   Climbed we bank and rocky height,
   Bore her through thick woods, where light
   Fell dappling those green haunts of Night.

4. O'er the rush of billows hurled,
   Where they tossed and leaped and curled,
   Past each wave-worn boulder whirled,
   How fast we sailed, no sail unfurled !

B

5. Laughs from parted lips and teeth
    Hailed the quiet reach beneath,
    Damascened in ferny sheath,
    And girt with pine and maple wreath.

6. Oh, the lovely river there
    Made all Nature yet more fair ;
    Wooded hills and azure air
    Kissed, quivering, in the stream they share.

7. Plunged the salmon, waging feud
    'Gainst the jewelled insect-brood ;
    From aerial solitude
    An eagle's shadow crossed the wood.

8. Flapped the heron, and the grey
    Halcyon talked from cedar's spray,
    Drummed the partridge far away ;—
    Ah ! could we choose to live as they !

LEGEND OF THE CANADIAN ROBIN.

Is it Man alone who merits
  Immortality or death ?
Each created thing inherits
  Equal air and common breath.

Souls pass onward : some are ranging
  Happy hunting-grounds, and some
Are as joyous, though in changing
  Form be altered, language dumb.

Beauteous all, if fur or feather,
  Strength or gift of song be theirs ;
He who planted all together
  Equally their fate prepares.

Like to Time, that dies not, living
  Through the change the seasons bring,
So men, dying, are but giving
  Life to some fleet foot or wing.

Bird and beast the Savage cherished,
  But the Robins loved he best ;
O'er the grave where he has perished
  They shall thrive and build their nest.

Hunted by the white invader,
 Vanish ancient races all;
Yet no ruthless foe or trader
 Silences the songster's call.

For the white man too rejoices,
 Welcoming Spring's herald bird,
When the ice breaks, and the voices
 From the rushing streams are heard.

Where the Indian's head-dress fluttered,
 Pale the settler would recoil,
And his deepest curse was uttered
 On the Red Son of the soil.

Later knew he not, when often
 Gladness with the Robin came,
How a spirit-change could soften
 Hate to dear affection's flame:

Knew not, as he heard, delighted,
 Mellow notes in woodlands die,
How his heart had leaped, affrighted
 At that voice in battle-cry.

For a youthful Savage, keeping
 Long his cruel fast, had prayed,
All his soul in yearning steeping,
 Not for glory, chase, or maid;

But to sing in joy, and wander,
 Following the summer hours,

Drinking where the streams meander,
　Feasting with the leaves and flowers.

Once his people saw him painting
　Red his sides and red his breast,
Said : " His soul for fight is fainting,
　War-paint suits the hero best ; "

Went, when passed the night, loud calling,
　Found him not, but where he lay
Saw a Robin, whose enthralling
　Carol seemed to them to say ;

" I have left you ! I am going
　Far from fast and winter pain ;
When the laughing water's flowing
　Hither I will come again ! "

Thus his ebon locks still wearing,
　With the war-paint on his breast,
Still he comes, our summer sharing,
　And the lands he once possessed.

Finding in the white man's regions
　Foemen none, but friends whose heart
Loves the Robins' happy legions,
　Mourns when, silent, they depart.

WERE THESE THE FIRST DISCOVERERS OF AMERICA?

Milicete Legend of the Ouangondé, or River St. John.

Though the ebbing ocean listens
To Ugondé's throbbing roar,
Calm the conquering flood-tide glistens
Where the river raved before.*

So the sea-brought strangers, stronger
Than their Indian foes of old,
Conquered, till were heard no longer
War-songs through the forests rolled.

Yet the land's wild stream, begotten
Where its Red Sons fought and died,

* The Bay of Fundy tide rises to such a height that it flows up the St. John River channel to some distance, silencing the roar of the falls, which pour over a great ledge of rock left by the ebbing sea.   Taken very literally from a tale in the " Amaranth Magazine," 1841.

With traditions unforgotten
   Strives to stem Oblivion's tide ;

'Tells the mighty, who, like ocean,
   Whelm the native stream, how they
First in far dim days' commotion,
   Wrestling, fought for empire's sway.

Hear the sad cascade, ere ever
   Sinks in rising tides its moan,
True may be the tale, though never
   By the victor ocean known.

Now the chant rings softly, finding
   Freedom as the sea retires ;
Loudly now, through spray-tears blinding
   Throb and thunder silver lyres ;

Silenced when the strong sea-water
   To its great heart, limitless,
Rising, takes the valley's daughter,
   Soothes the song of her distress.

UGONDÉ'S TALE.

For a while the salt brine leaves me
   O'er my terraced rocks to fall,
And my broad swift-gliding waters
   Olden memories recall.

Ere the tallest pines were seedlings
  With my life-stream these were blent;
As a father's words, like arrows
  Straight to children's hearts are sent,

So my currents speeding downwards,
  Ever passing, sing the same
Story of the days remembered,
  When the stranger people came.

Men of mighty limbs and voices,
  Bearing shining shields and knives,
Painted gleamed their hair like evening,
  When the sun in ocean dives.

Blue their eyes and tall their stature,
  Huge as Indian shadows seen
When the sun through mists of morning
  Casts them o'er a clear lake's sheen.

From before the great Pale-faces
  Fled the tribes to woods and caves,
Watching thence their fearful councils,
  Where they talked beside the waves.

For they loved the shores, and fashioned
  Houses from its stones, and there
Fished and rested, danced at night-time
  By their fire and torches' glare.

Sang loud songs before the pine-logs
    As they crackled in the flame,
Raised and drank from bone-cups, shouting
    Fiercely some strange spirit's name.

Turning to the morning's pathway,
    Cried they thus to gods, and none
Dared to fight the bearded giants,
    Children of the fire and sun.

From their bodies fell our flint-darts,
    Yet their arrows flew, like rays
Flashing from the rocks where polished
    By the ice in winter days.

Then the Indians prayed the spirits
    Haunting river, bank, and hill,
To let hatred, like marsh vapour,
    Rise among their foes and kill.

And they seemed to heed, for anger
    Often maddened all the band,
Fighting for some stones that glittered
    Yellow on Ugondé's sand.

Seeing axe and spear-head crimson,
    Hope illumined doubt and dread,
And our land's despairing children
    Called upon the mighty dead.

All the Northern night-air shaking,
  Rose the ancients' bright array,
Burning lines of battle breaking
  Darkness into lurid day.

But the stranger hearts were hardened,
  Fearless slept they; then at last
Our Great Spirit heard, and answered
  From his home in heaven vast.

For his waving locks were tempests,
  And the thunder-cloud his frown;
Where he trod the earthquake followed,
  And the forests bowed them down.

As his whirlwind struck the mountains,
  Rent and lifted, swayed the ground;
Wingèd knives of crooked lightning
  Gleamed from skies and gulfs profound.

Floods, from wonted channels driven,
  Roared at falling hillside's shock;
What was land became the torrent,
  What was lake became the rock.

Now the river and the ocean,
  Whispering, say: "Our floods alone
See white skeletons slow-moving
  Near the olden walls of stone."

Moving slow in stream and sea-tide,
　There the stranger warriors sleep,
And their shades still cry in anguish
　Where the foaming waters leap.

THE GUIDE OF THE MOHAWKS.

For strife against the ocean tribe
   The Mohawks' war array
Comes floating down, where broad St. John
   Reflects the dawning day.

A camp is seen, and victims fall,
   And none are left to flee;
A maid alone is spared, compelled
   A traitress guide to be.

The swift canoes together keep,
   And o'er their gliding prows
The silent girl points down the stream,
   Nor halt nor rest allows.

"Speak! are we near your fires? How dark
   Night o'er these waters lies!"
Still pointing down the rushing stream,
   The maiden naught replies.

The banks fly past, the water seethes;
   The Mohawks shout, "To shore!
Where is the girl?" Her cry ascends
   From out the river's roar.

The foaming rapids rise and flash
   A moment o'er her head,
And smiling as she sinks, she knows
   Her foemen's course is sped;

A moment hears she shriek on shriek
   From hearts that death appals,
As, seized by whirling gulfs, the crews
   Are drawn into the falls!

THE STRONG HUNTER.

There's a warrior hunting o'er prairie and hill,
Who in sunshine or starlight is eager to kill,
Who ne'er sleeps by his fire on the wild river's shore,
Where the green cedars shake to the white rapids'
    roar.

Ever tireless and noiseless, he knows not repose,
Be the land filled with summer, or lifeless with
    snows ;
But his strength gives him few he can count as his
    friends,
Man and beast fly before him wherever he wends.

For he chases alike every form that has breath,
And his darts must strike all,—for that hunter is
    Death !
Lo ! a skeleton armed, and his scalp-lock yet streams
From this vision of fear of the Iroquois' dreams !

MON-DAW-MIN;

OR, THE ORIGIN OF THE INDIAN-CORN.

CHERRY bloom and green buds bursting
 Fleck the azure skies;
In the spring wood, hungering, thirsting,
 Faint an Indian lies.

To behold his guardian spirit
 Fasts the dusky youth;
Prays that thus he may inherit
 Warrior strength and truth.

Weak he grows, the war-path gory
 Seems a far delight;
Now he scans the flowers, whose glory
 Is not won by fight.

" Hunger kills me; see my arrow
 Bloodless lies; I ask,
If life's doom be grave-pit narrow,
 Deathless make its task.

" For man's welfare guide my being,
 So I shall not die

Like the flow'rets, fading, fleeing,
  When the snow is nigh.

"Medicine from the plants we borrow,
  Salves from many a leaf;
May they not kill hunger's sorrow,
  Give with food relief?"

Suddenly a spirit shining
  From the sky came down,
Green his mantle, floating, twining,
  Gold his feather crown.

"I have heard thy thought unspoken;
  Famous thou shalt be;
Though no scalp shall be the token,
  Men shall speak of thee.

"Bravely borne, men's heaviest burden
  Ever lighter lies;
Wrestling with me, win the guerdon;
  Gain thy wish, arise!"

Now he rises, and, prevailing,
  Hears the angel say:
"Strong in weakness, never failing,
  Strive yet one more day.

"Now again I come, and find thee
  Yet with courage high,
So that, though my arms can bind thee,
  Victor thou, not I.

" Hark ! to-morrow, conquering, slay me,
  Blest shall be thy toil :
After wrestling, strip me, lay me
  Sleeping in the soil.

" Visit oft the place ; above me
  Root out weeds and grass ;
Fast no more ; obeying, love me ;
  Watch what comes to pass."

Waiting through the long day ·dreary,
  Still he hungers on ;
Once more wrestling, weak and weary,
  Still the fight is won.

Stripped of robes and golden feather,
  Buried lies the guest :
Summer's wonder-working weather
  Warms his place of rest.

Ever his commands fulfilling,
  Mourns his victor friend,
Fearing, with a heart unwilling,
  To have known the end.

No ! upon the dark mould fallow
  Shine bright blades of green ;
Rising, spreading, plumes of yellow
  O'er their sheaves are seen.

Higher than a mortal's stature
Soars the corn in pride;
Seeing it, he knows that Nature
There stands deified.

" 'Tis my friend," he cries, "the guerdon
Fast and prayer have won;
Want is past, and hunger's burden
Soon shall torture none."

THE ISLES OF HURON.

Bright are the countless isles which crest
With waving woods wide Huron's breast,—
  Her countless isles, that love too well
    The crystal waters whence they rise,
  Far from her azure depths to swell,
    Or wanton with the wooing skies;

Nor, jealous, soar to keep the Day
From laughing in each rippling bay,
  But floating on the flood they love,
    Soft whispering, kiss her breast, and seek
  No passions of the air above,
    No fires that burn the thunder-peak.

Algoma o'er Ontario throws
Fair forest heights and mountain snows;
  Strong Erie shakes the orchard plain
    At great Niagara's defiles,
  And river-gods o'er Lawrence reign,
    But Love is king in Huron's isles.

THE MYSTIC ISLE OF THE " LAND OF THE NORTH WIND."

(KEEWATIN.)

A LAND untamed, whose myriad isles
Are set in branching lakes that vein
Illimitable silent woods,
Voiceful in Fall, when their defiles,
Rich with the birch's golden rain,
See winging past the wildfowl broods.

Blue channels seem its dented rocks,
So steeply smoothed, but crusted o'er
With rounded mosses, green and grey,
That oft a Southern coral mocks
Upon this Northern fir-clad shore,
'Neath tufted copse on cape and bay.

Here sunshine from serener skies
 Than Europe's ocean-islands know
Ripens the berry for the bear,
And pierces where the beaver plies
His water-forestry, or slow
The moose seeks out a breezy lair.

The blaze scarce spangles bush or ferns,
 But lights the white pine's velvet fringe
And its dark Norway sister's boughs;
At eve between their shadows burns
The lake, where shafts of crimson tinge
The savage war-flotilla's prows.

Far circling round, these seem to shun
An isle more fair than all beside,
As if some lurking foe were there,
Although upon its heights the sun
Shines glorious, and its forest pride
Is fanned by summer's joyous air.

For 'mid these isles is one of fear,
And none may ever breathe its name.
There the Great Spirit loves to be;
Its haunted groves and waters clear
Are homes of thunder and of flame;
All pass it silently and flee,

Save they who potent magic learn,
Who lonely in that dreaded fane
Resist nine days the awful powers :
And, fasting, each through pain may earn
The knowledge daring mortals gain,
If life survive those secret hours !

WESTWARD HO!

Away to the West! Westward ho! Westward ho!
Where over the prairies the summer winds blow!

Why known to so few were its rivers and plains,
Where rustle so tall in their ripeness the grains?
The bison and Red-men alone cared to roam
O'er realms that to millions must soon give a home;
The vast fertile levels Old Time loved to reap
The haymaker's song hath awakened from sleep.

Away to the West! Westward ho! Westward ho!
Why waited we fearing to plant and to sow?

Not ours was the waiting! By God was ordained
The hour when the ocean's grey steeds were up-reined,
And green marshes rose, and the bittern's abode
Became the Lone Land where the wild hunter strode,
And soils with grass harvests grew rich, and the clime
For us was prepared in the fulness of Time!

Away to the West! Westward ho! Westward ho!
For us 'twas prepared long ago, long ago!

There came from the Old World at last o'er the sea,
The bravest and best to this land of the free;
And, leal to their flag, won the fruits of the earth
By might that has given new nations a birth,
But found in our North-land a bride to be known
More worthy than all of the love of the throne.

Away to the West! Westward ho! Westward ho!
God's hand is our guide; 'tis His will that we go!

'To lands yet more happy than Europe's, for here
We mould the young nation for Freedom to rear.
Full strongly we build, and have nought to pull down,
For, true to ourselves, we are true to the Crown;
The will of the people its honour shows forth,
As pole-star, whose radiance points steadfastly north.

Away to the West! Westward ho! Westward ho!
Where rooted in Freedom shall Liberty grow!

Right good is the loam that for five score of days
Its rolling lands show, or its plains' scented ways:
Nor used is the pick, if the earth has concealed
The waters it keeps for the house and the field;
The spade finds enough, until burst on the sight
Our Rocky Sierras' sweet rivers of light.

Away to the West! Westward ho! Westward ho!
From mountains and lakes there the great rivers flow!

If told of Brazil or great Mexico's gold,
Of Cotton States' warmth and of Canada's cold,
Go say how we prize, like the ore of the mine,
The snows sapphire-shadowed in winter's sunshine;
—Our gayest of seasons! which guards the good soil
For races who won it through faith and through toil.

Away to the West! Westward ho! Westward ho!
Bright sparkles its winter, and light is its snow!

There gaily, in measureless meadows, all day
The sun and the breeze with the grass are at play,
In billows that never can break as they pass,
But toss the gold foam of the flower-laden grass,
The bright yellow disks of the asters upcast
On waves that in blossoms flow silently past.

Away to the West! Westward ho! Westward ho!
Where over the prairies the summer winds blow.

The West for you, boys! where our God has made
    room
For field and for city, for plough and for loom.
The West for you, girls! for our Canada deems
Love's home better luck than a gold-seeker's dreams.
Away! and your children shall bless you, for they
Shall rule o'er a land fairer far than Cathay.

Away to the West! Westward ho! Westward ho!
Thou God of their fathers, Thy blessing bestow!

THE SONG OF THE SIX SISTERS.*

At a feast in the east of our central plains,
Girt with the sheaths of the wheaten grains,
Manitoba lay where the sunflowers blow,
And sang to the chime of the Red River's flow :
" I am child of the spirit whom all men own,
My prairie no longer is green and lone,
For the hosts of the settler have ringed me round,
And his bride am I with the harvest crowned." ·

On her steed at speed o'er her burning grass
We saw Assiniboia pass :
" The bison and antelope still are mine,
And the Indian wars on my boundary-line ;
Where his knife is dyed I love to ride
By the cactus blooms or the marshes wide,
While the quivering columns of thunder fire
Give light to the darkened land's desire."

" To the North look ye forth," cried the voice of one,
Who dwells where the great twin rivers run ;—

* Manitoba, Assiniboia, Saskatchewan, Athabasca, Alberta,
and British Columbia.

"Or farther yet," Athabaska cried,
"Where mightier waters the hills divide:
'Peace' is their name, and the musk ox there
Still feeds alone on the meadows fair."
"Nay, stay," said the first; "the white man's word
Hath called me the kindest to horse and herd."

From on high where the sky and the snow-born rill
Each morn and eve to the rose-tints thrill,
Sang the fairy Sprite of the Fountain Land:
"A daughter of her, whose sceptred hand
With the flag of the woven crosses three
Hath rule o'er the ocean, hath christened me,
And my waves their homage repeat again,
And that standard greet in the loyal main."

And their lays in her praise then sang the four:
"Alberta has all we can boast and more:
The scented breath of the plains is hers,
The odours sweet of the sage and firs;
There the coal breaks forth on her rolling sod,
And the winters flee at the winds of God.
Columbia, come! for we want but thee;
Now tell of thyself and thy silent sea!"

"Clad with the silver snow, a pine
    Guarded the grot of a golden mine,
And dark was the shade which the mist-wreaths cast,
Though brightly they shone on the mountain vast.

Stars and sun o'er that cavern swept,
Where on the glittering sand I slept;
But none could behold me, or know where was
　　stored
More treasure than monarch e'er won with the
　　sword.
　　Floods in fathomless torrents fall
　　Through the awful rifts of the Alpine wall,
Where I passed in the night over forest and glen,
O'er the ships on the sea and the cities of men—
　　Swifter than morn!　His shafts of love
　　Behind me caught the peaks above,
But touched not my wings: I had gone e'er he came.
Where the vine-maple fringed the deep forest with
　　flame.
　　Strewn o'er the sombre walls of green
　　In saffron or in crimson sheen,
How lovely those gardens of autumn, where rolled
In smoke and in fire the red lava of old!
　　Soon I reached my sea-girt home
　　Sheltered from the breakers' foam.
Seek not for mine isle, for a thousand and more
Lie asleep in the calm near the mountainous shore.
　　Oft I roam in moon ray clear
　　With the puma and the deer;
From the boughs of Madrôna that droop o'er a bay
I watch the fish dart from the beams of the day.
　　Mine are tranquil gulfs, nor give
　　Sign to lovers where I live;

But the sea-rock betrays where my netting is hung,
When the meshes of light o'er its mosses are flung!"
    She ceased, and then in chorus strong
    The blended voices floated long :—

    " No sirens we, of shore or wave,
    To sing of love and tempt the brave :
    We fled their path, and freedom found
    Where blue horizons stretched around,
    And lilies in the grasses made
    A double sunshine on each blade.
    No wooers we, but, wooed by them,
    We yield our maiden diadem,
    And welcome now, no longer mute,
    Tried hearts so true and resolute !"

THE PRAIRIE ROSES.

The Noon-Sun prayed a prairie rose
   To blanch for him her blossom's hue,
But to the Plain all love she owes;
   Beneath that mother's grass she grew.

And sheltered by her verdant blades,
   Their tints of green she made her own;
But still the Sun sought out her shades
   And said, "Be my white bride alone!"

Then, sorrowing for his grievous pain,
   Her sister loved the amorous god,
And blushed, ashamed, as o'er the plain
   His parting beams illumed the sod.

So one sweet rose yet wears the green,
   And one in sunset's crimson glows;
Still one untouched by love is seen,
   And one in conscious beauty blows.

CREE FAIRIES.

" DID earth ever see
On thy prairie's line
Tribes older than thine,
Old Chief of the Cree ? "

.   .   .   .   .

" Before us we know
Of none who lived here :
The Blackfeet were near ;
Our shafts bade them go

" But others have share
Of lake and of land,
A swift-footed band
No arrow can scare.

" Their coming has been
When flowers are gay ;
On islet and bay
Their footprints are seen.

" There dance little feet,
Light grasses they break ;
Beneath the blue lake
Must be their retreat.

"We listen, and none
Hears ever a sound ;
But where, lily-crowned,
Floats the isle in the sun,

" Three children we see
Like sunbeams at play,
And, voiceless as they,
Dogs bounding in glee.

" Of old they were there !
Ever young, who are these
Whom Death cannot seize ?
What Spirits of air ? "

THE "QU'APPELLE" VALLEY.

MORNING, lighting all the prairies,
  Once of old came, bright as now,
To the twin cliffs, sloping wooded
  From the vast plain's even brow:
When the sunken valley's levels
  With the winding willowed stream,
Cried, "Depart, night's mists and shadows;
  Open-flowered, we love to dream!

Then in his canoe a stranger
  Passing onward heard a cry;
Thought it called his name and answered,
  But the voice would not reply;
Waited listening, while the glory
  Rose to search each steep ravine,
Till the shadowed terraced ridges
  Like the level vale were green.

Strange as when on Space the voices
  Of the stars' hosannahs fell,
To this wilderness of beauty
  Seemed his call "Qu'Appelle? Qu'Appelle?"

For a day he tarried, hearkening,
  Wondering, as he went his way,
Whose the voice that gladly called him
  With the merry tones of day?

Was it God, who gave dumb Nature
  Voice and words to shout to one
Who, a pioneer, came, sunlike,
  Down the pathways of the sun?
Harbinger of thronging thousands,
  Bringing plain, and vale, and wood,
Things the best and last created,
  Human hearts and brotherhood!

Long the doubt and eager question
  Yet that valley's name shall tell,
For its farmers' laughing children
  Gravely call it "The Qu'Appelle!"

THE BLACKFEET.

I.

Where the snow-world of the mountains
    Fronts the sea-like world of sward,
And encamped along the prairies
   · Tower the white peaks heavenward ;
Where they stand by dawn rose-coloured
    Or dim-silvered by the stars,
And behind their shadowed portals
    Evening draws her lurid bars,
Lies a country whose sweet grasses
    Richly clothe the rolling plain ;
All its swelling upland pastures
    Speak of Plenty's happy reign ;
There the bison herds in autumn
    Roamed wide sunlit solitudes,
Seamed with many an azure river
    Bright in burnished poplar woods.

II.

Night-dews pearled the painted hide-tents,
    " Moyas " named, that on the mead

Sheltered dark-eyed women wearing
  Braided hair and woven bead.
Never man had seen their lodges,
  Never warrior crossed the slopes
Where they rode, and where they hunted
  Imu bulls and antelopes.
Masterless, how swift their riding!
  While the wild steeds onward flew,
From round breasts and arms unburdened
  Freedom's winds their tresses blew.
Only when the purple shadows
  Slowly veiled the darkening plain
Would they sorrow that the Sun-god
  Dearer loved his Alp's domain.

III.

Southward, nearer to the gorges
  Whence the sudden warm winds blow,
Shaking all the pine's huge branches,
  Melting all the fallen snow,
Dwelt the Séksika, the Blackfeet;
  They whose ancestor, endued,
With the dark salve's magic fleetness,
  First on foot the deer pursued.
Gallantly the Braves bore torture
  While their Sun-dance fasts were held,
While the drums beat, and the virgins
  Saw the pains by manhood quelled.

As each writhing form triumphant
  Called on the Great Spirit's might,
On his son, whose voice in thunder
  Summons airy hosts to fight.

IV.

" Star-Child," praised as bearing all things,
  Praised as Brave who never feared,
Young, but famed above his elders,
  Chief to man and maid endeared,
Went with comrades, quiver-harnessed,
  O'er the hills, and face to face,
Where the bright leaves trembled round them,
  Found the fearless huntress race.
Was it peace or was it warfare?
  Starting back, their bows they drew,
But a mystic power compelled them,
  And no word, no arrow flew.
Nearer to each other drawing,
  Strength and beauty beckoned " Peace,"
Each the other envious eyeing,
  Jealous lest their hunt should cease!

V.

" They are strong; could not they aid us?"
  Thought the maiden band amazed;
" Conquered, these could well obey us!"
  Dreamed the warriors as they gazed.

Falsely answered cunning "Star-Child,"
  Smiling as they slowly met,
While the women's frequent questions
  Were to laughter's music set,
" Who is chief among you, tell us ? "
  " He is far ! Is she your queen
With the shells and deer-teeth broidered,
  Decked with sheen of gold between ? "
" Yea ; she slays the bear, the grizzly :
  Light her empire on us lies ;
With the love she rules her courser
  Guides and guards us ' Laughing Eyes ' ! "

VI.

Vaunted then the men their " Star-Child : "
  " Peerless soldier, keen-eyed king !
From the girl he weds shall heroes
  Worthy war-god's lineage spring.
Know ye not how old enchantment
  Saw his storm-born sire appear,
Armed, upon a peak dark-lifted
  O'er the snows and glaciers drear ?
His the darts divine, whose breaking
  Thrice hath some disaster sent,
Shafts that killed and then returning,
  Kept his armoury unspent."
" Give us of these arrows. Bring him ! "
  Cried the maidens. " Nay," they said ;

"Come with us and share our hunting
  Ere the autumn leaves are shed."

VII.

Answered they : " In painted lodges
  Berries we have dried and meat ;
Come again ! e'er comes the winter,
  Let us hear your horses' feet."
And they sprang into their saddles,
  Swept, white-splashing, through a stream ;
Red and saffron hued, the pageant
  Crossed the blue translucent gleam.
Then unwilling, as they vanished,
  "Star-Child" slow to camp returned ;
Told the council of the Blackfeet
  All the marvels he had learned ;
Dressed him in his chief's apparel,
  Rode to where, within the glen,
Lay the trail that led him onward
  To the town, unknown of men.

VIII.

From each Moya thronged the dwellers :
  " Hath the chief the arrows sent ? "
" I am Chief ; behold me ; trust me.
  Lead me to your ruler's tent.'
" He hath not the shafts enchanted ;
  Thus unarmed came never chief ! "

Bent a thousand bows around him :
  " Back or die, impostor, thief ! "
Angry, yet afraid to anger,
  Lest he lose those " Laughing-Eyes,"
He, obeying, vowed to conquer ;
  Scorning to make vain replies,
Went ; and weary seemed the journey !
  All along the yellow plain
Red as rose-leaves in the grasses
  Flushed his dusky cheeks with pain.

IX.

Grave, in silent circles seated
  'Neath their Moya's smoke-tanned cone,
Round the fire his chieftains heard him,
  Holding each a pipe's red stone.
Pausing long, they gave their counsel,
  Different from their wont; for here
All the young men spoke for kindness,
  All the old men were severe.
But the Braves rode forth at morning,
  Half the magic darts they bore ;
Pledge so precious of their friendship
  None had thought to give before !
To the huntress nation welcome,
  Waking song in every tent,
Where the hours were passed in feasting
  And the days to love were lent !

X.

Thus the maidens were the victors,
  For to them the warriors came :
" Laughing-Eyes " but loved the " Star-Child "
  When his shafts her own became.
Ah ! but where is man or woman
  Who may boast of triumph long ?
Nought abides, and mighty nations
  Cannot ever more be strong.
So each huntress found a master,
  Yielding to her heart's new birth,
And no more along the prairie
  Beat her steed the sounding earth.
Yearly yet the Blackfeet women
  Meet and dance and sing the day
When through love they won, and, winning,
  Freedom passed with love away !

SAN GABRIEL, ON THE PACIFIC COAST.

GREY-COWLED monk, whose faith so earnest
　　Guides these Indians' childlike hearts,
As their hands to toil thou turnest,
　　Teaching them the Builder's arts,
Speak thy thought ! as now they gather
　　Round the white walls on the plain,
Rearing them for God the Father,
　　And the glory of New Spain.

"Thou, St. Gabriel, knowest only
　　Why thy holy bells I raise,
To no turret proud and lonely,
　　There to sound the hours of praise ;—
Why I keep them close beside me,
　　Framed within the church's walls,
Here where heathen lands shall hide me
　　Until death to judgment calls."

Then St. Gabriel in high heaven
　　Told the saints this mortal's lot,

As the Angelus at even
  Rose to day that dieth not;
And from out the nightly wonder
  Of the darkened world would float,
Mingling with the near sea's thunder,
  Yonder belfry's golden note.

"Two there were, whose loves were blighted
  By the Spanish pride abhorred,
And their vows and wealth they plighted
  To the Missions of the Lord.
For his church these bells she gave him,
  When within their glowing mould,
She had cast what were her treasures,
  —All her ornaments of gold.

"So do these, that to his seeming
  Were but good as touched by her,
Ring to seek for love redeeming
  All who sorrow, all who err.
Yes, though human love be ever
  Heard upon the throbbing air,
This shall make his life's endeavour
  Stronger through a woman's prayer.

"God is not a Lord requiring
  Sacrifice of memories dear,
And their love in life untiring
  To His life hath brought them near.

Thus his wish to have beside him
   That which seems her voice, is good :
Lovingly the Lord hath tried him,
   And his heart hath understood !"

NIAGARA.

A CEASELESS, awful, falling sea, whose sound
   Shakes earth and air, and whose resistless stroke
   Shoots high the volleying foam like cannon smoke !
How dread and beautiful the floods, when, crowned
By moonbeams on their rushing ridge, they bound
   Into the darkness and the veiling spray ;
   Or, jewel-hued and rainbow-dyed, when day
Lights the pale torture of the gulf profound !
So poured the avenging streams upon the world
   When swung the ark upon the deluge wave,
And, o'er each precipice in grandeur hurled,
   The endless torrents gave mankind a grave.
God's voice is mighty, on the water loud,
Here, as of old, in thunder, glory, cloud !

ON CHIEF MOUNTAIN,

**A GREAT ROCK ON THE AMERICAN NORTH-WEST
FRONTIER.**

AMONG white peaks a rock, hewn altar-wise,
   Marks the long frontier of our mighty lands.
   Apart its dark tremendous sculpture stands,
Too steep for snow, and square against the skies.
In other shape its buttressed masses rise
   When seen from north or south ; but eastward set,
   God carved it where two sovereignties are met,
An altar to His peace, before men's eyes.
Of old there Indian mystics, fasting, prayed ;
   And from its base to distant shores the streams
Take sands of gold, to be at last inlaid
   Where ocean's floor in shadowed splendour gleams.
So in our nations' sundered lives be blent
Love's golden memories from one proud descent !

CUBA.

Spake one upon our vessel's prow, before
  The sinking sun had kissed the glittering seas:
  "'Twas here Columbus with his Genoese
Steered his frail barks toward the unknown shore,
With hope unfaltering, though all hope seemed o'er;
  Calm 'mid the mutineers the prophet mind
  Saw the New World to which their eyes were blind,
Heard on its continents the breakers' roar,
Told of the golden promise of the main,
  While cursed his crew, and called a madman's
      dream
The land his ashes only hold for Spain!
  It rose on dim horizon with the gleam
Of morn, proclaiming to the kneeling throng
All treasures theirs, because one heart was strong."

ON THE NEW PROVINCE "ALBERTA."*

In token of the love which thou hast shown
   For this wide land of freedom, I have named
   A province vast, and for its beauty famed,
By thy dear name to be hereafter known.
Alberta shall it be ! Her fountains thrown
   From alps unto three oceans, to all men
   Shall vaunt her loveliness e'en now ; and when,
Each little hamlet to a city grown,
And numberless as blades of prairie grass,
   Or the thick leaves in distant forest bower,
Great peoples hear the giant currents pass,
   Still shall the waters, bringing wealth and power,
Speak the loved name,—the land of silver springs—
Worthy the daughter of our English kings.

* This Province was called after the Princess, one of whose
Christian names is Alberta.

VERSES

CHIEFLY FROM HIGHLAND STORIES.

GAELIC LEGENDS.

Oft the savage Tale in telling
   Less of Love than Wrath and Hate,
Hath within its fierceness dwelling
   Some pure note compassionate.

Mark, if rude their nature, stronger,
   Manlier are the minds that keep
Thought on rightful vengeance longer
   Than on those who can but weep.

Better sing the horrid battle
   Than its cause of crime and wrong;
Sing great life-deeds! the death-rattle
   Is too common for a song.

Lays where man in fight rejoices
   Sang our Sires, from Sire to Son;
Heard and loved the hero voices,
   " Dare, and more than life is won!"

COLHORN.

Lo, a castle, tall, lake-mirrored,
   Ringed around by mountain forms,
Roofless, ruined, still defying
   Summer's rains and winter's storms.

Every shattered lifeless window,
   Every stone in every wall,
Keep and gable, broken stairway,
   Woman's faithful love recall.

Colin, called " the Swarthy," famous
   In the annals of Lochow,
When a child, was gently fostered
   Near where Orchy's waters flow.

The Black Knight, his sire, could value
   Vassal's love and hardy fare ;
To a gudewife gave him, saying,
   " Train him with the sons you bear."

Strong he grew, and brave, till armies
   Praised in him a man of men.
Came a peace—then love ;—a lady
   Ruled with him the Orchy's glen.

But afar from over Ocean
   Rose a cry for Christian aid :
Blessed of Pope, 'neath holy banners
   Sailed he for the great crusade.

Leaving with his weeping lady
   Half their marriage ring, whereon
Written stood his name, and taking
   Half where hers, engraven, shone.

" If no tidings reach thee, darling,
   Blame my death." But she through tears
Answered : " I'll believe thee living
   Though I hear not seven years."

Lonely lived the lady, lonely :
   Riches grew, and brought her all
Save the loving words whose echo
   Seemed to linger in his hall.

Voiceless passed the years ; and Rumour
   Falsely slew him, whose steel mail
Flashed o'er white walls, azure sea girt,
   Watched, and feared by Moslem sail.

Rhodes' fair island saw his valour;
  'Mid her gardens he had bled;
Glowing as her sun, his love-words
  Homeward to his lady sped.

Ah, they reached her not, to banish
  Days of care, and nights of woe;
Their warm sunshine never parted
  Clouds that darkened o'er Lochow.

Weary is her lot whose favour
  For her wealth is held a prize;
Oft she finds no truthful homage,
  Sees no love in pleading eyes.

Man gains strength from gold, but woman
  Worse than dross her wealth may call;
Avarice is her haunting suitor,
  Giving naught and seeking all.

Messages from the Crusader
  Fell into a Baron's hands;
Who, with subtle treason working,
  Coveted dark Colin's lands:

Spread the base and cruel rumours,
  Preyed upon the aching heart,
Asked her year by year in marriage,
  Falsely played the lover's part.

And the heartless seasons vanished,
  Other twain were nearly sped;
Then at last his suit seemed answered,
  Silently she bent her head.

Gaily, loudly, laughing o'er her,
  Named the Baron hour and day.
But she said: " No, for this wedding
  First I'll build a castle gay.

" When its halls are built, we'll tarry
  Where our guests can praise our cheer;
When the feast-smoke from its chimneys
  Rises, then the day is near."

So the building rose, and slowly
  Walls and stairway, keep and tower,
Stone by stone completed, sadly
  Heralded the wedding hour.

Shall it come, and never mercy
  Shown of God avert the doom?
Shall the longing for the absent
  Turn to feasting o'er his tomb?

Yes. The Castle's new possessor
  Soon shall follow thronging guests:
As the Lake reflects the turrets
  Men shall second his behests.

Mournful, where they laughed so gladly,
 A poor beggar, haggard, grey,
Trod with pain the stony roadside,
 Often halting by the way.

He too reached the Castle's portal,
 Stood within its archway grim,
Loitering in the path of others;
 Who would step aside for him?

Pushed a henchman rudely, saying,
 "Get you hence," but still he stood:
Then they gave him bread and water,
 "Loiter not, you have your food."

Twice came others, in his wallet
 Thrusting bread and meat, and said:
"Now away, why stand you troubling,
 Here you cannot make your bed."

"Drink from her own hands imploring,
 Tell your Lady here I wait!"
Wondering went she where the beggar
 Shadowed stood within the gate.

Now she pours the crystal water,
 Quickly he the cup returns;
Oh! what golden circlet broken
 Sees she there that gleams and burns?

Eagerly she grasped the token,
 Turning to the light away;
Came again, and crying " Colin ! "
 On the beggar's breast she lay.

Spoke he sadly : " Hast thou truly
 Still the heart I loved ?   I know—
They have told me—that thou takest
 To thy love my deadly foe.

" The gudewife, my foster mother,
 Unto whom I made me known
When I reached the Orchy, told me
 How the rumour base had grown :

" I was dead, or cared not for thee
 Who received no word of mine ;
'Twas thy lover's doing, woman,
 Hungering for my wealth and thine !

" ' Take,' the gudewife said, ' a beggar's
 Old attire ; and see the mist
Where the wedding smoke is ordered
 By the lips which thou hast kissed.'

" Thou hast put our ring together
 Can it be as one again ? "
Then she raised her face, and proudly
 Spoke unto her serving-men :

"See you where the Baron's people
  Come with him along the road?
Go and tell them quickly, 'Colin
  Rules again his own abode.'"

Fled the traitor, pulses beating,
  Not with love, but craven fear;
And the beggar found the treasure
  That to noble hearts is dear.

Found the love no time had altered,
  Honoured lived, and honoured died;
And in Rhodes and in Glenorchy
  Honoured shall his name abide.

LOCH BÚY.

PART I.

DARK, with shrouds of mist surrounded,
  Rise the mountains from the shore,
Where the galleys of the Islesmen
  Stand updrawn, their voyage o'er.

Horns this morn are hoarsely sounding
  From Loch Búy's ancient wall,
While for chase the guests and vassals
  Gather in the court and hall.

Hounds, whose voices could give warning
  From far moors of stags at bay,
Quiver in each iron muscle,
  Howl, impatient of delay.

Henchmen, waiting for the signal,
  At their chief's imperious word
Start, to drive from hill and corrie
  To the pass the watchful herd.

Closed were paths as with a netting,
   Vain high courage, speed, or scent;
Every mesh, a man in ambush
   Ready with a crossbow bent.

" Eachan, guard that glade and copsewood,
   At your peril let none by ! "
Cries the chief, while in the heather
   Silently the huntsmen lie.

Shouting by the green morasses
   Where the fairies dance at night,
Yelling 'mid the oak and birches
   Come the beaters into sight.

And before them, rushing wildly
   Speeds the driven herd of deer,
Whose wide antlers toss like branches
   In the winter of the year.

Useless was the vassal's effort
   To arrest the living flow;
And it passed by Eachan's passage
   Spite of hound, and shout, and blow.

" Worse than woman ! useless caitiff !
   Why allowed you them to pass ?
Back, no answer !   Hark, men, hither !
   Take his staff and bind him fast."

Hearing was with them obeying,
    And the hunter's strong limbs lie
Bound with thongs from tawny oxen,
    'Neath the chieftain's cruel eye.

"More than twoscore stags have passed him,
    Mark the number on his flesh
With red stripes of this good ashwood,
    Mend me thus this broken mesh!"

Ah, Loch Búy! faint and sullen
    Beats the heart, once leal and free,
That had yielded life exulting
    If it bled for thine and thee.

Deem'st thou that no honour liveth
    Save in haughty breasts like thine?
Think'st thou men, like dogs in spirit,
    At such blows but wince and whine?

Often in the dangerous tempest,
    When the winds before the blast
Surging charged like crested horsemen
    Over helm, and plank, and mast,

He, and all his kin before him,
    Well have kept the clansman's faith,
Serving thee in every danger,
    Shielding thee from harm and skaith.

'Mid the glens and hills, in combats
    Where the blades of swordsmen meet,
Has he fought with thee the Campbells,
    Mingling glory with defeat.

But as waters round Eorsa
    Darken deep, then blanch in foam,
When the winds Ben More has harboured
    Burst in thunder from their home,

So the brow fear never clouded
    Blackens now 'neath anger's pall,
And the lips, to speak disdaining,
    Whiten at revenge's call!

PART II.

Late, when many years had passed him,
    And the Chief's old age begun,
Seemed his youth again to blossom
    With the birth of his fair son.

Late, when all his days had hardened
    Into flint his nature wild,
Seemed it softer grown and kinder
    For the sake of that one child.

And again a hunting morning
　Saw Loch Búy and his men,
With his boy, his guests, and kinsmen,
　Hidden o'er a coppiced glen.

Deep within its oaken thickets
　Ran its waters to the sea :
On the hill the Chief lay careless,
　While the child watched eagerly.

'Neath them, on the shining Ocean,
　Island beyond island lay,
Where the peaks of Jura's bosom
　Rose o'er holy Oronsay.

Where the greener fields of Islay
　Pointed to the far Kintyre,
Fruitful lands of after-ages,
　Wasted then with sword and fire.

For the spell that once had gathered
　All the chiefs beneath the sway
Of the ancient Royal sceptre
　Of the Isles had passed away.

Once from Rathlin to the southward,
　Westward, to the low Tiree,
Northward, past the Alps of Coolin,
　Somerled ruled land and sea.

Colonsay, Lismore, and Scarba,
   Bute and Cumrae, Mull and Skye,
Arran, Jura, Lew's and Islay
   Shouted then one battle-cry.

But those Isles that, still united,
   Fought at Harlaw, Scotland's might,
Broken by their fierce contentions
   Singly waged disastrous fight.

And the teaching of forgiveness,
   Grey Iona's creed, became
Not a sign for men to reverence,
   But a burning brand of shame.

Still among the names that Ruin
   Had not numbered in her train,
Lived the great Clan, proud as ever
   Of the race of strong Maclaine.

And his boy, like her he wedded,
   Though of nature like the dove,
Showed the eagle-spirit flashing
   Through her heritage of love.

Heir of all the vassals' homage
   Rendered to the grisly sire,
He had grown his people's treasure,
   Fostered as their heart's desire.

Surely Safety guards his footsteps ;
   Enmity he hath not sown :
Yet who stealthily glides near him,
   Whose the arm around him thrown ?

It is Eachan, who has wolf-like
   Seized upon a helpless prey !
Fearlessly and fast he bears him
   Where a cliff o'erhangs the bay.

There, while sea-birds scream around them,
   Holding by his throat the boy,
Eachan turns, and to the father
   Shouts in scorn and mocking joy:

" Take the punishment thou gavest,
   Give before all there a pledge
For my freedom, or thy darling
   Dying, falls from yonder ledge.

" Take the strokes in even number
   As thou gavest, blow for blow,
Then dishonoured, on thine honour
   Swear to let me freely go."

Silent in his powerless anger
   Stood the Chief, with all his folk ;
And before them all the ransom
   Was exacted stroke for stroke.

Then again the voice of vengeance
    Pealed from Eachan's lips in hate:
"Childless and dishonoured villain,
    Expiation comes too late.

"My revenge is not completed!"
    And they saw in dumb despair
How he hurled his victim downward
    Headlong through the empty air.

Then they heard a yell of laughter
    As they turned away the eye;
And they gazed again where nothing
    Met their sight but cliff and sky;

For the murderer dared to follow
    Where the youthful spirit fled,
To the Throne of the Avenger,
    To the Judge of Quick and Dead.

THE HARD STRAIT OF THE FEINNE.

Now of the hard strait of the Feinne this legend's verse
    shall tell :
When Fionn's men had fought and won, and all with
    them was well,
And victory on Erin's shores had given spoil which
    they
Alone could win whose swords of old were mightiest
    in the fray :
For in those days the bravest hand, and not the
    craftiest brain,
Got gold, and skill in gallant fight was found the surest
    gain.
Great Fionn's wont it was to give, when foes had bled
    and broke,
A feast to nobles and to chiefs and all the humble
    folk :
Upon the plain they sat, and ate the meat which
    smoking came
From layers of stone, well laid on pits half filled with
    charcoal flame,
Where 'neath the covering roof of turf that kept the
    heat aglow

The boar was quickly roasted whole, with many a
stag and roe.
And while the feast, with laugh and jest, gave careless
time to most,
Two watchers bold kept guard the while, and gazed
o'er sea and coast—
Two watchers good, and keenly eyed, sent out by
Fionn to mark
If danger rode upon the sea, with Norway's pirate bark.
Full well they watched, although behind they heard
the shouted song,
And knew the wine was bathing red the fair beards of
the strong,
While chanted verse, and music's notes, arose upon
the air,
And the briny breeze itself half seemed a savoury steam
to bear ;
Nor left their post, when from the clouds the hail-
stones leaped to ground,
And plaids were wrapt o'er shoulders broad, and o'er
deep chests were wound.
But Fionn's plaid untouched lay yet upon the earth
outspread,
And white it grew as lichened rock, or Prophet's hoary
head.
"Oh would it were all ruddy gold, there lying thickly
strewn ;
What joy were ours to share alike, and bear away each
stone."

And laughingly each filled his hands, forgetful of the
    twain,
Their comrades good, on guard who stood to watch
    the moor and main.
But when their lonely vigil o'er, they, Roin and Aildé,
    came,
And found how little friendship counts, when played
    the spoiler's game,
Sore angered that no hand for them had set apart a
    prize,
They murmured. " With such men of greed all faith
    and kindness dies !
When thus they deal with us in peace, how shall we
    fare when blood
Runs from the wounds to blind the eyes to aught but
    selfish good ? "
They swore that they forgotten thus were better far
    away,
And sailed to Lochlin's distant shore, and served in
    her array.
Their fame was great in Norway's realm, and love for
    Aildé came
To melt the heart of Norway's queen, a sudden quench-
    less flame.
She fled with Aildé from the King, and soon on Scot-
    land's coast
She trod, a messenger of ill, a danger to the host.
Great Eragon, far Lochlin's King, was not the man
    to know

The blood mount hot at insult's stroke without an
    answering blow,
His dragon keels were rolled to waves that shouted
    welcome loud
To glittering helm and painted shield beneath each
    spar and shroud.
Oh! strong was Eragon in war, in battle victor oft,
From many a rank, from many a mast his banner
    streamed aloft;
With forty ships he set to sea, and scores of glancing
    oars
Streaked white his wake on fiord and loch along the
    echoing shores.
The Shetland Islands saw them pass, where on the
    tides, their sails
Shone like a flight of mighty swans, fast borne on
    wintry gales:
Hoarse as the raven's note their oath rang over all
    the seas,
False Fionn's host should bend and break before the
    Northern breeze.
And southward, onward still they steered, and up Loch
    Leven bore,
As you may know, for one great ship was lost upon
    the shore:
The sunken rock on which she drove and inlet where
    she lay
Were called the Galley's Crag and Port, and bear the
    name to-day.

They left her, taking all her crew, and landing near
    Glencoe,
On level ground their tents were set, thick planted
    row on row.

To Fionn of the Feinne that day, King Eragon sent
    word,
To yield him homage or abide the hard doom of the
    sword.;
But grievous then was Fionn's strait, for thrice a thou-
    sand men,
His best and bravest, far away were hunting hill and
    glen.
The wives, the old and feeble folk alone were left, and
    these
He gathered, asking how to blind the strangers of the
    seas?
Then gave they counsel: "We are weak. By thee
    must peace be sought,
E'en though with massy store of gold the boon to-day
    be bought;
And if all this do not avail," they said, "O Fionn,
    thou
Shouldst yield thy daughter as the price, our ransom
    on her brow!"
Their messenger then offered these before the set of
    sun;
When flamed the wrath from Norway's King: "I ask
    not what I've won,

Your master stands before you now, my vengeance is
    my own;
For Aildé's deed the Feinne as slaves in Norway shall
    atone."
Back went the messenger in haste, and sadly Fionn knew
The threat was uttered by the strong, against the old
    and few.
But homeward from the forest soon he saw each hero's
    hound
Come swiftly back, in front of all he saw his Oscar
    bound;
And when the foremost hunters came, he told their
    noble band
How fight was sought with them this day upon the
    Northern strand.
Then looked they for some ground whose strength
    would quickly hide and save
Their little force, till gathering might gave fortune to
    the brave.
They dug four trenches deep, where firs above the
    birches flung
Red gnarléd limbs that glowed at eve the dark green
    plumes among;
There hidden silently they watched, while rugged,
    scarred, and high,
Just at their rear a peak appeared to move against the
    sky.
Steep were its rocky ledges, strewn with jagged stones
    that lay

So loose one hand might send a mass on its resistless
    way,
While from the neighbouring hills the mount was sun-
    dered by a glen,
Where lightly crossed the grey cloud mists, but never
    mortal men.
Such was the chosen fort. The Feinne into the trenches
    went ;
For succour through all Alban's realm their messengers
    were sent ;
To the green slopes of deep Glencoe the warriors
    summoned came,
Alas, too few to brave in fight the men of Norway's
    name.

They held long counsel, and the chief sent forth that
    hostage fair
His daughter, with a chosen band, his words of peace
    to bear ;
And Fergus, his young son, to speak on his behalf,
    that they
Might change to love the king's black thought, and all
    his wrath allay—
For Fergus' speech, like ivy wreath, o'er heart of rock
    could wind
Till tender thoughts, like nestling birds, would come
    and shelter find.
Wealth to awake the Northmen's greed should weight
    his tempting word

For quaichs of gold, and precious belts, and magic stones
    which stirred
The torpid blood of all disease to vigorous life once
    more,
And fivescore mares of iron grey, and hunting hawks
    threescore,
Were gifts to promise, with good herds, and cows with
    calves at side.
They placed the maid upon a horse, and bade her
    boldly ride;
With Fergus marching at her rein, his comrades close
    at hand,
They came to where the fleet and camp thick covered
    sea and land.

And halting there, young Fergus spake across a space
    of ground
Unto the king, who foremost stood with mailéd men
    around;
He offered all the tribute rich, and that fair lady proud.
But when he ceased a silence fell, and then the answer
    loud
In Eragon's deep voice rang forth : " Let Fionn bring
    me all,
All that he hath on earth, and here let him before me
    fall,
Him and his wife before me here upon the shore, that I
May see them on their knees to me swear troth and
    fealty,

While as they homage make I shall above them rear
    my blade
To spare, or slay them at my feet, if so their debt be
    paid."

Then called in scorn the lady's voice, " No, Eragon,
    your might
Hath not across the broad salt seas brought such a
    host to fight
As e'er shall cause my father's knees to bend to you in
    prayer,
Nor shall you ever call me bride, or spoil of Erin wear."
She quickly turned her horse and went, but Fergus
    stood and waved
The signal banner for the chief, and for a while he
    braved
The onset of the foe, and fought until the evening fell.
Then gave the council their advice to Fionn. " It
    were well
That Aildé should himself defy the king, and man to
    man
With sevenscore 'gainst sevenscore contend before the
    van."
And thus they fought, and Aildé fell, and Eragon
    defied
An equal band to equal fight, for great had grown his
    pride.
Then paused and pondered Fionn long, and doubted
    whom to ask

To lead in such a venture great, and dare so grave a
  task.
But Goll, the son of Morna, named at Fionn's call, went
  forth
And matched with equal force, back drove the boasters
  of the North.
And yet again a band as strong was overcome and
  made
To own our heroes' swords were best, when man to man
  arrayed ;
But Eragon in fury cried his men should conquer yet.
For eight days more aye sevenscore 'gainst sevenscore
  were set,
And when the blood had flowed in streams, to utter
  madness urged
Against the trenches of the Feinne their baffled army
  surged.

Then sparkled swords like gleams of light upon the
  ocean's spray
When tossed aloft to wind and sun where battling
  currents play.
In that fierce fray did Eragon the son of Morna greet,
And, striking fast their mighty blades ascend and flashing meet ;
Then sank the stranger king in death, and Goll sore
  wounded fell,
Against the Northmen went the day ; and of their slain
  they tell

That from Glen Fewich to the shore they lay, and of
    the host
So few escaped that galleys twain alone left Scotland's
    coast.
Nay, even they ne'er reached a port, so that in Norway
    none
Could tell how Eragon revenged the deed by Aildé
    done.
But sorrow came upon the Feinne for all their strongest,
    dead ;
And Fionn found that from that time his fortune waned
    and fled,
For ne'er again in equal strength the Feinne in arms
    were seen
Since the dark days of Aildé's love, and Norway's evil
    queen.

Note.—This story was taken down by J. Dewar in prose from
oral recitation in Gaelic in 1860. Translated by H. McLean,
of Islay. It is rendered here nearly literally.

TOBERMORY BAY.

1588.

In the vapour and haze on the ocean,
  Where the skies and the waters meet,
There's a form that drifts, phantom-like, onward
  As it follows the grey clouds' feet.

O'er the sea come the winds and the billows,
  And they howl to the rocks, and they cry,
They will bring them a wreck on the morrow,
  Ere the joy of the tempest die.

The shade looming dark in the distance
  Is naught but a galleon proud;
And the spray has long battered her turrets,
  And loosened each yard and each shroud;

But not on the surf-beaten islands,
  Nor yet upon Morven's land,
Does she drive, for her rudder, unshattered,
  Is firm in the steersman's hand.

No mist wreath, no cloud, was the shadow
  That moved on the height of the seas ;
Like a castle how steep are her bulwarks,
  Her spars like a forest of trees !

She is safe from the gales for a season,
  In the shelter and calm of the sound ;
A harbour named after the Virgin,
  The " Well of Our Lady " she found.

She may rest in that haven, hill-girdled,
  Near the shade of the woods on the shore,
Where the hush of the forest is deepened
  By the waterfall's song evermore.

How grandly her masts rise to heaven,
  How glitters the blest Mary's form,
High placed o'er the stern, and upholding
  The Prince of our Peace through the storm !

Now waters their orisons murmur
  As they fold her bright robes to their breast,
Where they mirror the galleried windows,
  And the flag and the face of the Blest.

Again with that sign and the banner
  Of the gold and the crimson of Spain,
Shall this ship front the foes of the Virgin,
  And the English be chased from the Main.

Yes, again on the heretic Saxon
  Her cannon shall thunder in scorn,
Till in triumph through insolent England
  Shall the Faith and King Philip be borne.

But the rows of dark mouths that have spoken
  Defiance with sulphurous breath,
Glisten black, stretching forth in the silence,
  And in vain ask the presence of death.

Yes, repose and surcease of all hazard,
  A truce to all war for a time !
The cliffs and the pines only echo
  The laugh of a sunnier clime.

And gaily the dark-visaged seamen
  Quaff, cursing the mists and the rain ;
Gravely drinking from goblets of silver
  Sits their chief, Don Fereija of Spain.*

But the souls of the men to whose nostrils
  Had risen the smoke of the fight,

* This galleon was said to have been " The Florida," commanded by Don Fereija. A search at Madrid among the
archives shows that the only vessel named the " Florida " in
the Armada, was a small ship which came safely back to Sant-
ander Roads after the destruction of the fleet. No commander
had the name assigned to the captain of the vessel sunk at
Tobermory. The identity of this galleon remains, therefore, a
mystery.

Soon tired of the shore and of slumber,
  Soon yearned for the red battle light.

And courtesy fled from the weary,
  From idleness arrogance grew ;
And all they received as a favour
  They haughtily claimed as their due.

Then answered the Islesmen in anger,
  " The food you demand as your own,
By our people's free favour long given
  Shall be bought by your gold now alone."

" Now, down with the savage's envoy,
  Set sail and away on our track !
Carthagena's sweet girls shall deride him,
  And jeer the red locks on his back."

Below, in the dark narrow spaces,
  The Islesman gropes, down in the hold ;
Unnoticed, and one among many ;
  What harm can his hatred unfold ?

Swarm the men to the rigging, and swiftly
  Shine clouds of white canvas, and clank
The links of the anchor's great cable,
  Creaks, trampled on deck, every plank :

G

Swings round the huge bowsprit, and slowly
   With motion majestic and free,
The galleon, vast, gilded, and mighty,
   Passes on, passes forth, to the sea.

Her colours still paint all the ripples,
   Repeated her banners all seem,
Her sails, and her gold, and her cannon
   Float on like a gorgeous dream.

Came a flash, and a roar, and a smoke-cloud
   Rushed up, and spread far o'er the sky;
Sank a wreck, black, and rugged, and blasted,
   While the sound on the winds swept by.

And the mountains sent back the dull thunder
   As though to all time they would tell
The vengeance that pealed to the Heavens
   From the Harbour of " Mary's Well."

LOCH UISK, ISLE OF MULL.

Yon vale among the mountains
   So sheltered from the sea,
That lake which lies so lonely,
   Shall tell their tale to thee.

Here stood a stately convent
   Where now the waters sleep,
Here floated sweeter music
   Than comes from yonder deep.
Above the holy building
   The summer cloud would rest,
And listen where to heaven
   Rose hymns to God addressed ;
For the hills took up the chanting,
   And from their emerald wall
The sounds they loved, would, lingering,
   In fainter accents fall.

Hard by, beside a streamlet
   Fast flowing from a well,
A nun, in long past ages,
   Had built her sainted cell :

To her in dreams 'twas given
  As sacred task and charge,
To keep unchanged for ever
  The bright Spring's mossy marge.
" Peace shall with joys attendant
  For ever here abide,
While reverently and faithfully
  You guard its taintless tide."

And when she knew her spirit
  Was summoned to its rest,
To all around her gathered
  She gave that high behest;
And many followed after
  To seek the life she chose,
Till, like a flower, in glory
  The cloistered convent rose.

Through Scotland's times of bloodshed,
  Of foray, feud, and raid,
Their home became the haven
  Where storm and strife were stayed.
Men blessed each dark-robed Sister,
  And thought an angel trod,
Where walked in love and meekness
  A lowly maid of God !

Right happy were they, lighting
  With love those days of doom ;

For heart need ne'er be darkened
  By any garment's gloom.
Yes, often life thereafter
  Was here with gladness crowned,
For, sad as seemed their vesture
  The peace of God was found.
His holiness in beauty
  Made every trial seem
A rock that lies all harmless
  Deep hidden in a stream.
While life was pure there never
  Was wish in thought to gain
The world, where far behind them
  The black nuns left their pain;
And time but flew too quickly
  O'er that friend-circle small,
Where each one loved her neighbour,
  And God was loved of all.

Still from its beauteous chalice,
  That well's unceasing store
Poured forth, through whispering channels,
  The crystal load it bore.
Hope seemed to bring the fountain
  To seek the light of day;
Faith made it bright; Obedience
  Smoothed, hallowing, its way.

Full many a gorgeous Summer
  Woke heather into bloom,
And oft cold stars in Winter
  Looked on a Sister's tomb;
Before the joy had withered
  That virtue once had nursed;
Before their Lord and Master
  Grew love for things accursed.
Lo! then the stream neglected
  Forsook its wonted way;
In stagnant pools, dark-tainted,
  Its wandering waters lay.

There choked by moorland ridges,
  Black with the growth of peat,
Beneath the quaking surface
  The fetid floods would meet;
Till rising, spreading ever
  Above the chalice green
Of that fair Well, they covered
  The place where it had been.
Then, near the careless convent,
  Within the hill's deep shade,
The Fate which works in silence
  A lake had slowly made.
As evil knows not halting
  When passions strongly flow,
So daily deeper, deeper
  Would those dark waters grow;

Till on an awful midnight,
  When red the windows flamed
And song and jest and revel
  The Vesper hour had shamed,
And wanton sin dishonoured
  The time Christ's birth had crowned,
They burst their banks in darkness,
  And with their raging sound
The rocks of all the valley
  Rung for a few hours' space;
Then the wide Loch at morning
  Reflected heaven's face.

Few voices now are heard there,
  Around the wild deer feed;
And winds sigh loud in Autumn
  Through copse, and rush, and reed.
Men say that when in darkness
  They pass the water's verge,
Each hears, mid sounds of revel
  The "Miserere's" dirge;
That faintly, strangely, ever
  Upon the Loch's dark breast,
Beneath, above, around it
  Shine lights that never rest.

Of all such ghastly phantoms,
  Bred of the night and fear,

By hope of our salvation
   None meets the noontide clear !
The blue sky's tender beauties
   Upon the strong floods shine,
As God's eternal mercy
   Dwells with His might divine !
Pure as their mystic fountain
   They sleep and flow unstained,
Although the hue of sorrow
   Hath in their depths remained.

The swallow, swiftly passing
   Flies low to kiss the wave
When rippling gently over
   Some pure saint's holy grave :
The hunter's eyes discover
   Beneath those waters still
The walls of that proud convent,
   Where God hath worked His will.

THE LADY'S ROCK.

A brother's eye had seen the grief
    That Duart's lady bore;
His boat with sail half-raised flies down
    The sound by green Lismore.
Ahaladah, Ahaladah!
    Why speeds your boat so fast?
No scene of joy shall light your track
    Adown the spray-strewn blast.

The very trees upon the isle
    Rock to and fro, and wail;
The very birds cry sad and shrill,
    Storm driven, where you sail;
O when for yon dim mainland shore
    You launched your keel to start
You knew not of the load 'twill bear,
    The heavier load your heart.

See what is that, which yonder gleams,
    Where skarts alone make home;
Is that but one oft-breaking sea,
    Some frequent fount of foam?

The morn is dark and indistinct,
　　Is all through drift and cloud ;
Around the rock white waters toss,
　　As flaps in wind a shroud.

It cannot be a leaping jet,
　　Nor form of rock or wave
There stands some being saved by God
　　In mercy from the grave !
" Down with the sail, out oars ! the boat
　　Can reach the leeward side :
Mother of Heaven ! look you, men,
　　Where breaks that roaring tide."

" A living woman, do I dream
　　Or stands my sister there,
Where only at the middle ebb
　　The shelving ledge is bare ? "
O white as surf that sweeps her knee,
　　She falls, but not to die ;
Ahaladah is at her side,
　　He bears her up on high.

Away from Duart now he steers ;
　　Why curses he its lord ;
Why flee to Inveraray's strength,
　　As though he feared his sword ?
Proud triumph's notes were often heard
　　Where Aray's waters sing,

And mourners there have often wept
　　The slain for faith and king.

But never would that lady's lips
　　There speak her grievous woe,
Though in her chamber in the night
　　Her frequent tears would flow.
She dreamt of wrong where love was sought,
　　Of crafty cruel eyes,
Of one steep stair, of grasping hands
　　That stifled piteous cries;

Of wind which tore the hissing waves,
　　And howled o'er mountains bare;
Where swollen burns in feathery clouds
　　Were dashed into the air.
Of one wet rock, of horror wild,
　　When she was left alone,
Till madness seemed to whelm her thought
　　And, with a shuddering moan,

Again she heard the surges rush,
　　And, where she shrinking turned,
The seaweed there, like woman's hair,
　　The murderous billows spurned.
Again the night and wind were joined
　　To mock her hope of aid,
Till shrieking, she awoke, where once
　　She slept a happy maid.

But none would she accuse, and dumb
　　Rebuked the vengeance call,
Till one dark eve at supper-time
　　Within the old dim hall,
She heard some whisper, and she saw
　　Her brother leave his place,
Go forth, and entering, beckon out
　　A band, with stern set face.

Again he came, and o'er her bent,
　　And whispered "Sister dear,
Let fall your veil about your head,
　　Nor tremble when you hear
That Duart comes in mourner's guise!
　　Lo, there he takes his seat.
Chief, tell us why your mien is sad,
　　When friends and kinsmen meet?"

"My woes are great, my wife lies dead,
　　But yester week these hands
Closed her sweet eyes, and now I bring
　　Her body to your lands."
Then was the arras drawn aside
　　And girt with wake lights drear,
Beneath the archway's carven vault,
　　Was borne a white-crossed bier.

And Duart rose; his shifting eye
　　Moved like a marsh-fire pale,

But circling back, still restless scanned
   The lady of the veil.
Then through the silence broke a voice,
   " Know you that lady, chief?
She too, a guest with us, like you,
   Well knows the pangs of grief.

You come from far, bring wine." To each
   The ruddy goblet passed.
The lady raised her hand, and back
   The heavy veil she cast.
Strong Duart reeled as from a stroke;
   He stared as at the dead:
How could her glance o'er that dark face
   Such deathly palor spread?

"Your play is out, ah cursed fiend!"
   Ahaladah cried loud;
"Your death shall be no phantom false,
   No empty mask your shroud:
If hospitality's high law
   Here shields your life awhile,
By all the saints you yet shall feel
   The vengeance of Argyll."

  .   .   .   .

In Edinburgh Duart's Lord
   Strides down the shadowed town;
The white moon glints on roofs o'erhead,
   And on St. Giles's crown.

Another step is on the street,
 The watchmen hear no cry ;
But drenched in blood lies Duart, where
 Ahaladah passed by.

THE POOL OF THE IRON SHIRT.

Colin, Chief of Diarmid's kin,
Strode alone to Ederlinn.

Night, and heath, and deep morass
Hear the chain-mailed warrior pass.

Ambushed lay the treacherous foe,
Ear to earth, and dart on bow.

Vain their arrows' ringing hail
Fell on pointed helm and mail.

As he backward leaped, there flew
Moonlight down the sword he drew.

In his front the lonely man
Saw approach the hostile van :

Near him on the moor a tarn ;
On a knoll a wattled barn.

Refuge bad, yet near its door
·Sank the hot pursuit's uproar.

For, unsheathed his battle brand,
There they saw great Colin stand.

Dauntless cried he : " Here within
Rest I, then to Ederlinn ! "

Yelled the circling hounds in ire,
Set the woven wall on fire.

Sword in hand he stood, the light
Gleaming on his limbs of might.

Like a cloud-built column high,
Red, in sunset's flaming sky.

All too hot for mortal frame
Glowed his armour, wrapped in flame.

Hidden by the wreaths of smoke,
Hewing through the wall, he broke,

Felling seven, onward sped
Plunging through the lake's reed-bed.

Hiss the waters where he springs,
Hatred's yell again forth rings.

But he throws his mail away,
Dives, and darkness hides his way.

Smiling hears their lessening din ;
Onward strides to Ederlinn.

Ages since have passed, yet still
Tales recount his dauntless will.

" Pool of the Iron shirt," thy name
Keeps, in Erse, the hero's fame.

Look you, race of ancient Gael,
Never let such memories fail !

Set them far o'er gems and gold,
For your sons to have and hold.

Steadfast Will its goal shall win
Fairer e'en than Ederlinn !

INVERAWE.

Does death cleanse the stains of the spirit
　　When sundered at last from the clay,
Or keep we thereafter till judgment,
　　Desires that on earth had their way?
Bereft of the strength which was given
　　To use for our good or our bane,
Shall yearnings vain, impotent, endless,
　　Be ours with their burden of pain?

Though flesh does not clothe them, what anguish
　　Must be known in the world of the dead,
If the future lies open before them,
　　And fate has no secret unread.
And yet, oh how rarely our vision
　　May know the lost presence is nigh;
How seldom its purpose be gathered,
　　Be it comfort, or warning to die!

With mute or half-breathed supplication
　　Permitted to utter their prayer,

Demanding earth's justice, but ever
  Poor phantoms of mist and of air;
If in aught our belief may be certain
  Where founded on witness of man,
They come; and no tomb e'er imprisoned
  The shade when corruption began.

They come: and oh swiftly they follow
  The track of the murderer vile;
He is haunted for ever; his refuge
  A hell on far ocean or isle!
Though he fly as once fled from Barcaldine
  Young Donald's assassin, to claim
Guest-right, where all mercy a treason
  To kinship and justice became.

" Inverawe, Inverawe, give me shelter,
  I have shed a man's blood in a fray;
Oh swear that you will not betray me,
  By your dirk, by the dear light of day!"
And the prayer in his kindness he answered,
  But aghast heard the voices that cried;
"Your cousin lies slain! Can a stranger
  Have passed by the steep river side?"

Then bound by his oath he deceived them;
  But night brought a dream full of fear,
His cousin's pale image stood o'er him,
  Came a voice he had loved to his ear:

"Inverawe, Inverawe, give no shelter
　　To the man by whom blood has been shed:"
And he went to his guest, saying, "Leave me,
　　I obey the dear voice of the dead."

"By your oath, by the light of God's heaven
　　Your word has been passed for your guest."
"Then sleep in the cave in the mountain,
　　If Donald allow you to rest!"
Again shone the vision more awful,
　　Ere the hours of the darkness had fled;
"Inverawe, Inverawe, give no shelter
　　To the man by whom blood has been shed."

But empty the cave was at morning,
　　When searched for the murderer's trace,
And the ghost came again in the darkness,
　　The gore on its breast and its face.
"Inverawe, Inverawe," again whispered
　　The shade of the echoless feet,
"My blood has been shed, I await thee,
　　At Ticonderoga we meet."

And often in wonder repeated
　　That warning to many was known,
The strangely named place for the trysting
　　Men said was in dreamland alone;
"Why cherish a dismal illusion?
　　War summons gay hearts to the strife:

All share in the prizes of glory,
  The chances of death or of life."

In camp, on the march, in the battle,
  His thought would repeat evermore,
" At the place fore-ordained in the vision
  I shall pass to the Dark River's shore."
And often awaiting the summons,
  He asked for the wild Indian name,
When curled o'er American hamlets
  The smoke from the guns' sudden flame.

The forest one evening was silent
  As though in the calm of a trance
Yet within it two armies were resting,
  The soldiers of Britain and France.
Our Highlanders slumbered, march-wearied,
  Their sentries at watch in the wood :
Behind their long lines of entrenchment
  The French in their bivouacs stood.

" Inverawe, take your sleep ere the morning,
  When our praise or our death shall be sung,"
A comrade cried ; " soon for Carillon
  A chime that is new shall be rung !"
But the air of that night of midsummer
  Seemed chilly, and sleep fled away ;
And he wandered to where, near Carillon,
  The charge would be sounded at day.

To the North a pale ray of Aurora
　　Shot white o'er the black forest spars,
A lake through the pines softly gleaming
　　Lay calm in the radiance of stars.
It seemed a sweet heaven, whose brightness
　　Life's dark prison-bars could not hide:
As he gazed, lo, he thought that a figure
　　Advanced from that silvery tide.

Distinct as a luminous shadow,
　　It moved in the starlight alone,
Till it came to him close, and he shuddered,
　　For the face that he saw was his own!
The cloak of the dread apparition
　　His own, but bedabbled in blood!
Inverawe stretched his hand, but the spectre
　　Had vanished like mist in the wood.

To the fires of his comrades returning,
　　" Ah! friends, you deceived me," he said ;
" Why conceal from my ears that Carillon
　　Has the name that was named by the dead?
'Tis Ticonderoga, the fortress
　　We march on the morrow to storm,
Where Death and the Phantom stand watching
　　The hour when our column shall form."

The morn brought the hell of the onset,
　　When bayonet and Highlanders' blade

Sank crushed where the trenches were flashing
   In the roll of the long fusillade.
Repulsed ! O how sadly at night-fall
   The remnant was gathered and told !
In silence they thought of the wounded,
   And mourned the brave hearts that were cold.

Ere thundered again the dim battle
   Saluting the deathless in God,
A truce found that Leader all gory,
   Yet gasping his breath on the sod.
They bore him to camp, where around him
   They pressed as he beckoned in pain :
His voice seemed a breath in the forest,
   "I die—I have seen him again."

AN ISLESMAN'S FAREWELL.

Ah! must we part, my darling?
    O let the days be few,
Until your dear returning
    To one who loves but you!
Where'er your ship be sailing,
    Think on your own love true;
The back of the wave to you, darling,
    The back of the wave to you!

The witch, who oft at midnight
    Above Ben Caillach flew,
Told me she dreamed no danger
    Athwart your vessel drew;
For you she said the breezes
    Aye strong and fairly blew;
The back of the wave to you, darling,
    The back of the wave to you!

Ah! waiting here, and trembling
    When dark the water's hue,

I'll long for the dear pleasure
    That in your glance I knew ;
And pray to Him who never
    Can lose you from His view.
The back of the wave to you, darling,
    The back of the wave to you.

PREFACE TO DIARMID'S STORY.

Best beloved of ancient stories
    Are our Diarmid's woes to me.
Like a mist, by breezes broken,
So this tale of olden glories
Floats in fragments, as a token
    Of the song of Ireland's sea.

Through long centuries repeated
    Lived the legend told in Erse,
But a change comes swift or slowly
Fades the language, and defeated
Flies the faith, once counted holy,
    Old-world ways, and oral verse.

Not from men of note or learning
    May we gather now these tales,
Heard beneath the cotter's rafter,
Or where smithy sparks are burning,
Or at sea, when hushed the laughter
    Of the breeze on hull and sails.

Then with Ossian's rhythmic measure
  Comes upon the fancy's sight,
One with golden locks resplendent,
Great and strong with eyes of azure,
And, again in the ascendant,
  Magic reasserts her might.

Nought can wound him, sword or arrow,
  Only powerless are the spells
Where on the footsole implanted
There is hid a birth-mark narrow,
But this hero's brow enchanted
  Every woman's love compels.

Woe to him, that she whose glances
  Won the king on Denmark's shore,
Evil, beautiful, imperious,
Born where wheel the grisly dances ·
Through the glen of ghosts mysterious,
  Love's first passion for him bore.

For she saw his forehead bending
  O'er the snarling dogs at strife
At the wedding-feast of greeting;
And at dusk unto him wending,
"Come," she said, "let this our meeting
  Pledge my soul to thee for life."

"If, O queen, we go together,
  Not with friends, nor yet alone
Must thou be, nor sheltered ever,
Housed, nor braving wind and weather ;
If on horse or foot, then never
  Can thy love to me be known ! "

Flight were shield and fence far surer
  'Gainst a wily woman's ways
Than the wit of man ; for seated
Ere the dawn, his fair allurer
At his open door repeated
  All his words, with longing gaze.

"Go with me, O Diarmid ; see me
Not on horse, or foot ; with friends,
Nor alone ; not night or morning
Reigns : O come ; thou wilt not flee me ?
Never lived a warrior scorning
  Every joy that loving lends ! "

Then at last by her caresses
  Into flight and guilt beguiled,
Diarmid loathed his life, abiding
In the caves' or woods' recesses,
Like a thief or coward hiding,
  To his fate unreconciled.

Thus the mightiest magician
  Warped the true and loyal heart,
And he fled with her, forsaking
Friends and kinsfolk, while contrition
Gnawed into his life's days, making
  Sad his journey, hard his part.

He, a fugitive, whose valiance
  Made the Feinne fair Erin's boast !
Where the red cascade descended,
Lovely Grinie's evil dalliance
Held him thrall as though were ended
  Noble warring with the host.

He a slave ! whose oaths had ever
  Bade him "champion the oppressed,"
Pledged him to "confound the clever,
Aid the losing man's endeavour,
Be the first in fight, and never
  Heedless of the king's behest."

Once upon a rock, tree-shrouded,
  Hungry they had climbed to eat
Where the scarlet berries clustered :
Suddenly below them crowded
Dogs and huntsmen, 'til were mustered
  All the Feinne beneath their feet.

Fionn, then, their grim commander,
  Dreaming not his wife was near,
Had a giant chess-board graven
On the sod, and played; and under
The green leaves which gave him haven
  Diarmid watched the game in fear.

Oscar lost, with Fionn playing,
  Until Diarmid, from on high
Dropped the scarlet seeds to guide him,
Thus his presence there betraying:
And the friends of Fionn eyed him,
  Shouting, "Thou shalt surely die!"

But all Diarmid's comrades for him
  Fought, each venturing his life:
And amid the dread commotion
Fled the twain, until before him
To the peaceful sands of ocean
  Ran a woodland stream of strife.

Dwelling on its banks he made him
  There the wooden bowls that none
Fashioned with the dirk so deftly.
But the chattering stream betrayed him:
From the secret forest swiftly
  Flashed white shavings in the sun.

Then the king cried, " Grinie's lover
　Near us hath his lurking place !
Sound the hunting horns around him !
See if from the thickets' cover
By the ancient vows that bound him
　He shall come to join the chase ! "

．　　　．　　　．　　　．　　　．　　　．

How the queen bore his upbraiding ;
　How his death in hunting came,
Tell the verses here translated :
Lights are they, in transit fading,
Scattered sparks, oblivion fated,
　Memories from a mighty flame !

GRINIE'S FLIGHT WITH DIARMID.

(FROM THE GAELIC.)

THE Hern at early morning cries,
Where at Sleve-gail the meadow lies.

Say, Dúin's son, whom I love well,
Canst thou thereof the reason tell?

O ! Gormla's daughter, thou whose sire
Was named from tireless steeds of fire;

Thou evil-working one ! thy feet
Tread treacherous ways of ice and sleet.

Grinie ! of lovelier hue than Spring
To flower, or bloom on bough can bring,

More fleeting far your love that flies
Like the cold clouds of dawning skies.

Because of thine ill-chosen part
My fortune's firm set rivets start.

Yes, thine the deed, brought low to pain,
My grievous woe thine only gain .

From palaces of kings beguiled,
For ever outcast and exiled :

Like night-owl mourning, as she strays,
Her joy through dark and distant ways.

Like timid hind or hunted deer,
Through secret glens I tread in fear.

Shunning the loving friends who hold
The house of hosts so loved of old.

Their forms shone glorious as the lights
On the deep snows of frosted heights.

All these I left—mine own—whose love
Was generous as the Sun above.

But they are now hate-filled as though
Hate's sea would never ebbward flow.

Yes, since beguiled by you I fled,
Misfortune follows where I tread.

I

Lost now my white sailed fleet's array,
Through you my band is lost for aye.

Gone all my wealth, my gems, my gold,
All for the tale of love you told !

To me my friends are lost, to me
No more my country mine shall be.

Lost are my men whom none e'er found
Weak behind shield on battle ground.

Lost is their kindness evermore
The love for me the Feinne once bore.

Lost to mine honour mine own right,
Lost music's joy and lost delight ;

Erin and all I there have known,
For your ill-omened love alone.

Return I dare not,—may not,—never
Know their great friendship, gone for ever.

More than the beast of sharpest beard
My deed in hate by Fionn is feared.

Yes, fairest Grinie, thou hast done
Ill to thyself in love thus won.

Thou, winning hatred, wentst with me,
And kingly joys were spurned by thee.'

GRINIE.

O Diarmid! O Diarmid! of face far more fair
Than the new-fallen snow, or the hill flowret rare,
The sound of thy voice was more dear to my breast
Than all the bright satin the Fianti possessed.

More belovéd to me is the hue of thine eyes,
Those eyes like the morning's bright dew of the skies,
Ay, dearer to me than all strength or all gold
The great hall of the king of the Feinne shall e'er hold.

Love's mark is more sweet on thy beautiful brow
Than honey that drops where the green grasses bow;
Ah, when I beheld it above me, how pale
Seemed the glory and power of the Monarch of Fail.

My heart seemed to fall as I looked at thy face,
Adoring thy might ever blended with grace,
And wert thou not mine, to be gained to my side,
Not one day in this world would my spirit abide.

Oh! white-handed hero, so handsome, so strong.
Although it is I who have wrought all thy wrong,
Yet stay, stay again with me, wife would I be,
Vowing never on earth to be faithless to thee.

DIARMID.

Why love a woman mild in speech,
And yet a traitoress to each ?

GRINIE.

'Twas misery sundered my life from the king's,
I left thee awhile, for love, torturing, stings ;
Never more will I leave thee—my tender love round
    thee,
Like fresh boughs for thy life, would have sheltered
    and crowned thee.

DIARMID.

Fulfil then thy word, though so faithless, how fair !
Thy love, oh my Grinie, no giant shall share.

Note.—From Gaelic verse, printed by J. F. Campbell, Esq.,
in " Leabhar na Feinne."

THE DEATH OF THE BOAR.*

OSSIAN.

This vale of Peace, this glen close by,
Where deer and elk would often cry,
Of old saw the fleet-footed Fianti bound
In the strath of the west as they followed the hound.

List if you wish to hear a lay
Of gentle folks long passed away,
Of him who was Prince ; of Gulban's blue hill,
And sorrow-cursed Diarmid's sad legend of ill.

AUDIENCE.

Loved Ossian, sweetest voiced, what day
But sees us listeners to thy lay ?
Such strains from no birds of the shoreland can float,
Though dawn give each leaf in the woodland a note.

* Taken from "Leabhar na Feinne," and a prose version
written down from oral recitation by J. Dewar.

OSSIAN.

My own good king was hunting gone,
They whom no deerlike terror won,
His Feinne, through the secret glens followed, and we
Descended the slopes that lead down to the sea.

Then saw our own great king, whose word
The Feinne, the brave, obeying heard,
A nine folded shaving of wood brightly curled,
Shining white, as to seaward the swift waters swirled.

He grasped it, scanning it, the coil
Hid five feet and a span of soil;
Then loudly he cried, "Ah, Diarmid is here,
No swordsman of Cormac, but Diarmid is near!"

In truth, my own good king then swore
To break his fast and drink no more,
Until were unearthed the vile face of his foe,
If the caves of all Erin should refuge bestow.

Our hounds we sent, and shouting went
Where o'er the vales the branches bent;
The wild-cat we chased from the glens, that the cheer
And cries of our hunting might fall on his ear.

He who was never weak in fight
Heard the loud voices strike the height;
To Grinie he cried, "Though the hounds do not bay,
I wait not their voice, to the hunt I'll away."

GRINIE.

O Diarmid ! wait until they cry,
That hunting shout is but a lie,
Where grieves for his wife Cùall's son, there for thee
Thou know'st thy peril for ever must be.

DIARMID

Ere hounds can open on the scent,
To every chase my steps are bent,
And shame were it now for the king's evil will
To lose a good hunt as it sweeps o'er the hill.

OSSIAN.

Then down came Diarmid to the vale,
To the famed sons of Innisfail,
And glad was the king, for his foe in his sight
Came aidless and powerless to baffle his might.

Where o'er his red straths Gulban soars,
Were haunts well loved by savage boars,
And fine were the knolls on the blue mountain's face,
Where oft for King Fionn resounded the chase.

There Grinie's love brought her to shame,
'Twas there the king, with cheeks of flame,
Commanded the hunt, and 'twas there Diarmid stood
To watch for the boar if he broke from the wood.

Deceit a grievous evil wrought!
The monster's ear our tumult caught;
He moved in the glen, as from east and from west,
The shouting grew louder as nearer we pressed.

Envenomed, old, rage-filled, his jaw
Foamed as his eyes the heroes saw,
And faster he went, his strong bristles and mane
Erect, sharp as darts, strong as wood of the plain.

High reeds that fringed a marsh he found,—
Turned on the dogs all baying round,
And killed in a moment the bravest, and glared
As though to the combat their master he dared.

FIONN.

A huge old boar hastes yonder, mark
Of wounding full and bloodstains dark,
Now follow yourself, noble Diarmid, there goes
A monster of evil and terrible woes.

OSSIAN.

As quick his way the warrior took,
No trembling hand the javelin shook,
And hurrying fast as he closed with the boar
He rushed as in floodtide the wave to the shore.

Shot gleaming from white hand the spear,
Straight through the flank its path to shear,
But splintering there, left the head buried deep;
The shaft fell in three as it whirred o'er the steep.

The sword, the olden, he unsheathed
That victory in each battle breathed,
Then died the great beast on its blade's dripping length;
Unweakened, unharmed rose the youth in his strength.

But gloom the monarch's heart oppressed,
For from the hillside to the west,
He saw how fair Diarmid, unhurt by the tooth,
A conqueror stood in the beauty of youth.

*He saw the Feinne's loud wondering band,**
Deep-ringed around the carcass stand,
And heard as they praised the good courage and might
That vanquished so soon the grim beast in the fight.

But Diarmid went apart, lest he
To praise of self should listener be ;
That praise was to Conan's vile envy a sting,
Whose eye looked for gain to the hands of the king.

A dart in deadly poison dipped
Among the rough black hair he slipped,
And none could have seen where the bristles o'erlaid
The point firmly set of the venomous blade.

* The verses in italics are from the prose version received
from J. Dewar.

Then silent long, the king at last
Spake, all his thought to hatred cast,
"O Diarmid, now measure the Boar, snout to heel,
What length on the ground may the dark hide
  conceal?"

What man among the Feinne e'er saw
The youth from friend or foe withdraw?
He measured the back barefooted, and passed
Unharmed down the rugged spine, rigid and vast.

FIONN.

"O youth, whose weapons wound so sore,
I pray thee prove this yet once more,
Whate'er thou desirest I'll give thee, but see,
From foot to the snout what the measurement be?"

OSSIAN.

Again his sandals he unlaced,
And 'gainst the hair he slowly paced,
And bare was the foot where alone mortal harm
Could strike his limbs guarded by magic and charm.

There at one spot, life's crimson well
Was fenced by no enchanted spell.
Ah! if on that death-spot but one vein were rent,
How staunchless the flow of life's fountain unpent!

And fear was on him : as he stepped,
A keen pang through his senses swept,
For, pierced by the venomous bristle, his sight
Saw gloom shroud the mountain, and darkness the
    light.

Full soon the poison through his veins
Ran like a fire with fever's pains,
Then sank the bright locks of the warrior brave,
Whose face bore in anguish the hue of the grave.

His blood ran fast, as down a hill
From some high spring a slender rill ;
Ah, piteous it was on the brae to behold
How the guileless youth lay in his torture untold.

The cheek which shared the berry's hue
Which flushes red the hillside's dew,
Now blanched, was as cold as a cloud when it lies
Blue-shadowed at noon in the vault of the skies.

DIARMID.

A drink, one drink, O Fionn, give,
One cup to let me drink and live !
My blood flows so fast, give me drink from the spring,
Oft kind were thy words, the good words of a king !

FIONN.

No ! not one cup your lips shall drain,
To quench your thirst, to cool your pain !
What good is your life to me ? what has it won,
That the deed of one hour has not more than undone ?

DIARMID.

Not mine the wish to cause you care,
In East or West, not here or there !
But Grinie's the evil, when, captive, I found
Her love but a shadow, her word but a sound !

A drink, one drink, O Fionn, give,
One cup to let me drink and live !
My blood flows so fast, give me drink from the spring,
Oft kind were thy words, the good words of a king.

FIONN.

No cup of mine your lips shall drain
To quench your thirst, to cool your pain,
What good is your life, can its fair deeds o'erpower
The guilt of one act, and the curse of one hour ?

DIARMID.

If you could think of Sween's dread day —
No ! vain that memory passed away ! —

When fell the eight hundred and three, and my sword
In the narrow pass drank of their blood as it poured!

When prisoned in the Rowan Hold,
Of gratitude your words once told,
When the white teeth were wounding your limbs, and
    your breath
Came quick, for the fray brought you near unto death.

And yet again your friend was I
In Tara when the strife waxed high,
Not vainly you sought in that hour for a friend,
I fought for thee, king, making Enmity bend.

And Innse's sons, the three, the brave,
From lands far hidden by the wave:
I killed them for thee, who oppressest me sore;
Hard died they, O ruthless one, washed in their gore!

Remember Connell! see again
Carbúi front thee with his men,
To the host of the Feinne see how threatening their
    gaze:
Ah, Gulban, I burn, as I look on thy braes.

If known to Oigé's women fair
How snared and trapped I here despair,
Their mourning would rise, and their men would lament
The friend whose sad eyes on Ben Gulban are bent.

I, Diarmid of Newry named,
Of Connaught, of Béura famed—
Foster son to that Angus of Broá whose stride
Revealed the best man on the far mountain side :—

"The Eagle of the Red Cascade"—
"The blue-eyed Hawk whom no man stayed"—
They called me—"the strongest of all who could throw
The stone, or the spear, at our game or our foe."

Then knew he, as his strength grew less
That death would end his sore distress ;
The Feinne stood around, and they pitied the man
So weak, once the strongest who fought in their van.

They searched for water, and they found
A spring, clear-eyed, in mossy ground,
But cup had they none, and their hands, as they went,
Let fall every drop ere o'er Diarmid they bent.

In bitterness of soul he thought,
" They mock me, now that I am naught,
Your kind hands all leak ! of your deed men shall tell,
The ' spring of holed palms ' shall they name yonder well.

Yet would I ask you, now I die,
To lay me where the stream flows by
The water of Lunnan, for there in my grave
I'll hear, though I see not, its cold shining wave.

There place a pillar stone, and bear
My Grinie some day to me there,
And well to the traveller the words shall be known,
'Tis Diarmid who lies 'neath yon Pillar of Stone."

Oh woe is me! a foul swine's prey,
The victor lord of battle's day!
I faint, done to death, let me turn, let me lie
With my face to Ben Gulban, to see it, and die."—

OSSIAN.

In tears, and mourning sore,
Then to his grave we bore
That brave and hardy one;
On a green knoll alone,
Beneath a mighty stone
That sees the western sun.

When Grinie coming there,
At last of all aware,
Beheld his narrow bed;
As though her life took flight,
Bereft of sense and sight,
She fell, above the dead!

Then from her swoon awoke,
Her voice in cries outbroke,
And in this song of woe,

Wherein his praise was heard
In every mournful word,
Above the river's flow.

GRINIE.

Two in a fastness of rock were concealed,
Oft we lay there for a year unrevealed,
Though hidden from Fionn by the stream as it leapt,
Where it wet not the head of my love as he slept.

In the hunt's contest the keenest to share,
Hard was that bed for thy thick golden hair!
Never thought he of fear as he sprang to the cry,
When the chase was afoot, and he joined it, to die!

Hour of my torture, ochone, how the pain,
Sore, and sharp, as at first, smites again and again,
Sightless dear eyes, voiceless lips, and the breath
Sweet as honey, now lost in the chambers of death!

Sister's son of a king, a monarch high-placed,
Victor and friend, once with courtesy graced!
Ah what a generous heart to have nursed
Vengeance so causeless, a plot so accursed!

Diarmid, O Love, the best sword of them all,
Victory flew to the field at thy call;
Strongest arm in the games, thou wast ever the best,
Whether called to the fight, or to aid the distressed.

Bluer your eye than the blaeberry kissed
On the high mountain's shoulder by sun and by mist ;
Gentler your eyelids' soft motion, than where
The upland grass waves to the breezes of air.

Whiter your teeth than the blossoming spray
Danced in the winds 'mid the brightness of day ;
Never harp was so sweet, never bird-song above,
As the voice that is hushed on the lips of my love.

Like to the sun-nurtured sparkles of air
Were the fair yellow waves of the locks of thy hair,
Pure as foam the soft skin of the one of our race,
Who was mighty in mind as majestic in grace.

Sad is my heart, to no joy-shout replying,
Restless, lamenting in grief never-dying ;
Oh, the mavis calls sweetly in drear deserts lone,
But in vain I must yearn for the notes I have known.

Now shall my soul find its calm nevermore
In the depths—the blue depths—of your eyes as of
     yore,
Overborne by a perilous flood I shall know
Surcease of no sorrow, no lightening of woe.

Dark is your dwelling-place under the mould,
Narrow your frozen bed, songless and cold ;
Never morn shalt thou see, till the day of God's doom,
When awakened, O hero, thou'lt rise from the tomb.

K

Dead in the earth, and there hidden away,
Who shall not yearn for thee, fairer than day?
Be my blessing now thine, be it thine evermore,
Let it rest on the beauty 'twas mine to adore.

OSSIAN.

Each bard prepared his harp for singing
   That calm and lofty hero's praise ;
Deep sorrow through the long notes ringing,
   How wild their dirge, how sad their gaze !

THE BARDS.

Mayest thou be blessed, O thou our fairest
   Beloved, once to fortune dear,
If still for Ireland's Feinne thou carest,
   See how they wail thine absence here.

O strength, like flood on foemen pouring,
   Or swoop of eagle from the sky,
Or as the rush through ocean roaring
   When myriads from leviathan fly !

Béura's lord ! thy fair locks, waving
   Hath ceased, pressed down beneath the soil :
Thou'rt seen no more the billows braving,
   No more thou'lt know the hunter's toil.

When blows are rained thy blade no longer
  Shall strike where clear thy war cry rose,
O man, whose love than man's seemed stronger,
  Whose voice no more high Tara knows.

For thee our eyes are red with weeping,
  No beauty like to thine have we ;
Our solace gone, our best are keeping
  The death watch, bravest soul, with thee.

OSSIAN.

Yes, fallen all, to leave me living,
  A leafless tree decayed and grey,
Old oaks and young, their green life giving ;
  The strong must fall, the weak must stay !

Yet though to-day so frail, what glory
  Around my youth once shone of old !
Changed world ! this poor man, weak and hoary,
  Was great in war and rich in gold.

KING ARTHUR AND THE CAPTIVE MAIDEN.

(TRANSLATED FROM THE GAELIC.*)

KING Arthur on a journey went,
His men and he on hunting bent.

Came to the hill for victories known;
He, and Sir Balva, armed alone.

The King of Britain dreamed at night
Of fairest maid 'neath Heaven's light.

Her face's beauteous hues so clear
More than all gold to him were dear.

Yet all unknown where dwelt the maid,
His doubt and awe the search delayed.

For better were a battle stern
Than, blindly wandering, still to yearn.

* Taken down in Gaelic by Dewar.

Then spoke Sir Balva, kindly, meek,
" It is my wish this maid to seek.

Let me now take my Squire and hound,
And search until the maid be found."

Then seven weeks, with toil and pain,
We travelled wearily. the main.

No harbour gave our ship a home,
No land kept off the drifting foam.

But high above the rough sea wave,
We saw a smooth-walled castle brave.

Its gables shone with glass.   We laughed,
" Ah many a drink-horn there is quaffed."

Then sailing to its base there fell
A chain that lashed the ocean swell.

I seized it, fearless, hand o'er hand
I climbed upon the frowning land,

And seated on a golden chair,
I found a maiden wondrous fair,

Holding a mirror on her knee,
Her vesture beautiful to see.

I blest her, whose sad voice replied,
" Grief here thy blessing doth betide.

O comer from the sea, thou'lt feel
The heart of stone, the blade of steel."

Though merciless he be, yet know,
His sword can deal my heart no blow.

His love or hatred I despise
If gained the favour of thine eyes.

" The giant's star-white sword alone,"
Said she, " can wring from him a groan.

O hide thee in some place secure,
Or, gallant knight, thy death is sure."

Sir Balva heard the giant roar,
" What wave-thrown stranger climbed our shore ?"

Her voice replied, " Now come, nor wait,
My soul, for thee my love is great.

Put thou thy head upon my knee,
I'll sweetly play the harp to thee."

He rested, and a laugh displayed
The white teeth of the blue-eyed maid.

The wild harp-music sweetly rung,
And sweeter still her tuneful tongue.

And on his eyes, by sea winds fanned,
Sleep laid full soon his tranquil hand.

Then took they off his star-white sword
And slew the Castle's Giant Lord.

Thus how the captive maid was found,
Oft heard they of The Table Round.

SEANN ORAN GAILIC.[*]

Do reir beulaithris ann an linn Righ Artair bhi ann an Dun-
eidean, bha Triath urramach Eirinneach, a chuir tigh dìdean air
a chraig ris an abairte Aill-séid-chuan, agus ghoid e na braighde
rìomhfhinne uasal, agus thug e i do'n Dun a thog e air Aill-séid-
chuan, s bha e ga gleidh an sin na braighde.   Bha Righ Artair
latha anns a bheinn a sealg, luidh e a' leigeadh a sgìtheas dheth,
chaidil e agus bhruadair e air an rìmhfhinne a bha ann am braigh-
deanas, agus ghabh e toil a cuir saor, ach cha robh fios aige c'aite
an robh i.   Ghabh sir Bhalbha os laimh dol g'a h iarraidh na'm
faigheadh e long o'n Righ.   Thug an Righ long dh'a, agus sheol
sir Bhalbha gus gun d'fhuair e air thuileamus i, agus thug e
dh'ionnsaidh Righ Airteir i, agus b'ann do'n chùis chaidh an t
óran a leasas a dheanamh.

> Turus a chaidh Righ Arstair s a shluagh
> Gu tullach na'm buadh, a shealg ;
> Gun duine mar-ris an Righ
> Ach Sir Bhalbha, fo a lion arm.
> > Gun duine, &c.

> Chunnaic Righ Bhreatun s e na shuain
> An aon bhean a b'aillidh snuadh fo'n ghrein
> 'S b fhearr leis ro na bh'aige a dh'or
> An òg-bhean bhi aige fein.
> > 'S b fhearr leis, &c.

[*] The Gaelic spelt as by Dewar.

Ach b'fhearr leis tuiteam ann an sin
Le comhrag fir, mar bha e fein.
No dol a dh'iarraidh na mnà
S gun fhios aige cia an t'aite fo n ghréin.
   No dol a dh'iarraidh, &c.

Thubairt Sir Bhalbha suairce cuin,
'S e mo rùn dol a dh'iarraidh na mnà,
Theid mi fein mo ghille s mo chù
Nar triuir 'g a sireadh gun dàiL
   Theid mi fein, &c.

Seachd seachdainnean le strì
Bha sinn sgìth a sinbhal cuain
Gun chala gun talamh gun fhonn
Gun ionad amis an gabhadh an long tàmh.
   Gun chala gun, &c.

Chuannacas an iomall a chuain Ghairbh
Caisteal mór mìn-gheal ghuirm,
Uinneagan gloine air a stuagh
S bu lìon-mhor ann cuaich coirn.
   Uninneagan gloine, &c.

Air dhuinn bhi seoladh stigh ri bhun,
Chaidh slabhraidh a chuir a nuas ;
S roimh an t slabhraidh cha do ghabh-ar crith
Ach chaidhearurra na m'ruith suas.
   S roimh an t slabhraidh, &c.

Cuanna'cas an ighean eididh òg
Air cathair òir na suidhe a steach
Sgàthan gloine air a glùn,
S bheannaich-eam do a gnuis gheal.
Sgàthan gloine, &c.

Fhir a thainig oìrun o'n chuan
S truagh brìgh do bheannachadh ann.

.   .   .   .

Ged thigeadh am fear mor na m dhàil
Gun iochd gun bhàigh le a chlaidheamh cruaidh,
Air do ghuidh-se a bhean bhlath.
S coingeis leam a ghradh seach fhuath.
Air do ghuidh-se, &c.

Arm cha deargadh air an fhear,
Ach a chlaidheamh run-geal fein.
Agus is fhearr dhuit dol fo-chleith
Do aite air leith tearruinnt' o'n eug.
Agus is fhearr, &c.

Chaidh Sir Bhalbha fa-chleith
Agus a steach thainig am fear mor
Tha boladh an fhar-bhalaich a steach
Oirrinn iar teachd o thuinn na traigh.
Tha boladh an, &c.

Anamain, a sheircein, s a rùin
Is mor an gaol a thug mi dhuit,

Cuir thusa do cheann air mo ghlùin,
Agus seinnidh mi ciùin duit a chruit.
　　　Cuir thusa do, &c.

Chuir e a cheann air uchd an ighinn ùir,
Bu ghuirme sùil, s bu ghile deud,
S ge bu bhinn a sheinneadh i a chruit,
Bu bhinneadh an guth bha teachd o a beul.
　　　S ge bu bhinn, &c.

Air dhuinn bhi cuairteachadh na'n cuan
Chaidil e suain, na thruim sheamh fann,
S thug iad an claidheamh a chrios
S ghearr iad gun fhios d'dheth an ceann.
　　　S thug iad an, &c.

Ghoid iad a bhraighdeach s gu leir
S bha a bhean fein fo chumha thruim
Siod agaibh aithris mo sgeul
S mar a leugh iad am bòrd-cruinn.
　　　Siod agaibh, &c.

Latha do Righ Arstair s a shluagh
Bhi air Tullach na'm buadh, a shealg.
Gun duine mar-ris an Righ
Ach Bhalbha, fo lion arm.

DUNOLLY'S DAUGHTER.

Oʜ, dear to old Dunolly's heart
   His darling daughter seemed,
Yet when she fled, how pitiless
   His bitter curse was deemed.

To death he doomed her lover true,
   And swore his lowly blood
Should stain the land, whose soil would blush
   At wanton womanhood.

But leaves were thick, and woods were green,
   Where summer saw their love,
And none could tell Dunolly where
   Was nesting his wild dove.

Two years had sped, and all unchanged
   Dunolly's mood remained ;
When tired with hunting, late at eve
   A forest hut he gained.

A cheerful scene ! for hung on trees
  On either side the door
A stag and roe, and salmon there
  Lay strewn the hut before.

There pausing silently he heard
  Light laughter, O well known ;
And, looking through the wattled wall
  Stood motionless as stone.

He saw a happy woman lie
  Her true man's form beside ;
And laugh as on the bed they tossed
  A smiling child in pride.

No word Dunolly spoke, but went,
  An altered man, and said ;
" Go bring them home, for rich are they,
  Love shows them nobly wed."

THE ARMADA GUN.*

AN ancient cannon, finely cast
    Of bronze, all smooth and green with age,
    A by-gone actor on the stage,
Yet fit to take, as in the past
A role in war, and be the last
    Dread argument of kings !

The daisies grew around, and brought
    The homage of young spring to praise
    This stately relic of old days,
When France with Spain for mastery fought ;
And Philip over England sought
    To spread the Papal wings.

Initialed with King Francis' name,
    With Gallic lilies sculptured o'er,
    Above the vent the metal bore
A Salamander crowned, in flame ;
The massive breech could even claim
    A sheath of lotos bloom.

* This cannon was recovered in 1740 from the wreck of a
vessel of the Spanish Armada sunk in Tobermory Bay, and is
at Inveraray.

This goodly weapon, forged where Seine
　　By Fontainebleau and Paris flows,
　　And many a painted Palace shows
These emblems of the Valois' reign,
For centuries unseen has lain
　　Within the sea's dark tomb.

How came it there? A Spanish keel
　　One of the Great Armada gay,
　　Was blasted in Our Lady's Bay;
One of the Fleet the floods conceal,
Though o'er the waves was wont to peal
　　The thunder of their pride.

But how came France's lilies there
　　Beneath the flag of red and gold?
　　And o'er the ancient gun we told
The story which the legends bear,
How in defeat it bore its share
　　And stemmed the Victory's tide.

We thought the winds of hollow sound
　　Spoke from its mouth in solemn tone,
　　Of great events its life had known,
That thronged, as with the nearly drowned,
To recollection, ere it found
　　Beneath the sea a grave.

"'In flame I live, I quench its glow;'
    This motto at the foundry fire
    Was given me by his desire,
The king, whose crest and lilies show
How love and valour could bestow
    Their favour on the brave.

" My form was fashioned in each part
    By him who wrought in gems and gold,
    Whose glory, trumpet-tongued, is told
In fearful wars, in peaceful Art,
Cellini of the ardent heart,
    And Benvenuto named !

" The silver-voiced and laughing crowd
    Of ladies praised his fair design
    And asked if on the German Rhine,
Or English coasts of fog and cloud,
Would soon be heard my challenge loud
    For rights our country claimed ?

" To conquer fair Milan I threw
    My shot against the Swiss array
    On Marignano's dreadful day :
On sledges hardy soldiers drew
My weight through snows, where eagles knew
    Alone the Alpine way.

" And warring for the emperor's crown,
    I saw around me fall and die
    The noblest of our chivalry:
When peerless Bayard's high renown
Quenched not his blood, that streaming down
    Fell on me where I lay.

" Pavia felt my iron hail,
    When traitor Bourbon won the fight,
    Yet glad was I no foreign knight
Alone had made our siege to fail,
When wrote our king the dismal tale,
    'Save honour all is lost!'

" The impious victor hurled my fire
    Against the walls of holy Rome,
    But there the devil took him home!
For at the storm my artist sire,
Cellini, felled him, for the ire
    Of God his path had crossed.

" To nobler masters still a slave,
    I felt the fame of Doria mine;
    Saw Venice o'er her channels shine;
Pursued the Moslem on the wave,
And shattered them, when victory gave
    Her palm to Malta's isle.

L

" When Naples sent her ships to swell
  The swarming armaments that bore
  'Gainst England from each southern shore
In fleets whose numbers none could tell;
I saw how Drake upon us fell,
  How fortune ceased to smile.

" For tempests gathered o'er our track,
  The little English hornets stung,
  My heavy shot against them flung
Passed o'er their barks, so swift to tack,
And every ball they gave us back
  Upon our galleons told.

" Soon drifting o'er the Northern main
  Grey shores unknown were quickly past;
  Our consorts on the rocks were cast,
It was our fate alone to gain
The peaceful haven where MacLaine
  Set fire unto our hold.

I sank: a hundred years past by,
  And diving bells with searchers keen
  For treasure in the wreck were seen.
They took the gold, but let me lie
To sleep another century,
  Then raised and brought me here.

  . . . . . .

"Valois is dead, and Bourbon's Line
    No longer fills my country's throne .
    But death dear France shall never own !
Once more of late her joy was mine,
Once more for her my flames could shine,
    My thunder echo clear.

" For when the tide of battle rolled
    Against the far Crimean shore,
    And France and Britain downward bore
The Russian in his chosen hold,
-My last salute of victory told
    For France, as oft of yore !"

CAVALRY CHARGE—KÖNIGGRÄTZ.

We stood, as the helmeted horsemen
    Formed up in the light of the sun ;
We knelt, stretching bayonets towards them
    As they charged, ere the battle was won.

I marked their young leader apparelled
    As daintily as for parade,
A cigarette smoking, advancing
    He laughed, as he pointed his blade.

He played with his yellow moustaches,
    And looked on our ranks with a scorn
Such as mantles 'gainst mist and night-vapour
    On the brow of the Son of the morn.

He led a bright host where the glitter
    Of armour illumined the vale ;
As a flood rises slowly, so, coming,
    They rode with the sun on their mail.

Thus he steadied his men, and none wavered
   As the steeds settled down to their stride,
And we heard the first rush of the squadrons,
   Like the gathering roar of the tide.

Their order was perfect and splendid,
   And his voice, that at first held them in,
Had rung down their ranks for the onset,
   As though it were fate they should win.

I felt I half liked him as onward
   The lines of his cuirassiers came,
Like breakers wind-driven from seaward,
   Dark tossed in a whirlwind of flame.

I hated the shot that must enter
   That steel-girt and confident breast,
And quench that brave spirit for ever,
   That light on the cataract's crest.

But I gave forth the word, and our volley
   Rang clear o'er the thunder of feet
That rolled not to us, for Destruction
   Rejoiced their proud splendour to greet.

And the leader who laughed at our columns,
   At the ranks that bid gaiety die,
On his red bed of honour at even
   Lay smiling his scorn at the sky.

THE IRISH EMIGRANT.

1880.

Look not for me at eventide,
   I cannot come when work is done;
I go to wander far and wide,
   For 'tis not here that gold is won.
Perchance where'er I go, these hands
   May find me what I need to live;
Whate'er they win, if house, or lands,
   I'd yield for what they cannot give.

For who can turn away his face
   From home and kin and be at rest?
What country e'er can take the place
   That Ireland fills within my breast?
More kindly smile the distant skies,
   They say, beyond yon angry sea;
I know not what they mean, mine eyes
   Have never seen these frown on me.

To me these hills beside the wave
  With every year have dearer grown ;
Is it so great a thing to crave
  To call my native land, mine own ?
But why these useless plaints renew ?
  Farewell !   That word, it seems a knell !
If still I'm dear, kind hearts, to you,
  'Tis all I ask, Farewell, Farewell !

THE IRISH EMIGRANT.

1883.

"THEY sow in tears who reap in joy,"
    Was truly said of old ;
We wandered far, but round us still
    Stretched God Almighty's fold.

'Twas He who led us forth ; our grief
    Discerned His chastening hand,
And saw not, though before our eyes
    Shone bright His promised land.

O bless Him for the love that made
    The parting greeting sore,
But for the bold heart that He gave
    We bless our God yet more !

He gave us hope, He gave us strength ;
    For us His prairies smile,
The new world's untouched soils for us
    Spread boundless, mile on mile.

The richest heritage on earth
  For us His mercy saved ;
For ages Nature's harvests here
  Unknown, ungathered, waved.

Ours now the grain which decks the plains,
  Ours all their wondrous yield ;
Our children, and our kin possess
  Their own, in house and field.

What wonder then if many laugh,
  And wonder joy was dumb !
To friends in older lands with less
  Our happy hearts say " Come."

SONG.

OSBORNE, 1882.

Here Rose and Magnolia
Our dearest enshrine,
The prayer of the south wind
Is thine and is mine,
    For Child and for Mother
      Here sweetly twice isled,
     Brave Seamen are praying
     For Mother and Child.

Where State must surround them
Beneath the Great Keep,
And green oaks of Windsor
Shade River and Steep,
    For Child and Queen-Mother
     The choristers aisled,
    With armed men are chanting
     For Mother and Child.

Away where the Heather
  Blooms far o'er the Pine,
The Highlander's blessing
  Is mine and is thine,
    For Child and for Mother
      Beloved and mild;
    What heart does not bless them,
    Dear Mother and Child.

SONNET.

LORD F. DOUGLAS KILLED ON THE MATTERHORN,
SWITZERLAND, 1865.

Not home to land and kindred wast thou brought,
Nor laid 'mid trampled dead of battle won,—
Nor after long life filled with duty done
Was thine such death as thou thyself had'st sought !
No, sadder far, with horror overwrought
That end that gave to thee thy cruel grave
Deep in blue chasms of some glacier cave,
When Cervins perils thou, the first, had'st fought
And conquered, Douglas ! for in thee uprose
In boyhood e'en a nature noble, free,—
So gently brave with courtesy, that those
Old Douglas knights, the " flowers of Chivalry,"
Had joyed to see that in our times again
A link of gold had graced their ancient chain !

SADOWA.

JULY 1866.

WET, cheerless was our bivouac last eve, but still we
    spoke
Of fighting and of winning, to-morrow, when day broke:
That day the thundering echoes of cannon in our front
Had louder grown until around had raged the battle's
    brunt.
At last the carnage ended, and our regiment's retreat
Was marked by many wounded, who shrieked beneath
    our feet!
But here in closer order rides past a Lancer Troop—
They had but late been charging like falcons when they
    swoop.
How few there are remaining! Now the river's bank is
    gained;
The Trumpeter's white charger with blood on neck is
    stained.
His snowy flanks are heaving; he shudders on the
    brink,
Then, gently urged, he halts again, and stoops his head
    to drink.

He cannot ford the river, for lost are strength and
　　speed :
The Trumpeter, dismounted, now swims beside his
　　steed.
Together they have struggled ; he will not let him die,
And soon he stands beside him though the balls are
　　rushing by.
He takes him by the bridle ;—would lead him to the
　　town,—
Too late,—for life is ebbing,—the gallant steed is down !
Ah ! long I saw that horseman kneel by his charger's
　　head,
And when at last he left him, I knew the horse was dead.
How fiercely as he passes that comrade on the plain,
Remounted on the morrow, shall sound the " charge "
　　again !

ON A FOREIGN WAR SHIP'S SALUTE TO THE QUEEN'S STANDARD AT OSBORNE.

WITH their deep voice, monotonous and slow,
   The cannon's thunders roll along the sea ;
   But 'tis in reverence, and to work no woe
Those sounds here reach the shore and onward flee
Past the oak woods that climb the grassy lea,
   To strike thy terraces, and palace fair
   With stately salutation offered thee
   Who of these potent realms the crown dost wear.
So to the fabric of our future fame,
   Set in the green oak of our Empire's might :
Shall history's voice, with measured praise, proclaim
   Thy life-long love of justice and of right,
   And the good era that thy reign hath been,
   To hail thee, reverently, Victoria, Queen.

SPEECHES AND ADDRESSES.

*Some of the Speeches, and a few of the answers to
    Addresses, delivered during Lord Lorne's term
    of office in the Dominion, are printed in the
    following pages.*

On taking leave of his constituents in 1878, in a speech delivered at
Inveraray, Lord Lorne said :—

Judge of the wishes of our colonies, not from your
own point of view only, but from that of their interests
also, and from that of the well-being of the whole
Empire, whose glory and power is at once the best
result and the surest guarantee of the freedom which
is yours, and which the colonies inherit from you.
Many of you know well, because many of your
relations are settled there, the great British Colonies
of North America.   The Dominion now stretches
from ocean to ocean across that vast continent, em-
bracing lands of every nature—some valuable for
corn, some for pasture, for timber or for other treasures
which will in future centuries make the country one
of the richest on the earth—for coal and other minerals.
As your former member is about to join the number

of your friends who are already there, you will allow him to say a good word for those provinces of the Dominion, the threshold of which civilisation has already passed, and whose fair vacant chambers tempt the settler from the Old World to enter further and to occupy.

Some years ago, at a public meeting in Glasgow, I took the opportunity to describe the temptations offered by the Canadian Government to men employed in agriculture here to settle in Manitoba, and since that day, as before it, hundreds of happy homesteads have risen, and the energies of the Dominion have been directed towards the completion of that railway which will make Manitoba as accessible as is Inveraray. Now, let me again invite attention to this great Province and the vast territories beyond. In Argyleshire we have too few men, and we want more to settle with us, but Canada is a formidable competitor even to this fair country; and in other places, in the towns of this land, there are plenty of men who would do well, if they can hold the plough, to follow the gallant example of their countrymen who have added glory to Britain by forming another great British nation. Instead of leading an unhealthy city life, it were well that many of our townsmen should take to the life-giving work of a settler in the agricultural regions of Western Canada, where they are likely to live longer and to be happier than is the lot of the great majority of mankind.

On embarking at Liverpool in 1878 for Canada, Lord Lorne spoke
as follows in reply to an address presented by the Mayor of
that city :—

We shall not forget the attention we have received,
nor the great demonstration made by the people of.
Liverpool, of the interest entertained by them in the
good of Canada, and of the love borne by the whole
country for her children across the Atlantic. You
who dwell at this great port, and see so many leave
their native land for distant climes, will not misunder-
stand me when I say that we do not lightly leave you.
The heart is often sad at leaving home when the ship is
about to start and the anchor is being weighed, however
cheery the voices of those who raise it, and hearty the
farewell greetings of friends on shore. It is, however,
the duty of those who go, to look forward and not
back, and it is pleasant to think that across the water
we shall find ourselves among our own countrymen
and in our own country, among the same institutions
as those we know here and under the same flag. We
shall find the same laws and the same determination
to uphold and abide by them, the same love of liberty
as we have here, and the same ability to guard it in
honour and order, the same loyalty to the Throne
for the same cause, because it is the creation of free-
men, the bond of strength, and the symbol of the
unity and dignity of the British people. Where in
the British North American provinces we do not find
men of our own stock, we are fortunate in finding
those who descend from the noble French race—that

race whose gallantry we have for ages learnt to respect and to admire—the friendship of whose sons to the Empire and their co-operation in the public life of Canada, which is adorned by their presence, are justly held to be essential. Nowhere is loyalty more true and more firmly rooted than among the French Canadians, enjoying, as all do, the freedom of equal laws and the justice of constitutional rule. In conclusion, I will only say that nothing has struck me more than the enthusiasm manifested towards Canada among all classes of the community in England and Scotland, wherever I have of late had an opportunity of hearing any expression of the public mind. Crowds at any public gathering have always given cheers for Canada. The great gathering of to-day is a renewed symptom of the same favourable augury, for a good augury I hold it to be, that men in the old country are ready to call " Hurrah for Canada ! " On the other side of the ocean they are as ready to call " Hurrah for the old country ! " and these cries are no mere words of the lips, but come from the heart of great peoples. So long as the feelings which prompt these sayings endure —and endure, I believe they will—we may look forward with confidence to the future, and know that those bonds of affection which have been knit by God through the means of kinship and justice will not be sundered by disaster or weakened by time. (Great cheering.)

In reply to an address from the Liverpool Chamber of Commerce, which was read by Mr. W. B. Forwood, President of the Chamber, the Marquis said :—

You may well believe how highly I value the sentiments which have prompted you to come forward to-day with the address to which we have all just listened with interest, for Liverpool represents not only much of the trade of England, but much of the commerce of the world. It is perhaps the port more intimately connected than any in Europe with the American continent. It is between your quays and those of New York, that a steam service is conducted with the certainty and regularity which tells of the ablest seamanship, and it is by your river that the fine Canadian vessels of the Allan Line come, the magnificent representatives of the prospering mercantile marine of the Dominion, and proud may that country be of such a fleet. Your address shows how highly you value the friendship of the Canadian people, in what regard you hold their esteem, and with what interest and sympathy you watch the progress they are making. It seems to me but a short while ago since I last visited Canada ; but in twelve years there is a great change to be seen. Twelve years ago the British North American provinces were only isolated colonies, bound together by no Federal union, and lacking in the strength and deprived of the advantages of unity. Now the decrees of the Central Parliament at Ottawa are passed by the representatives of peoples whose mandates are obeyed through all that broad zone of productive land which crosses the

mighty continent, and the name of our Sovereign is
hailed with the same affection as before, but by no
mere collection of colonies, for we see a great Federal
people.   It is for their welfare that you, on behalf of
the merchants of Liverpool, express your just and confident hope; and the feelings of sympathy you have
shown will, I know, find a response on the other side
of the Atlantic.   I consider it of the highest value
that such a true expression of the affection entertained
by the great commercial centres of England should be
heard and known.   The sentiments which make the
hearts of the natives of these isles beat fast with the
just pride of nationality, when they see in far distant
countries the flag of St. George, St. Andrew, and St.
Patrick, is felt to the full by your colonists, who uphold
the flag as speaking to them of the great days of old
of which they, with us, are the heirs.   This common
loyalty to the Queen and pride in her ensign is a sure
guarantee for the continued greatness of our country.
You, gentlemen, have at heart the interests of commerce,
and, as merchants, the peace and prosperity of the
world.   There is no better hope for this than in the
unity between these kingdoms and the great dependencies of the Crown.   You know well how real that
unity is, and you will, I believe, join me in the confident expectation thật the eyes of men may long see,
beneath our Western sky, the bright apparition of Peace
speeding the beneficent navies of commerce as they
bear to all lands the fruits gathered from the great
harvest which is earned by industry and wisdom.

On passing Londonderry the representatives of the municipality
came on board "The Sarmatian," and in reply to the "God
speed" of the visitors, the Marquis of Lorne said :—

It is most cheering to receive from you the expression of your sympathy with our mission. We shall
feel, after seeing and hearing you, that we leave the
Irish shore bearing with us a precious message of good-
will given on the part of its people to their fellow-
subjects in Canada. The Dominion of Canada owes
much to Ireland. Who does not recall with gratitude
to the country that gave him birth, the rule of the late
Governor-General of Canada, the Earl of Dufferin?
Canada will never forget him, or fail to remember that
it was an Irish noble whose career has given her so
bright a page in her history. And from the Governors-
General, on through a long list of rulers whose presence was a benefit to the Dominion, we know also
that Canada is indebted to Ireland for many a hardy
agriculturist and many a clever artisan. It would be
difficult to speak of any part of our Empire which is
not in a similar case, and which does not point with
pride to the services of Irishmen, for on what field of
honour has the genius of the Irish race not contributed
to our power? on what path of victory has not an Irish
hand carried forward among the foremost the banner
of our union? It is under that ensign alone, of all in
the world, that an Irishman stands beneath the cross
of the Royal saint of Ireland, and each patriotic effort
made by a son of Erin adds another leaf to the wreath
of renown which, for so many centuries, has made the

piety and gallantry of the race a household word among the nations. In parting from you we shall not forget your kind words, and our visit to the neighbourhood of your city will always be a pleasant recollection. We thank you again, and ask you to convey to your fellow-townsmen the expression of our regret that circumstances have prevented us from receiving your address within their walls.

Arriving at Montreal, the Princess and Lord Lorne attended the " St. Andrew's Ball," and replying to Colonel Stevenson, who tendered the welcome of the committee, Lord Lorne said :—

Colonel Stevenson and Gentlemen, the Members of the St. Andrew's Society,—To me, I need hardly say, it is a great pleasure to find myself to-night among so many of my countrymen who hail from Scotland, and in saying this I am certain I shall have with me the sympathy of all Canadians of whatever race— English, French, or Irish. For all these nationalities wish you well. As for the English, it is impossible for them to feel anything but good-will, for they have as a people been so grateful for the last two centuries to Scotsmen for giving them a king, that they have ever since been only too happy to see Scotsmen getting their way everywhere. The French population shares in the goodwill felt towards you, for they remember that in the old days it was a Scotch regiment, the King's Bodyguard, which was the most popular corps at Paris, and that the French troops who guarded Edinburgh were there as the allies of Scotland. It is impossible for Irishmen to feel anything but the most cordial feeling of love for you, for what is Scotland but an Irish colony? But it is a colony of which Ireland, as a Mother Country, may well be proud. Gentlemen, as one bearing the name of one of the first of those old Irish colonists and civilisers of Scotland, I feel I have a right to be proud of the position taken by Scotsmen in Canada. We have had the good fortune since leaving England to be constantly under the guidance or tutelage of Scotsmen. The owner of the great line of steamships, in one of whose vessels we came here, is a distinguished Scotsman, well known to all in this hall. I am happy to say that the captain of our steamer was a Scotsman, the chief engineer was a Scotsman, and, best of all, the stewardess was a Scotswoman. Well, as soon as we landed we were met by a Scotch Commander-in-Chief and by a Scotch Prime Minister, who had succeeded a Prime Minister who is also a Scotsman. What wonder is it that Canada thrives when the only change in her future is that she falls from the hands of one Scotsman into that of another? Our countrymen are fond of metaphysical discussion, and are apt to seek for subtle reasons for the cause of things. Here it is unnecessary for them to do more in inquiring the reasons of the prosperity of the country, than to look around them and to note the number of their countrymen, and the existence of such societies with such chiefs as the St. Andrew's Society of Montreal. But it is time to put an end to such light discourse, and to proceed to the graver terpsichorean duties of the evening.

At Montreal, where a most cordial and memorable welcome was given, the following reply to the Mayor's address was made:—

TO HIS WORSHIP THE MAYOR, AND TO THE CITIZENS OF MONTREAL:—Mr. Mayor and Gentlemen,—In the name of our Queen I ask you to accept our thanks for your loyal and eloquent address. I need hardly say with what pleasure the Princess and I have listened to the courteous expressions with which we are now greeted—and for your most hearty and cordial welcome. We consider ourselves fortunate that so soon after our arrival in the Dominion, we have an opportunity of passing this great city; and while halting for a short time within its walls, on our journey to Ottawa, to make the acquaintance, at all events, of some among the community which represents so large and important a centre of population and industry. Your beautiful city sits, like a queen enthroned, by the great river whose water glides past in homage, bringing to her feet with the summer breezes the wealth of the world. It is the city of this continent perhaps the best known to the dwellers of the old country; and not only is it famous for the energy, activity, and prosperity of its citizens, but it is here that the gigantic undertaking of the Victoria Bridge has been successfully carried out; and the traveller in crossing the mighty stream feels, as he is borne high above it through the vast cavern, that such a viaduct is a worthy approach to your great emporium of commerce. Its iron girders and massive frame are worthy of the gigantic natural features around, and it stands, spanning the flowing sea, as firm and as strong as the sentiment of loyalty for her whose name it bears—a love which unites in more enduring bonds than any forged with the products of the quarry or the mine, the people of this Empire. It seems but a short time ago since the Prince of Wales struck the last rivet in yonder structure ; and yet what wonderful strides have been made in the progress of this country since that day ! Every year strikes a new rivet, and clenches with mighty hand that enduring work—that mighty fabric—the prosperity of the Dominion. Long may your progress in the beautiful arts and industries continue, and far be the day on which you may point to any marks but those which tell of the well-earned results of indomitable energy and determined perseverance. The people of this country may be well assured that the Earl of Dufferin has carried home with him ample proofs of the profound love Canada bears to the Mother Country, and these assurances have been conveyed by him personally to Her Majesty. We wish, in answering your address, to acknowledge the extreme loyalty exhibited by the French-Canadian populations, as well as the populations of the Maritime Provinces, through whose country we have, during the last two days, travelled, and to thank them once again, as we had the opportunity this morning, for the kindness shown toward us personally. This scene, the magnificent reception of your great city, we shall ever remember with pride and gratitude.

It is with the greatest satisfaction that I accept your loyal address, and hear in it those expressions of devotion to Her Majesty the Queen, which indicate the feelings which rise so truly in the hearts of every man, woman, and child in Canada, and which not only prove the natural impulses of all who enjoy the birthright of British citizens, but demonstrate the convictions of a people who, by the knowledge they have acquired of the political institutions of the world, cling with a tenacity and firmness never to be shaken, to the constitution which their fathers moulded, and under which they experience now the blessings of freedom and the tranquillity of order, beneath the sceptre of a Gracious Ruler, whose Throne is revered as the symbol of constitutional authority, and whose person is honoured as the representative of benignity and virtue. The attachment which binds the provinces of British North America to the British flag has never been more strikingly shown than during the past year; and we know that the readiness displayed to share the dangers and to partake of the triumphs of the Mother Country is no fleeting incident, but a sure sign that the people of this Empire are determined to show that they value, as a common heritage, the strength of union, and that the honour of the Sovereign will be upheld with equal loyalty by her subjects in every part of the globe. We have now traversed, in coming here, some parts of the important Provinces of the Dominion. In all places we have visited—and I regret it was not in our power, at this season of the year, to visit more—we have met with the same kindness and the same hearty cordiality. I can assure you we are deeply sensible of all that is conveyed in such a reception; and it has been, and will be, a pleasant duty to convey to the Sovereign a just description of the manner in which you have received her representative and her daughter. It is with a peculiar feeling of pride in the grandeur of this Dominion that I accept, on the part of the Queen, the welcome given to us at Ottawa, the capital of the greatest of the colonies of the Crown. It is here that we shall take up our abode among you, and the cordiality of your words makes me feel that which I have known since we landed: that it is to no foreign country that we come, but that we have only crossed the sea to find ourselves among our own people, and to be greeted by friends on coming to a home. In entering the house which you have assigned to the Governor-General, I shall personally regret the absence of the distinguished nobleman whom I have the honour to call my friend, and whose departure must have raised among you the sad feelings inseparable from the parting with one whose career here was one long triumph in the affection of the people. A thousand memories throughout the length and breadth of the land speak of Lord Dufferin. It needs with you no titular memorials, such as the names of streets and bridges, to commemorate the name of him who not only adorned all he touched, but, by his eloquence and his wisdom, proved of what incalculable advantage to the State it was to have in the representative of the Sovereign, one in whose nature judiciousness and impartiality, kindness, grace, and excellence were so blended that his advice was a boon equally to be desired by all, his approbation a prize to be coveted, and the words that came from his silver tongue, which always charmed and never hurt, treasures to be cherished.   I am confident that the land he served so well knew how to value his presence, and that you will always look upon his departure with a regret proportionate to the pleasure Ottawa experienced from his sojourn among you.   I am confident that we shall find with you a generous and kindly desire to judge well of our effort to fulfil your expectations, and although you speak of the recent growth of your city, and contrast it with places which have become famous in the world, I need not remind you that there is a special interest and significance in casting in our lot with those whose fortune it is not to inherit history but to make it.   I accept your expression of confidence, and promise that I shall do my best to deserve it.

The following is a report of the speech delivered by His Excellency the Governor-General, after distributing the prizes at the school entertainment in the Opera House, on Friday last, December 23, 1878.   His Excellency said :—

Ladies and Gentlemen, and my young friends, the pupils of the Public Schools, —Let me express to you the pleasure I feel in being with you to-night, in being able to wish you all a merry Christmas and a happy New Year, and in having an opportunity of giving to the successful candidates for honours the prizes which they have so well won in the competitions which have taken place. I congratulate them upon their laurels, and I wish, after handing to them the proof of their success, to say to them how fortunate I consider them to be, in that their lot has been cast in a land where education is so much prized, and where, both in the Public Schools and in the Separate Schools, it is so well known how to give effect to the value set by all the community upon the thorough and universal training of the youth of the country. I have heard men who have come from England and from Scotland say, on learning of the manner in which schools are sown broadcast in Ontario, and on understanding the system of education adopted here, and the nature of the tuition given, " I wish that I in my time had had only the tenth part of the schooling which is given to the boys and girls in Canada." Let me tell you what lately brought home to my mind, in the most striking way, the consideration and care the Canadians bestow upon their schools. At the great Paris Exhibition this year, where the things in which each nation took an especial pride were paraded before the eyes of the world, the space allotted to Canada was largely occupied with the books, the atlases, and the furniture of all kinds used here in the schools, while no other country seemed to have thought of exhibiting anything of the kind. It was remarked how wise it was of this young country to show these things, for it told the world that she does not only invite to her fair and untilled lands the self-reliant and honest among the crowded populations of Europe, but it told how well the sons of the emigrant, as well as of the resident, were cared for, and educated in the Provinces of the Dominion. I am afraid that with many of the books shown at Paris, our young friends are much better acquainted than many of us, their elders, can now pretend to be ; and I am sure that many of the clever young Canadians whom you see before you, could give us, whose learning has become rusty, many a bit of knowledge which might still stand us in good stead. The exhibition at Paris from your schools filled up what some said was a blank, namely, the absence of any of the fruits of your wonderful harvests, and of any machinery from Canada. It was said, I remember, that the fruit could not be carried, but perhaps it was owing to a wish not to wound the susceptibilities of the Old World that none of the beautiful products of your orchards were there, and because you did not wish that any of your modest-looking but unapproachable *pommes grises,* or blushing and splendid Pippin apples, should appear in the character of apples of discord. It may have been owing to the same wish not to excite unduly and unnecessarily the envy of others, that no machinery was exhibited from Canada, and that while other nations were making the great building resound and vibrate to the whirr of wheels driven by steam ; you did not, even by so much as a picture, remind the Parisians of your wealth in water power as well as in steam, and there was nothing to show the citizen of London or of Paris, who supposes the Thames or the Seine to be the greatest streams on earth, why he should be ashamed of himself if he could but look upon the Ottawa or the St. Lawrence. But the school display made up for any blank, and under the shadow of the magnificent Canadian lumber trophy which adorned the palace, reaching to the roof, and which demonstrated the wealth of your forests, were the implements you use for the cultivation of your greatest treasure—the ready brains and quick intelligence of your youth. I am glad to meet some of those to-night for whom all that preparation is made; and first, I would say to those who have not this year been among the prize winners, that I shall hope to see some of their names in the opposite category another year. "Better luck next time" is a good saying, but "Never say die" is perhaps a better. Try again, and yet again, and you will succeed. Many a man begins, and has begun in all times of the world, at the first rung of the ladder, who finds himself, if he will only give his own gifts their due, at the top at the end. I do not know that I need recommend to you that most delightful book of history, "The Tales of a Grandfather," written by Sir Walter Scott. He describes, as few can, the despair of the Scottish king, who lay, tired to death, and pondering whether he should or should not try again the apparently hopeless task to deliver his country from her strong and terrible enemies; and how a spider, spinning her web in the rafters over his head, was seen by him to fail again and again, and yet

again, until eight times she had endeavoured to fix a
thread, and eight times she had found the space too
great to span; and how he said within himself, "If
she try again and fail, I too shall deem my task hopeless;" but the ninth time the attempt was made and
did not fail, and I need not pursue the story further,
or tell you how Scotsmen look back, through more
than five centuries, on the resolve then taken by Bruce
with feelings of gratitude and pride which can never
fade and die.   But there are other cases of men who
had become famous for their ability to do that which
at first seemed impossible.   Let me mention one (to
come down to our own times) because his name is
widely known and honoured as one of the greatest
financiers of our day.   I allude to Mr. Gladstone, who,
as you know, was the last Prime Minister in Great
Britain and was acknowledged by both parties in the
State to be one of the best Finance Ministers who
ever presided over the National Exchequer.   When
Mr. Gladstone was a young man, and was about to go
to the university (as several of you are about now to
leave school for college), he told his father that there
was one branch of learning in which he must not expect his son to distinguish himself, and that was in
mathematics, as he had no turn for figures.   He went
to the university, and he came out as what is called a
"double first," that is, he proved himself to have become as superior to others in mathematics as in the
classical studies, and took first honours in both.   I
need not tell you here, in this free and happy country,
that it is quite unnecessary for any one to have any

artificial advantage in getting to the head of a profession. Industry will find a way, here perhaps more easily than in the old country, though there it is open to all to rise to the highest places. I will only cite one other instance of remarkable success, because it is within my knowledge. It is the case of a man who was one of the greatest shipbuilders on the Clyde, and who built, among many other vessels, the splendid war-ship, the *Black Prince*, which was lately at Halifax, under command of one of the Queen's sons, the Duke of Edinburgh. The builder of that vessel died lately, one of the wealthiest and most successful of Glasgow's great shipbuilders, and had furnished more fine vessels to the mercantile and war marine of Great Britain than perhaps any one in his time, for he lived to a good old age. His fortune was made by his own strong hand, good head and honest heart. His name was Robert Napier, and I cannot wish you a better career than his, or that you should seek your fortune with greater uprightness and courage. I heartily wish continued success to you who have received prizes this evening. Allow me to hint to you that you must not relax your exertions. If I may use the metaphor, you have learned to swim, but many a stroke is necessary before you can hope to reach your goal. Determine what your goal shall be, and strike out straight for it. You have a variety of pursuits in this country. Determine to be of use to the land which has given you birth. Determine to be a credit to it. Remember that you are Canadians, and remember what this means. It means that you belong to a people who

are loyal to their Queen, whom they reverence as one
of the most perfect of women, and as their Sovereign;
and who see in her the just ruler under whose impartial sway the various races, creeds, and nationalities of
this great Empire are bound together in happiness and
unity.   But to be loyal means even more than this.
It means that you are true to your duties to your fellow-countrymen, and that you will work with and for
all, for the common weal in brotherhood and tolerance.
It means, finally, that you will be true to your self-respect, that you will do nothing unworthy of the love
of your God, who made you in His image, and set you
in this fair land.   I believe that you will each and all
of you be loyal and true Canadians, that you will de-
vote your energies throughout your lives for the good
of your native province, and for the welfare of this
wide Dominion, and I feel in speaking to you that I
address those whose children will assuredly be the
fathers of a mighty nation.

During a visit to Kingston in 1879, the degree of Doctor of Laws of
    Queen's College was conferred upon the Governor-General, and
    an address was presented by the Trustees. His Excellency, in
    acknowledging the honour conferred, said :—

Mr. Chancellor, Principal Grant and Gentlemen,—
Believe me I am deeply sensible of the honour
you have conferred upon me by conferring on me the
degree of Doctor of Laws at this time and in this
place.   I say at this time, because it is a time in which
we have been sent here to represent her Majesty; and

at this place, because here I see represented every section, creed, and class of the great community of Canada. I accept the honour, if you will allow me to do so, not because I myself am worthy of it, for I feel deeply my own unworthiness, but as a recognition of the position which has been conferred upon me by the grace of the Sovereign. (Cheers.) I am glad that it has taken place here, because it has just been pointed out to me we are in front of that building in which formerly met the Parliament of Canada, and which, good building as it is, when compared with the great and handsome Parliament buildings now at Ottawa, gives a just impression of the progress and advancement made in a short while in this great country. The only personal claim I have to represent her Majesty in this country, is that I have had some experience in that great law-making assembly in Great Britain, her House of Commons. But here I occupy a position unknown in the constitution of foreign countries, as a political doctor, because whatever prescriptions I give must be such that they can hardly be visible to or appreciated by the public. (Laughter.) They must be written in invisible ink—(laughter)—and I can only give a prescription at all when I meet with other physicians in consultation; and any remedy given must be given, not by myself, although it may be administered by any others of those whom I meet in consultation. (Great laughter.) This is a peculiar position, and one which is totally incomprehensible to many foreign doctors. (Loud laughter.) But I am glad to see by your presence and by the kindness

of your reception to-day, and by the manner in which
you are working out your political destinies, that you
know the value and importance of such a position.
(Applause.) I thank you for the kindliness of your
reception, and I assure Mr. Chancellor and Principal,
that I shall always look back with pride and pleasure
to the day on which I received this academical distinction at the hands of the authorities of Queen's College.
(Loud cheering.)

In acknowledging the address he said :—

TO THE TRUSTEES OF THE UNIVERSITY OF QUEEN'S
COLLEGE :—Gentlemen,—I am much rejoiced at learning from you of the large number of students at present
attending the Queen's College, and hail this as a proof
that the high tone of the instruction here imparted, and
the excellence of all matters connected with the organisation and management of this seat of learning, have
challenged the attention and won the entire confidence
and approbation of the people of this part of the Province. I don't know whether a general holiday is the
best occasion on which to enter an abode of learning.
But you will agree with me that it is not only learning
which makes a man wise, but that his heart and his
affections have also something to do in the promotion
of wisdom. To-day your preparation for the future,
in the matter of labour in gathering knowledge, is laid
aside in order that you may let the heart speak and
show gratitude for the blessings you now enjoy, and

that your fathers have bequeathed to you in the liberty enjoyed under our gracious Queen, the best interpreter of the best constitution ever perfected by any nation. (Cheers.) We thank you in her name for the welcome accorded to us, and we identify ourselves with you in the satisfaction you must experience in the ceremonial of to-day, for in the achievement of the task of raising so large a sum of money, the inhabitants of Kingston show that they wish their children to follow the loyal, prudent footsteps of those who are proud of the name of this city, and are resolved that the next generation shall receive their instruction from no foreign hands, but at home. (Cheers.) Just as Kingston in former days knew how to defend herself and keep her own, so will you on the field of learning ensure that no ground gained by the genius, the labour and the science of former days be lost, but that, strong in the conquests of the past, your students may be free to undertake fresh work, and that each man for himself may advance on new paths of progress. (Loud cheers.)

Ladies and Gentlemen,—Now that the first stone of the new college has been laid, let me congratulate you who have met here on this auspicious day. My observations will not take much time, and shall be brief, because, with the best voice I can command, I fear it is perfectly impossible for me to make my utterances reach over so large an area and be audible to so great an audience as that I have the honour of seeing before me to-day. Indeed, if it were probable that some of those young men who are here as students would, in after life, have the honour of addressing so great a multitude of their fellow-countrymen, I should certainly advise the authorities of the college to erect a chair for teaching the art of elocution—(applause)—so that the volume of the voice might be increased to reach much further than I am afraid is possible for me to-day.   But let me join with you in wishing continued success to the Queen's College University at Kingston—(applause)—to associate myself with you in the hope that this new building will long stand as a monument to the generosity of the townspeople of this generation—(applause)—and to the talent of the architect who has designed so handsome and imposing a structure.   (Cheers.)   I shall not inflict upon you many observations upon the subject of education, for I know no ears to which such observations would sound more trite than those of the people of Ontario, who have shown by the ample and magnificent pro-vision which they have made for education in this province, how all-important they consider it is, that this growing population, extending as it is so rapidly, and being recruited from almost all quarters of the world, should receive a thorough and well-grounded training, and be well instructed in all learning and knowledge.   (Applause.)   I trust that this college may be a home of happy memories to all who shall receive their education here and who will go forth to spread its renown far and wide.   (Loud cheers.)   This place is already comparatively old, and I must consider this town of Kingston, which has already made its mark in the history of this country, as fortunate in possessing a university—for certainly by the possession of such an institution, one of those wants is supplied which is rather too apt to be visible in a new and enterprising country. (Applause.) Where many are rather apt to suppose that sufficient is done by a school education for the practical and rougher life, which is the lot of many here, I am sure that all present value the higher training to be alone obtained in a university. (Applause.) It would be superfluous to dwell upon the value of the completion and of the elaboration of education imparted by such an institution, for large as Canada is, the world is even larger—(applause)—and by such a higher training avenues are opened throughout every profession in England and her great dependencies, for there is no office in this vast Empire which is not open to Canadian talent. (Loud applause.) It is on this ground that I believe we can confidently appeal to the generosity of the wealthy, that generosity which is the mainspring of every institution in a free country. (Cheers.) It was in 1836 that it was said by those who founded the college, that "a deep and wide foundation had been laid, a foundation capable of extension," and I rejoice that now in the lifetime of the generation which has succeeded to that in which those words were spoken, there is so fair a promise of the completion of the work, and that those aspirations will be realised. (Applause.) And now let me mention one other bond of union between the students of this college and myself, and another cause of sympathy, for with your honoured and learned Prin-

cipal I have this bond of fellowship, that we were
both friends—and I may almost say pupils—of a great
preacher and a very beloved man, not the least of
whose merits in your eyes will be that it was owing to
his persuasion that your late Principal undertook the
charge of this college. (Loud cheers.) And I believe
it was also owing to his initiative that your present
Principal undertook a charge in Canada, an action
which ultimately led up to his present position where
he is honoured and revered by you all. I allude to
the late Rev. Norman Macleod. (Loud cheers.) And,
gentlemen, I have one other cause for feeling a fellowship with you, and that is, that I had the advantage
for sometime of being a student at a Scottish university,
and in very much I trace points of resemblance between
the system of your university and that which obtained
at home, and especially in this that, although founded
by a Scotchman, this institution of Queen's College is
one absolutely free and open to every denomination.
(Applause.) Indeed this institution is in its features
so much like the great universities at home, the great
University of Edinburgh, for example, to whose proportions I hope you will in course of time attain, that I
almost expect to see some gentleman make a proposal
which will fill the only serious want I detect in your
organisation, and that is, that there is no provision here
for a Celtic chair for the teaching of the Gaelic language.
I am sure that in this opinion all our Irish friends
will join, for what is a Highlander but an Irishman?
(Laughter and applause.) What is he but a banished
Irishman?—(renewed laughter)—speaking a language

which I am sure would be pronounced by the ancient Four Masters to be a mutilated form of the old Irish language. (Great laughter and cheers.) And now that I have mentioned Scottish students, I am sure you will not think that I am making any invidious comparison when I allude to the noble example I have seen set by them in the determination and energy with which I have known them prosecute their studies. (Hear, hear.) I have known at St. Andrew's men go up to the university so little able to afford the necessary money for their stay there, that they have apprenticed themselves to resident tradesmen in the town, and have risen at I do not know what hour of night or morning, and have gone through the whole of the manual labour necessary for their temporary profession—(loud applause)—and after this exhausting labour have attended throughout the day at their classes in the university and have managed there to take a high place with their fellow-students. (Loud applause.) I am sure you will not think I mention this because I imagine that anybody is not capable of the same effort, for although wealth is much more evenly divided here than it is in Scotland, I believe you are here animated by the same spirit. (Cheers.) I remember mention-ing the example of the Scottish students to a famous and learned professor of Cambridge, the late Professor Whewell, of Trinity, and he thought that an invidious comparison was intended, for he sharply replied to me, "Well, there is nothing to prevent you working here." (Great laughter.) This is not the way in which you will take my little story. I am sure there is not only nothing to prevent you working here, but that there is everything to make you do so, and I am confident the students here will take advantage of their opportunities, and do their best to make the name of a Canadian an honoured designation throughout the world.   (Loud and long-continued applause.)

At the Royal Military College, Kingston, the Governor-General attended the distribution of prizes, and, at the close, his Excellency rose and delivered the following speech :—

Gentlemen Cadets of the Royal Military College,— On the Princess's behalf I must first express her pleasure in giving you the prizes awarded for mental worth and also for physical exercises—(applause)— and I cannot say how much satisfaction I have had to-day in seeing the manœuvres so well executed during the very pretty little field day you have gone through, and in thoroughly examining into every part of this Institution, and seeing myself the place which, I believe, will hereafter be as famous in Canadian history as the training place of the officers in whom Canada puts her trust as is Woolwich in England, or the Academy at West Point, among our neighbours.   (Applause.)   In being here I confess I think your lines are cast in pleasant places, and it is well that it should be so, for to judge from my own experience when going through a course of training at Woolwich, it may be possible that in future years you will re-visit this scene of your early labours.   It is often the case that after some years' service, students of the military art find that owing to the constant progress made in military science, they have fallen a little behind, have perhaps become a little rusty, and have to go back for a time to drill. This may be the case here as well as in other armies, and if ever I have the pleasure in future years again of visiting Kingston, I may find some of the young and soldier-like body whom I have now the pleasure of addressing, again going through " repository " work as stout captains or as weighty majors—(laughter)—here again for a while to polish off any little rust that may have accumulated in their minds. It is certainly a matter of surprise to find what wonders have been accomplished by this school in a short time, and how under the able, energetic, and genial leadership of Col. Hewitt, and of the instructors, to whom you owe an uncommon debt of gratitude, for their work has been very hard, and like the British Infantry, they are excellent, but they are too few—(applause)—a school of arms has arisen which will bear comparison with some of the oldest of similar institutions in other countries. The good which has been done in this school is evident to all who visit it, and this is recognised by those who have not had that advantage, but who, hearing of your progress, and reposing, with good reason, confidence in the able board of officers who guide your studies, have afforded their support to an experiment which may be already pronounced a great success. It is not only one Province that is represented amongst you, but the Dominion at large, and we may look forward to having many from the gallant Province of Quebec—(applause)—whose famous military annals will, I am confident, should necessity arise, be repro-

duced in the actions of her sons. (Applause.) The life
that you have led in this place and the spirit of com-
radeship here engendered will be a bond of union for
our Canadian Dominion—(applause)—and many of
you when you leave this will feel for your Alma Mater
that sentiment of affection which Napoleon felt for St.
Cyr. May this Kingston Military Academy be a fruitful
mother of armed science—(applause)—and a source
of confidence and pride to her country. You will go
hence after your studies are completed as men well
skilled in many of those acquirements which may
be looked upon as wont to lead to success in civil
life; but above all, you will be officers to whom can
be entrusted with confidence the leadership of our
Canadian Militia. (Applause.) It will be your duty
to command those who are called out for service first
of all for the defence of your own homes; but I doubt
not that you will always remember that in belonging
to the Canadian Militia you belong to an auxiliary
force of the Imperial army, whose services are constantly illustrating anew, in distant and various climes,
and against every kind of foe, the qualities of the
British valour and the virtues which have made Britain
what she is. (Applause.) It may never be your fate
to have any share in war's convulsions, and you may
have no opportunity of doing what the Zulus would
call, "Washing your spears." Do not on that account
think that your time has been misspent, or regret the
preparation which is the best means of preventing any
disaster falling upon your country. The training you
have here received will certainly not only pay well in

giving you those habits of mind and knowledge which will be of advantage to you whatever line in life you pursue, but will help you to become good citizens, and will make you worthy representatives of that home army which is so essential for the defence of the land. It is the proud fortune of those who follow that profession, of which it has been finely said that "it is their trade to die," to know that by their life they not only foster those feelings of manliness and hardihood without which life is not worth having, but that it is also under their protecting arm that every profession pursues its even way, and arts and commerce flourish, and wealth increases in security. (Loud applause.)

On the 24th May 1879, after an interesting review at Montreal of a militia force, comprising one regiment of American Militia from New York State, a dinner was given at the Windsor Hotel, and, in reply to the toast of his health, the Governor-General rose and said :—

Gentlemen and Officers of the Canadian Militia,— Allow me to thank you from the depth of my heart for the extreme kindness of your reception, but you must allow me to ascribe that reception to my official position, for I am fully conscious that I have been too short a time among you to be able to do more than to claim your kindness and consideration. With the Princess it is different, and I believe I can claim for her personally a warmer feeling. (Tremendous applause.) I cannot tell you enough on her behalf of her feelings as to the manner in which she has been received by every section of the Canadian people. I am often asked how she likes this country, and I can only reply to the numerous inquirers by repeating what I have said to those who have asked personally, that although she likes this country very much, she likes the people a great deal better. (Great cheering.) I must not forget to thank Sir Edward Selby Smyth for the extreme cordiality with which he was so good as to propose this toast, and I can assure him that it is not only here amongst Canadian officers, but anywhere else, I should have been proud to hear from him the words he has used. (Cheers.) He has, I am sure, earned the gratitude of every militia regiment in Canada during the time that he has been here, and he speaks, I am sure, as your representative, with the full voice of your authority. (Renewed cheering.) He has held before your eyes a high standard, he has held that standard up with a most efficient hand, and I believe you thoroughly well know how valuable his services have been, and what an advantage it is to have an officer at the head of the Canadian militia who has had experience in active warfare. (Loud cheers.) The manner in which the manœuvres were performed to-day show how much value you have attached to his teaching—what full advantage you have taken of all the opportunities given to you. And while I am speaking on the subject of the review, allow me to congratulate you on having in your midst to-day, and forming so splendid a part of your spectacle, the gallant American regiment, many of whose officers I have the pleasure of seeing in this hall. (Great cheering.) I wish to repeat to them to-night what I had the honour of saying to the regiment at large, that I thank them most sincerely for having come this journey to honour our Queen's Birthday—(tremendous applause)—and I regard their having undertaken the journey, and having come here, as a proof of the amity of feeling and sentiment for us which is as strong in the breasts of the American people as is their community with us in that freedom in which we recognise our common heritage. (Cheering.) I believe I am not wrong in saying that they have paid us an unusual compliment in allowing their band to play our National Anthem, while a part of their musicians were arrayed in our national colour. Some of the band wore the Queen's colour, and I believe I am not misinterpreting the feelings of the officers here present when I say, that the very many Americans, not only those of British race, but many others, wear in one sense the Queen's colour at their hearts—(loud cheers and applause)—not only because she is the Queen of that old country with which so many of their most glorious memories are for ever identified,—that old country of which they are in their hearts as proud as I can honestly say England is of them,—but also because the Americans are a gallant nation, and love a good woman. (Great applause.) They have lent us a helping hand to-day, and I believe they will always be ready to do so, should occasion arise on which we may ask them to stand by us. (Tremendous cheering.) We have had a very pleasant day together, which has been followed by a restful evening and a pleasant dinner—pleasant to all, I venture to say—but restful only to those whose fate it has not been, when the dessert has been put upon the table, and the wine has been passed round, to be obliged, by making speeches, to "open fire" again. (Laughter and applause.) If an army could always depend upon having such a good commissariat as our little force has enjoyed to-day, it is my belief that field days would be even more popular than they are—(laughter)—and I doubt if the finances of any people, no matter how many changes they should make in their tariff, could long stand the expense. (Laughter.) But if nations are happier when there is no need for them to squander wealth, and spread sorrow and disaster by the maintenance of large forces kept on foot for purposes of offence; yet it will be generally conceded that no nation should be content without a numerous, an efficient, and well-organised defensive force. This Canada and the United States fortunately possess—(applause)—and the motto which was proposed by Lord Carlisle as that which the volunteer force of England should take, viz., "Defence, not defiance," is one which is equally suitable to our kindred peoples. At our review to-day we have had one of the few occasions on which it has been possible of late to bring a fair number of men together for united drill. Good drill requires constant attention and work, and I believe it has certainly been the opinion of the spectators of the force to-day, that officers and men have made the best use of the opportunities which have been given them. (Loud cheering.) Our militia force is large in number, and we have had during the last two years the best proof of the spirit with which it is animated. I should be neglecting an important duty were I not to take this opportunity of tendering the warmest thanks of Her Majesty, and of the Imperial authorities at home, to those gallant officers of the Canadian Militia Force who have of late so often offered themselves for service in active warfare—(cheers)—and to assure them that although it was not necessary to take advantage of their offers, that their readiness to serve has been none the less valued, noted, and appreciated, and that the patriotic spirit which binds together all branches of our Queen's army in whatever quarter of the globe they may stand, and from whatever race they may spring, is seen with pride and satisfaction. (Loud applause.) And, gentlemen, although the bearers of commissions in our militia service have not been able to show their devotion personally to their Sovereign and country among the lofty ranges of Afghanistan, or on the bush-covered slopes of Zululand, yet the news of the distant contests waged in these regions has, we know, been watched here with as close an interest, as intense and hearty a sympathy, as in Britain itself—(applause) ;—and the sorrow at the loss of such gallant officers as Northey and Weatherley—(tremendous cheering)—has been shared with our comrades in arms in the old country, not only because the same uniform is here worn, but also because the honoured dead are united with our people by ties of the closest relationship. The dividing seas have not sundered the brotherhood which the love of a gracious Sovereign, and the passion for freedom, make the lasting blessing

of the great English communities—(great cheering) ;—
and just as our country shows that she can strike from
the central power whenever menaced, so will her
children's States, wherever situated, respond to any
call made upon them, and prove that England's union
with the great colonies is none the less strong because
it depends on no parchment bonds or ancient legal
obligations, but derives its might from the warm attachment, the living pride in our Empire, and the freewill
offerings of her loving, her grateful, and her gallant
sons.   (Long continued cheering.)

The opening of an Art Institute at Montreal in 1879 gave occasion
to the following reply to an address :—

Ladies and Gentlemen,—This is the first occasion,
I believe, on which a large company, representing
much of the influence and wealth of this great city,
has met together in order formally to inaugurate the
opening of the buildings of an Art Institute.   Through
the kindness of the President and Vice-President, I
have already had an opportunity to-day to inspect the
works with which this city, through the munificence
of Mr. Gibb, has been endowed.   I think Montreal
can be honestly and warmly congratulated, not only
upon the possession of a collection which will go far
to make her Art Gallery one of the most notable of
her institutions, but on having succeeded in getting
possession of funds enough, at a time by no means
propitious, to give a home to this collection in the
Gallery in which we are assembled, and to have erected

a building large enough to exhibit to advantage many other pictures besides those belonging to the bequest. It is perhaps too customary that the speeches of one in my position should express an over-sanguine view of the hopes and aspirations of the various communities in the country, and I believe the utterances of a Governor-General may often be compared to the works of the great English painter, Turner, who, at all events in his late years, painted his pictures so that the whole of the canvas was illuminated and lost in a haze of azure and gold, which, if it could be called truthful to Nature, had, at all events, the effect of hiding much of what, if looked at too closely, might have been considered detrimental to the beauty of the scene. (Applause.) If I were disposed to accept the criticisms of some artists, I should be inclined to endorse the opinion I have heard expressed, that one of the few wants of this country is a proper appreciation and countenance of Art; but the meeting here to-day to inaugurate the reign of Art in Montreal enables me to disprove such an assertion, and to gild over with a golden hue more true than that of many of Turner's pictures this supposed spot upon the beauty of our Canadian atmosphere. Certainly in Toronto, here and elsewhere, gentlemen have already employed their brush to good effect. We may look forward to the time when the influence of such associations as yours may be expected to spread until we have here, what they formerly had in Italy, such a love of Art that, as was the case with the great painter Correggio, our Canadian artists may be allowed to wander over the land scot free of expense, because the hotel keepers will only be too happy to allow them to pay their bills by the painting of some small portrait, or of some sign for "mine host." (Laughter and applause.) Why should we not be able to point to a Canadian school of painting, for in the appreciation of many branches of art, and in proficiency in science, Canada may favourably compare with any country. Only the other day Mrs. Scott-Siddons told me that she found her Canadian audiences more enthusiastic and intelligent than any she had met. Our Dominion may claim that the voices of her daughters are as clear as her own serene skies; and who can deny that in music, Nature has been most ably assisted by Art, when from one of the noble educational establishments in the neighbourhood of this city, Mademoiselle Albani was sent forth to charm the critical audiences of Europe and America? Canada may hold her head high in the kindred fields of Science; for who is it who has been making the shares of every Gas Company in every city fall before the mere rumours of his genius but a native Canadian, Mr. Edison, the inventor of the electric light? In another branch of Art her science must also be conceded. In photography it cannot be denied that our people challenge the most able competition. (Applause.) I have heard it stated that one of the many causes of the gross ignorance which prevails abroad with reference to our beautiful climate, is owing to the persistence with which our photographers love to represent chiefly our winter scenes. But this has been so much the case, and these photographs excite so much admiration, that I hear that in the old country the practice has been imitated, so that if there may have been harm at first the very beauty of these productions has prevented its continuance, because they are no longer distinctively Canadian, and the ladies in the far more trying climates of Europe are also represented in furs by their photographers, so that this fashion is no longer a distinguishing characteristic of our photography; in proof of this I may mention that in a popular song which has obtained much vogue in London, the principal performer sings :—

> " I've been photographed like this,
> I've been photographed like that,
> I've been photographed in falling snow,
> In a long furry hat."

No doubt these winter photographs do give some of our friends in the old country the belief that it is the normal habit of young Canadian ladies to stand tranquilly in the deep snow, enjoying a temperature of 33° below zero—(laughter) ;—and it would certainly give a more correct idea of our weather were our Canadian ladies and gentlemen to be represented, not only in bright sunshine, but also amongst our beautiful forest glades in summer, wearing large Panama hats, and protected by mosquito veils ; but I suppose there are obstacles in the way, and that even photographers, like other mortals, find it difficult properly to catch the mosquitos. (Renewed laughter.) I think we can show we have good promise, not only of having an excellent local exhibition, but that we may in course of time look forward to the day when there may be a general Art Union in the country ; a Royal Academy whose exhibitions may be held each year in one of the capitals of our several Provinces ; an academy which may, like that of the old country, be able to insist that each of its members or associates should, on their election, paint for it a diploma picture ; an academy which shall be strong and wealthy enough to offer, as a prize to the most successful students of the year, money sufficient to enable them to pass some time in those European capitals where the masterpieces of ancient Art can be seen and studied. Even now, in the principal centres of population, you have shown that it is perfectly possible to have a beautiful and instructive exhibition ; for besides the pictures bequeathed to any city, it may always be attainable that an exhibition of pictures be had on loan, and that there be shown besides the productions in both oil and water-colour of the artists of the year. It may be said that in a country whose population is as yet incommensurate with its extent, people are too busy to toy with Art ; but, without alluding to the influence of Art on the mind, which has been so ably expressed in your address, in regard to its elevating and refining power, it would surely be a folly to ignore the value of beauty and design in manufactures ; and in other countries blessed with fewer resources than ours, and in times which, comparatively, certainly were barbarous, the works of artists have not only gained for them a livelihood, but have pleased and occupied some of the busiest men of the time, the artists finding in such men the encouragement and support that is necessary. Long ago in Ireland the beautiful arts of illumination and painting were carried on with such signal success that Celtic decoration, as shown in the beautiful knotted and foliated patterns that still grace so many of the tombstones and crosses of Ireland and of the west of Scotland, passed into England, and, more strangely, even into France. The great monarch, Charlemagne, was so enchanted with the designs and miniatures of an Irish monk, that he persuaded him to go to work at Paris, and for nearly two centuries afterwards the brilliant pages of French Bibles, Missals, and Books of Hours showed the influence of the culture, the talent, and the tastes of Erin. Surely here there should be opportunity and scope enough for the production of the works of the painter's hand. The ancient states of Italy, her cities and communities of the Middle Ages, were those who cherished most their native painters, and the names of many of those who covered the glowing canvases of Italy with immortal work are known often from the designation of some obscure township where they were born, and where they found their first generous recognition and support. Here in this great Province, full of the institutions and churches founded and built by the piety of past centuries, as well as by the men now living, there should be far more encouragement than in poorer countries of old for the decoration of our buildings, whether sacred or educational. The sacred subjects which moved the souls of the Italian, German, Flemish, and Spanish masters are eternal, and certainly have no lesser influence upon the minds and characters of our people. And if legendary and sacred Art be not attempted, what a wealth of subjects is still left you,—if you leave the realm of imagination and go to that of the Nature which you see living and moving around you, what a choice is still presented. The features of brave, able, and distinguished men of your own land, of its fair women ; and in the scenery of your country, the magnificent wealth of water of its great streams ; in the foaming rush of their cascades, overhung by the mighty pines or branching maples, and skirted with the scented cedar copses ; in the fertility of your farms, not only here, but throughout Ontario also ; or in the sterile and savage rock scenery of the Saguenay—in such subjects there is ample material, and I doubt not that our artists will in due time benefit this country by making her natural resources and the beauty of her landscapes as well known as are the picturesque districts of Europe, and that we shall have a school here worthy of our dearly loved Dominion. It now only remains for me to declare this gallery open, and to hope that the labours of the gentlemen who have carried out this excellent design will be rewarded by the appreciation of a grateful public.

In June 1879, his first visit was paid to Quebec, and the answer to the Mayor's greeting is given below :—

Au Maire et à la Corporation de la Cité de Québec :—Messieurs,—C'est avec le plus profond sentiment de plaisir que nous nous trouvons au milieu de la population de Québec, et que nous entendons, des personnes autorisées à parler de la part de cette ancienne et fameuse cité, les mots de loyauté et l'assurance de dévouement exprimés dans votre adresse, et je vous prie de transmettre aux différentes institutions et sociétés que vous représentez ma reconnaissance de la cordiale et bienveillante réception qui nous a été offerte aujourd'hui.

La loyauté est une fleur précieuse qui ne se fane et ne se flétrit pas facilement, s'il lui est seulement donné de croître à l'air frais de la liberté. Elle fleurira ici aussi longtemps que le Canada existera, et sera chérie, comme aux anciens jours, le furent les lis-d'or, pour lesquels tant de vos ancêtres versèrent si noblement leur sang.

Comme représentant de la reine, permettez-moi de vous dire que sa majesté est assurée de la loyauté et du dévouement de ses sujets de la province de Québec, qu'ils soient issus de pères venant des Iles Britanniques, ou que l'ancienne France les réclame comme soutenant, dans un nouveau monde, l'honneur, le renom, la bravoure et la fidélité au souverain et au pays, qui distinguèrent leurs ancêtres.

J'exprime ces sentiments dans ce beau langage qui, dans tant de pays et durant des siècles, fut regardé comme le type de l'expression concise et nette et le plus habile interprète de l'esprit et de la pensée humaine.

Le monde entier en l'employant, se rappelle avec vous que c'est la langue qui, dans l'eglise, se répandit avec éloquence des lèvres de Saint Bernard et de Bossuet ; et qui, avec Saint Louis, Du Guesclin et l'héroïque Pucelle d'Orléans, résonna sur les champs de bataille.

Cette place sera toujours identifiée avec la race glorieuse qui produisit ces grandes âmes ; et cette cité, placée comme elle l'est, sur un des sites les plus imposants du monde, semble digne de ceux dont le langage est parlé dans tout l'ancien Canada, et qui couronnèrent de demeures civilisées le rocher élevé qui est aujourd'hui le Gibraltar de notre puissance.

Bien des changements se sont opérés depuis que la première flotte européenne jeta l'ancre sur les bords du Saint-Laurent, mais aucun événement ne souilla jamais les glorieuses annales de cette forteresse, de cette place si chère à l'histoire.   Car ne fut-ce pas d'ici que jaillirent ces influences qui changèrent en riches habitations de nations puissantes, ces vastes déserts inconnus ?   Ne fut-ce pas de Québec que les paroles de foi, les impérissables richesses de la science et de la civilisation se répandirent à travers un nouveau continent ? C'est d'ici que les grandes rivières furent découvertes, et que les flots, devenant les grandes voies du commerce, furent forcés de partager le travail de l'homme.

Qu'y a-t-il d'étonnant à ce que vous chérissiez tant ces souvenirs, et que, de l'avis et avec l'assistance de Lord Dufferin, vous ayez résolu de faire tout ce qui est en votre pouvoir, non seulement pour conserver ce qui rappelle au voyageur vos jours de gloire, mais encore pour embellir le plus possible la précieuse relique qui vous a été léguée en votre charmante cité.

Les mesures que vous avez prises au sujet de l'embellissement de votre ville, mises au jour tout récemment, créées par votre générosité, et encouragées par l'esprit sympathique de votre dernier gouverneur-général, à qui aucun effort noble et généreux ne fit appel en vain, prouvent que vous ne permettrez jamais que l'intérêt et la beauté qui attirent tant de milliers de visiteurs, chaque année, vers votre cité, soient détruits par un utilitairianisme mal entendu ; mais que vous tiendrez à conserver en son intégrité le seul grand et antique monument de la grandeur du Canada, que ce pays possède.

En conclusion, permettez-moi de vous assurer que nous souhaitons sincèrement que vos vœux les plus ardents, quant à ce qui regarde l'accroissement du commerce de votre port, se réalisent, et que les eaux de la grande rivière qui coule au pied de votre promontoire puissent constament être couvertes des vaisseaux, superbes et solidement construits, que vos artisans peuvent produire avec tant d'habileté et en aussi grand nombre.

Personne ne désire ce résultat plus sincèrement que la princesse, que vous avez si gracieusement acclamée et qui se joint à moi pour vous exprimer mes sincères remerciements ; elle qui en venant ici, doit être regardée comme la représentante personnelle de notre reine issue de cette maison royale, qui reçut comme fiancée Henriette de France, fille du grand monarque français, dont une des gloires de son règne fut l'honneur qu'il rendit au voyageur illustre, l'intrépide Champlain, ce nom à jamais identifié avec tout ce qui nous entoure.

At Laval University he said :—

Monseigneur et Messieurs,—La rivalité à laquelle vous faites allusion dans votre éloquente et bienveillante adresse, et qui, dites vous, existe encore entre les sujets de sa majesté au Canada, ne devrait jamais s'éteindre surtout quand cette émulation a pour origine le désir d'obéir aux lois dans leur libre et juste application, et les nobles efforts d'un chacun pour placer chaque province au premier rang dans la représentation de notre pays et faire ainsi progresser le Canada dans la voie de l'ordre et de la prospérité.

De même que votre magnifique édifice domine votre cité, de même la pensée dominante de votre université est d'être le phare sur lequel se dirige le peuple dans l'espérance que cette émulation tendra à nous diriger vers de hautes et nobles destinées.

Nous entrons avec le plus profond intérêt dans ces salles où vous avez entrepris cette tâche glorieuse, et nous concourrons de tout cœur dans les souhaits que vous venez d'exprimer, dans le vœu que nous formons pour votre prospérité.

Nous nous sommes réjouis, en débarquant il y a deux jours, de voir que vos autorités, avec un si grand nombre de population, manifestaient de la manière la plus énergique et avec une noble générosité la confiance qu'ils avaient placé dans le représentant de leur souveraine.

Soyez persuadé que je comprends toute l'importance de cette confiance. Ce n'est pas à moi personnellement que ces témoignages s'adressent, mais au représentant d'un gouvernement assurant une liberté à laquelle on ne songe pas dans d'autre pays, et qui se trouve unie aux anciens usages et à l'autorité modérée sous laquelle le peuple de notre empire a trouvé le bonheur, la puissance et l'union.

Permettez-moi de vous remercier de votre bienveillante reception, et de vous dire que je désire avoir ma part de l'approbation que le public accorde à vos travaux, en continuant l'octroi des prix inauguré par Lord Dufferin, qui savait si bien apprécier la valeur de votre université, et qui, en sa qualité de savant, connaissait tout le prix de l'enseignement qu'on y donne.

Ici les élèves placés sous vos soins, reçoivent tous les jours une large part des connaissances que vous avez puisées à des sources précieuses dans diverses contrées du globe ; car les voyages sont aussi propres à instruire que les livres eux-mêmes, et parmi vos professeurs il y en a qui ont parcouru beaucoup de pays et vu beaucoup de peuples différents, et qui ont suivi en Amérique la pratique des fondateurs du Christianisme, en apprenant les langues étrangères, en voyant l'ancien monde, ses habitants, tout en s'initiant à sa littérature immortelle.

Les fondateurs de cette institution ont pourvu aux moyens de faire suivre des cours complets de médecine, qui jusqu'ici n'avaient été ouverts qu'à un petit nombre de personnes ; car dans votre institution la médecine s'enseigne d'après une méthode digne de la nation qui a produit Broussais, Bichat, Corvisart et Pinel.

Les sciences naturelles sont enseignées à des hommes qui, en prenant part au développement et aux découvertes des richesses naturelles de ce vaste continent, continueront l'œuvre de leurs ancêtres, les pionniers du Canada.

Cette partie de la puissance renferme des richesses naturelles encore inconnues et qui n'exigent que l'esprit d'entreprise pour leur exploitation.

C'est aussi un pays où l'or, les marbres précieux et les serpentines aideront á augmenter par leur valeur les revenus de la population qui doit neanmoins compter principalement sur la culture du sol et qui dans l'elevage des bestiaux augmentera sa prospérité en approvisionnant les marchés de l'Europe.

Je suis très-honoré de votre réception, et mon désir le plus sincère est que la Divine Providence permette que l'Université Laval soit toujours le flambeau des arts et des sciences pour la noble et généreuse population de Québec.

At Toronto during the same year the Governor-General had
occasion to speak as follows :—

Gentlemen,—In rising to return you my heartfelt thanks for the loyal and cordial manner in which you have received the toast of the health of the Queen's representative, I thank my learned and honourable friend on my left for the manner in which he has proposed that toast, and you, gentlemen, for the way in which you have been good enough to receive it. I knew that in a Canadian company that toast would be received with all honours, because I believe there is no nation in this world which has more profound love for its Sovereign than the Canadian people. (Loud cheers.) With reference to the Prince of Wales, to whose visit you have made allusion, I know that he was delighted, as was also the Duke of Connaught, with the visit they paid to Canada, and they have both expressed a confident hope that during my term of office they may revisit Canadian soil. (Loud cheering.) With regard to ourselves personally, I shall accept with gratitude everything that has fallen to-night from your eloquent lips, sir, with regard to the Princess, my wife. (Great cheering.) But as for myself, I must demur to the excessive kindness of some of your expressions; and although it may be a bold opinion for a layman to lay down in the presence of so many distinguished in the law, I believe my learned friend has almost for the first time—and I hope for the last—in his life departed from that attitude of strict impartiality which it is his duty, as well as my own, to maintain. (Great laughter and cheering.) I have a theory on the subject, of which I will let you into the secret. My honourable friend has confided to me that it was his painful duty to make some very severe observations from the Bench to-day. I think that it may be possibly owing to a natural reaction of feeling, that he has found it almost obligatory to make some observations in my favour to-night, almost too kind. (Loud laughter.) We have been delighted with the reception we have met with in Toronto, and I must say that it has been a matter of good fortune, in my opinion, that we have been able to visit this great city at a time when its citizens are occupied with the great show which is being held within a short distance of its limits, and which is a most remarkable exhibition to have been set on foot and carried out by any city. (Cheers.)   And in a few days we shall not only have had the pleasure of inspecting the exhibits, but of seeing some of the live stock which is now enjoying such favour not only in Canada, but also, luckily for Europe, over the water.   That examination will be for me one of peculiar interest.   I look forward to that trade developing a new and—as I trust it will be—a permanent source of revenue to this country.   (Cheers.) I see you have Landseer's pictures of " Peace " and " War " upon your walls.   I know of no more striking contrast that can be seen between peace and war than at Quebec, for instance, where under the frowning guns of that magnificent fortress the air is daily full of the lowing of cattle and bleating of sheep, and vast numbers are to be seen being embarked upon the large and fine vessels of the Allan Line for transport to Europe.   (Cheers.)   We may congratulate Canada not only that she has begun that trade, but that she has done so in so energetic a fashion, that though the shippers expected there would be but little traffic so late this year, the trade has been carried on with increasing volume throughout the autumn, and depend upon it, it will bring you good return, not only to the farmers already here, but by bringing more people to Canada. These people are the class you want, and I believe that for every few hundred cattle or sheep you send to Liverpool, you have every prospect of getting in exchange a stout English farmer.   (Loud cheers.)   Gentlemen,

I hardly expected that upon this, my first official visit, I should have had the opportunity of expressing my gratitude to the Toronto Club for entertaining me in so friendly a fashion at so pleasant a banquet. In meeting you here to-night, I feel I am in the presence of a representative assembly of those who lead the intellectual and commercial life of this city, one of the greatest already, and at the same time one of the most promising, not only in the Dominion but on the American continent. Before you, then, gentlemen, I wish I could find words warm enough to give you an idea of the manner in which we have been touched by the efforts made in our behalf by the citizens of Toronto. (Loud cheers.) It would not be reasonable to seek any justification of such kind feeling, but, at all events, I can say to you that, if a hearty and earnest interest in every phase of your national life can be taken as any excuse for such welcome, this justification, at all events, exists to the full. (Loud and prolonged cheering.) In one sense, also, I am no stranger to your affairs, for I do not feel that in studying Canada I have embarked on a sea hitherto unknown to me. It is not only since my arrival here that I have watched with unflagging enthusiasm the current of events which is so surely leading this country to the full enjoyment of a great inheritance, for long before we landed on your shores much of your history and of your present condition was well known to me. A brief visit, paid many years ago, could give me but little real insight into your condition, but every man in England who has had anything to do with

public life has, since the Confederation of the British
North American Provinces, considered his political
studies as wholly wanting if a pretty thorough knowledge of your resources and position were not included
in his survey of the Empire. (Cheers.) Confederation
has had this advantage, that your destinies have been
presided over by men who had weight and authority
at home, and who were able to put before the English
people, in attractive form, the resources of this country.
Especially was this the case during the six and a half
years Lord Dufferin has been in this country; for his
speeches, giving in so poetical a form, and with such
mastery of diction and such a grasp of comprehension,
an account of your material and political condition,
were universally read and universally admired. (Loud
cheers.)   Perhaps in former days, and before the
country had become one, so much attention would not
have been given to your affairs, but since Confederation we all know in England—every politician in England knows—that he is not to consider this country as
a small group of disconnected Colonies, but as a great
and consolidated people, growing in importance not
only year by year, but hour by hour. (Great cheering.)
You now form a people for whom the Colonial Office
and Foreign Office alike are desirous to act with the
utmost strength of the Empire in forwarding your interests; and in speaking through the Imperial Foreign
Office, it is impossible that you should not remember
that it is not only the voice of two, three, or four or five
millions, as the case may be, that you speak, but the voice
of a nation of over forty millions. (Great cheering.) As

I said before, I believe that in former days perhaps the interest was not so lively, although perhaps it would be unjust to say that too strongly, because within the last few months, as well as in past years, we have had striking examples of how willing Great Britain is to undertake warlike expenditure for colonies by no means as united or as important as Canada. (Prolonged cheers.) But the feeling with regard to Canada as a mere congeries of colonies, and Canada as one people and Government, may perhaps be compared to the different feelings that a mother may be supposed to have in the pride with which she may regard a nursery full of small infants, and the far different pride with which she looks upon the career and stature of her grown-up and eldest son. (Laughter and cheers.) To be sure, as it is with all sons and all mothers, little passing and temporary misconceptions may occasionally occur, and which only show how deep in reality is their mutual love. (Laughter.) The mother may sometimes think it sad that her child has forgotten some little teaching learnt on her knee, and that one or two of the son's opinions smack of foreign notions—she may think that some of his doings tend not only to injure her, but himself also and the world at large. (Great laughter.) Perhaps, sometimes, he thinks on his part that it is a pity old people cannot put themselves in the place of younger natures. (Uproarious laughter.) But if such is the tenor of the thought which may sometimes occupy the mother and the child, let no one dream for a moment that their affection has become less deep, or that true loyalty of nature is less felt. (Loud cheering.) They are one in heart and mind; they wish to remain so, and shall remain so; and I should like to see the man who would dare to come between them. (Tremendous cheering.) In saying this, gentlemen, I express what may be regarded as my first impressions of the feelings which animate you, and I believe that when I leave you, my last impressions will be identical. (Loud cheering.) And now, gentlemen, the topics on which a Governor-General may speak without offence are somewhat limited—(laughter)—although he is expected to be the advertiser-general of one of the largest countries in the world—(great laughter and applause)—an empire so large that the study of its proportions is, I think, much more like the study of astronomy than the study of geography. (Laughter and applause.) It is perhaps best that he should speak on generalities; but in making my first appearance among you I may be expected to record other general impressions. I may perhaps be permitted to mention a subject which is generally understood as giving a good opening for conversation and acquaintance, and likely to lead to no serious difference of opinion, namely, the subject of the weather. (Roars of laughter.) I can now speak with some authority upon that momentous topic—(laughter)—because I have now spent a winter, a spring, a summer, and part of an autumn in Canada, and I believe that any one who has had a similar experience with me will agree that the seasons and climate enjoyed here are singularly pleasant and salubrious. (Cheers.) You have, gentlemen, real seasons—there is a real winter and a real summer. (Loud laughter.) You are not troubled with shams in that respect—(laughter)—no shoddy manufactures of that nature are imported over here from Europe, where winter is often like a raw summer and summer like a wet winter. How different has been the reality of your winter, for as an old woman once wrote home to her friends in Scotland, "All the children here may run about in the snow without wetting their feet." (Great laughter and cheers.) We have only to look at that column on which a splendid bunch of peaches is hanging to see a summer trophy which should bring many to our door; but it is only a small sample of a vast crop of a similar nature which you have in Western Ontario, for as I am informed by my honourable friend on my right, Mr. Mackenzie, the peaches are often given to the pigs. (Great laughter.) The pleasant and bracing seasons of Canada can be enjoyed in a country without its equal, for nowhere has the settler a more varied range of choice in the scenery, the locality, the soil which will finally determine him where to found a home. His fortune may be compared to that of a man entering one of those new houses where each may have his own flat—a magnificent abode, where, if he wish not to travel far, to be easily reached and visited by his friends, he may remain in the rooms of the ground floor—our spacious Maritime Provinces, where he will find himself very near his fishmonger—(cheers and laughter)—close to the old tradesmen with whom he has dealt in Europe, and warmed by a great kitchen well furnished with a store of Pictou coal.

(Laughter and cheers.)   If he prefer other apartments he may ascend to those great and most comfortable rooms, our ancient and populous Provinces of Quebec and Ontario—the first-floor rooms of our Canadian mansion, which are so amply provided with the old-fashioned associations which he may love ; while, if still more active, he may select accommodation in the vast chambers of the second floor—the wonderful districts of the North-West, which have been so bountifully furnished by beneficent Nature, that he will require but little capital to make his abode exactly according to his own taste.   (Loud cheers.)   And if he prefers another and still more airy location—(laughter)—he may go on again and inhabit our recently erected and lofty storey of the Rocky Mountain District, near which he would again find an ample supply of coal, nearly as good as that which he found " down below."   (Applause.)   He will be none the less fortunate when he makes the acquaint-ance of the master of this modern mansion, when he finds that everything is ruled in order and prosperity by him, and that his name is the Canadian House of Commons.   (Loud applause.)   And now, dropping all fanciful metaphors, I must speak in more serious terms for a moment, and express my admiration for that most able House, the excellence of whose debates would be a credit to any assembly.   (Cheers.)   During its session I have sometimes been reminded of an exclamation of the late Baron Bunsen, the German diplomatist and author, whose residence in London as Prussian Ambassador at the Court of St. James's has caused him to be affectionately remembered in England.

Chevalier Bunsen, looking on at the proceedings of the House of Commons, said that to him it was a marvel how an Englishman could ever rest until he had sought to become a member of that Assembly, where the Ministers of the Sovereign, and they who endeavoured to win a share in the government of a powerful people, met face to face as champions of different policies to discuss before the country the principles which should guide a mighty nation. As in England, so here, let no one turn his back on political life as too hard, as bringing too much contention, or as occasioning too much unpleasantness. One of the worst signs of a country's condition is, when they who have leisure, or property, or social influence look upon public life as too dirty for them, and hang back from the honourable rivalry, allowing other hands to have a commanding share in government. (Hear, hear.) I am confident that this will not be the case here, and long may it be before a Canadian prefers his ease, if he may command it, to that noblest labour to which he can be called by the voice of his fellow-citizens, a share in the government of his country, in her Parliament. (Cheers.)

In striving to be a member of the Dominion Parliament, or to have a potent voice in the election of such a one, each man, whatever may be his circumstances, must feel that it is a high and proper ambition to do what in him lies to direct the policy of this Royal Commonwealth, which sees its will expressed by the Cabinet—which is but a Committee of the Parliament elected by the people—carried out loyally and fully by

the Executive head of the Government.   (Cheers.)
To be sure you may say to me, you are speaking in
ignorance—the Governor-General is not allowed to be
present at the debates of Parliament.   (Laughter.)
Certainly, gentlemen, I am not allowed to be present
and never have been.   (Renewed laughter.)   I have
never even followed the example of my eminent predecessor, who has left me such a heritage of speeches
at the Toronto Club.   (Laughter and applause.)   I
have followed his example in making a speech, but I
have not followed his example in another case, for I
am informed that he has heard debates of the House
concealed by the friendly shadows behind the Speaker's
chair.   (Loud cheers and laughter.)   I have never
placed myself in that position, and of course my knowledge is entirely derived from reports—of course I do
not speak of newspaper reports.   (Roars of laughter.)
That is quite impossible—(renewed laughter)—because
I am fully conscious that we should not put our trust
in printers—(great laughter)—but I speak of other
reports which are more trustworthy, and for which, of
course, my responsible Ministers are responsible.
(Laughter.)

I shall mention a particular rumour that has
reached my ears, which is to the scarcely credible
effect that the current of discussion is often not
quite so tranquil as might be assumed by outsiders,
looking only at the harmonious outline of the buildings in which the members meet.   (Great laughter.)
Perhaps the reported occasional quickening of the
political current, and the hurried words to which it gives

rise, occur only because pure panegyric is distasteful, and a wholesome criticism is on the other hand preferred.

Believing this, I shall only venture to express the opinion, that if any spoken words fly too swiftly it is because one bad habit, and one only, exists among the politicians of Canada. It is this—and I am sure you will realise the melancholy significance of the fact to which I am so reluctantly compelled to allude—it is, that Canadian politicians do not bring their wives with them to Ottawa. (Uproarious laughter.) I hope the recently developed doctrines of constitutional duty may still allow a Governor-General to take the initiative in making a suggestion, and my suggestion would be that the ladies should favour us with their presence at Ottawa, for I am certain that an alteration in this practice would soon put a stop to the reports to which I have drawn your attention, which some people may think may detract from the position of our celebrated, and alas! at Ottawa, too often celebate politicians. (Roars of laughter.) And now, gentlemen, I have only to thank you repeatedly and most earnestly for your welcome, and the citizens of Toronto I would thank, through you, at large for the extreme kindness with which they have been pleased to receive us. But I believe, gentlemen, it is not mere kindness that is shown by such demonstrations as those we have recently seen. If it were that only, it would perhaps lose some of its significance. In the display made we have seen the outpouring of the heart of a people whose loyal passion is strong for the unity which binds a great

History to a greater Present, and which, under the temperate sceptre of our beloved Queen, is leading Canada and Britain together in freedom to an assured and yet more glorious Future.   (Cheers.)

During a visit in 1879 to St. John, a city then suffering from the effects of a disastrous fire, he said :—

Although there may be temporary pressure, and partial failure in trade, not a year elapses that does not indicate progress made in the material welfare of the country as a whole.   The Dominion is steadily and surely rising in wealth, in unity of feeling, in all that makes a nation.   Our territories are enormous, and no one need travel far in any Province, but he will find new clearings and fresh settlements ; while land in abundance and of great excellence, as compared with much in the old country, can be had almost for the asking.

Throughout our greater Britain, and steadily and surely upon these our eastern coasts, the people increase from decade to decade, notwithstanding the great attractions offered by the prairie lands of the interior.   No one can look at the district you inhabit without feeling certain that this increase will continue. Impatient, restless, and ignorant of his true interests would that man be, indeed, who, under such circumstances, would not desire to tread in the steps of his fathers, to face, with British pluck and spirit, any difficulties that may arise ; and to rejoice that his lot has been cast in that Empire which has withstood every danger, whose might has been moulded by centuries, and whose flag has never waved over any people whose character has not been ennobled by the free institutions it represents.

In reply to an address of the City Corporation, he said :—

TO THE MAYOR, ALDERMEN AND COMMONALTY, ST. JOHN, NEW BRUNSWICK :—Mr. Mayor and Gentlemen,—The dignified and truthful words in which you recall the trials through which many of your ancestors passed in this country, now the happy home of their descendants, remind me how strong to-day among you is the feeling of the duty of patriotism—a duty, the fulfilment of which I rejoice to think is accompanied by no burden, but brings with it the enjoyment of much political advantage. We have found with pleasure that sufficient time has been at our disposal during this, the first year after our arrival in the Dominion, when there have been necessarily duties which have demanded attention at the capital and journeys to be undertaken in other parts—to allow us to return to those Maritime Provinces where we were first welcomed by a loyal people, and to visit St. John, which must be regarded as the commercial capital of even a wider district than is contained in New Brunswick itself.

Accept our thanks for meeting us here, on behalf of your city, and for the genial reception tendered to us. I should indeed have considered our first survey of our Dominion most incomplete had we been unable to stay awhile among you.

Much we have been unable to see; many places in which we should wish to spend some days, and where we might observe mining and other industries successfully followed, we must hope to visit another year. In St. John we arrive at once at one of the centres of life and activity on these our eastern coasts. We observe with the greatest satisfaction the evidences of the energy you bring to the aid of our common country, and the important place you fill in promoting the welfare of our Federation. The British people and foreign countries alike look upon the Dominion as our Empire's eldest son, in whose life and character the nature which has made the mother country stronger, the older it has grown, is seen and recognised by all. You are entering on a glorious manhood, which will, in future ages, stand forth in the beauty of strength and pride of freedom, to be known in history as asserting a place among the mighty of the earth.

The district is the scene of events wherein widely different actors have played their parts, and interesting, indeed, is the development of the story of which your harbour and town have been the theatre. Two centuries ago the adventurer only knew this place— his company stealing along the coast in small and battered craft, seeking a settlement, obliged to guard against the savages of the forest, yet full of visions of a great future for his new home, and endeavouring, almost in vain, to interest Europe in his schemes. But the years peopled the shores with sturdy colonists, who pushed their way, although held down by difficulties of transport, by distance from other settlements,

by wars of race and by mutual jealousies. Now we
see a land whose natural loveliness and fertility is
turned to the best account, connected with all the life
of Europe and America by countless channels of communication, and using the arts of modern civilisation
to make the utmost of its political and geographical
position.

In expressing to you our gratitude for the welcome
you now give us, accept our best wishes for your welfare, and let us utter a fervent hope that the energy here
exhibited, which no depression in trade can master,
and which even the ruin of fire has only been able,
temporarily, to affect, may receive full reward in the
future prosperity of your loyal and flourishing city.

During His Excellency's visit to Fredericton, the capital of the
Province of New Brunswick, he replied as follows to an
address :—

To the Mayor and City Council of the City
of Fredericton : — Mr. Mayor and Gentlemen,—
This is not the first time, as you remind me, that the
Queen's children have visited your people, and have
received at their hands the proofs of an affection
for our Sovereign which animates all Her Majesty's
subjects. The Queen has now reigned for a longer
period than has been vouchsafed to most of our
monarchs, over a prosperous and united nation, whose
strength has, during her life, been greatly increased
by development and consolidation of this her great
Dominion. Her Majesty possesses here the love of

Q

a people more numerous than was the English nation
when it achieved the glories which the trumpet of
fame, moved by Shakespeare's breath, made a household word among all nations.

In Canada, I am able to receive with pride testi-
monials of respect, reverence, and love for her rule, from
men whose Government represents a force, if population and material resources be taken into account, far
greater than that possessed of old by England, even in
those days which ring with the deeds of her heroes,
and have been called the "spacious times of great
Elizabeth."

And while we must look upon this country as
rapidly becoming one of the moving influences of
the world, we cannot forget what an advantageous
variety of position and power, within the sphere of the
Dominion, is possessed by the various Provinces. Here,
in the Province of which this city is the capital, you have
the great ocean and highways so near you that your
brave and hardy maritime population can furnish your
mercantile marine with many of the best sailors in
America. In the territory, comprised within your
limits, you occupy a central position through which
much of the land traffic of this part of the American
continent is likely to be conducted, and your climate
gives to all who cultivate your soil abundance of
agricultural resources in corn and pasture land.

It may not be unappropriate now, when you give
us your kindly and hospitable welcome to the capital
of your Province, to ask you to receive with our thanks
the expression of our hope that the members selected

as the representatives of the Province, and who assemble here, may be granted wisdom by the Most High to further the welfare and promote the best interests of a true and loyal people.

During this visit to New Brunswick, he said, in reply to the Warden and Members of the Municipality of Kings County :—

Gentlemen,—The duties connected with the high office with which I am honoured cannot indeed be considered to impose any heavy burdens, when their performance leads me to visit populations so kindly in their sympathies as are those of this Province, where we meet men always glad to testify their affection for the institutions under which they live by their reception of the representatives of the Queen. Perhaps in no other country in the world is it possible for the representative of any sovereign to travel for thousands of miles, and to be everywhere greeted with the same assurances of contentment with political condition and affection for the throne. I thank you, especially on the Princess's behalf, for the words you have spoken in reference to her. She will always associate herself gladly in anything tending to the welfare of the people of this Dominion. In so doing she will fulfil the wish of her father the Prince Consort, whose desire it was that his children should identify themselves with the interests of our Colonal Empire. I hear with gladness the assurance you give of the firm and unswerving loyalty of the people of the county of Kings, and I desire to tender to them my sincere thanks.

The first visit to Toronto took place in 1879. A loyal and kindly address having been read, His Excellency replied :—

Mr. Mayor and Gentlemen,— I remember well that the first time I saw Toronto was when, a good many years ago, the city was pointed out to me, where far off, over the waters its houses were visible from a spot not distant from Niagara. This first gave me an idea of the size and importance of your town. Men who were then with me told me that thirty or forty years before there would not only have been nothing visible at that distance, but only a very small settlement when viewed much nearer. But just as the city can be seen from afar, so is its position now so important that you cannot think of Ontario, wide as are its limits, or indeed of Canada itself, without seeing in the mind Toronto, the capital of our most populous Province. Here are combined things rarely found closely united, namely, great commercial prosperity with great literary activity. If you are proving that you can lead the way in commerce, it is as great a distinction that you can, by the ability of your literary men, do much towards guiding and influencing the thoughts of your fellow-citizens of the Dominion. I thank you for your loyal words in our Queen's name. They express the feeling I expected to find among you, but I must speak my grateful acknowledgments for the cordial manner in which you have given utterance to them. Adhesion to our Empire and love for its Sovereign I knew I should find ; but the character of this great reception, the magnificence of your preparations to welcome the representatives of the Sovereign, form a demonstration for which I confess I was not prepared. It has been our fortune to be kindly received by great communities, both in the old world and in the new; but I never returned my thanks with a more heartfelt gratitude than I do now to you, the citizens of Toronto, for the manner, at once so splendid and so sympathetic, in which you have been pleased to receive us. In December last, delegates from many of the towns of Ontario came to Ottawa to give us their greeting. Accompanying the addresses presented to us was an offering which, while it showed a feeling of personal regard, might well, I believe, serve as an emblem of the patriotism of Ontario. It was a wreath of that plant which in the old country loads the air with perfume wherever moss and mountain are most green with moisture. Reared among morasses, it grows only where around its roots the soil is firm; and where it springs, the foot may safely tread and securely stand. It was therefore, in olden days, taken as my clan's badge to signify a firm faith and steady trust, and with this signification I looked upon the wreath of marsh myrtle given to us on the part of so many communities in Ontario last December, as a fit emblem and just expression of that steady, firm, and faithful support which our Queen will ever find wherever a citizen of Ontario lives to assert his rights and freedom in up-holding the honour, the dignity, and the power of our united Empire.

To an address in German, presented in 1879 at Berlin, Ontario, the Governor-General answered :—

Meine Herren und Damen!—Die Prinzessin und ich finden es eine unserer angenehmsten Pflichten, Ihnen einen Besuch hier zu machen, um uns von der Fruchtbarkeit, welche Ihre Kolonie charakterisirt, zu überzeugen.

Wir freuen uns um so mehr, da Ihre Zuschrift uns in der lieben deutschen Sprache ein Willkommen sagt, und die Versicherung deutscher Treue aus deutschem Munde kommt.

Wir wissen, daß Sie als Zeichen der Gesinnung Ihrer deutschen Bevölkerung in Canada den Spruch, der seit Jahrhunderten dem Sächsischen Hause angehört:—„Treu und fest," als ihr Motto nehmen könnten.

Obgleich Sie uns in so treuer Weise empfangen, und der Königin Ihre Ehrerbietung beweisen, bleiben Sie dennoch gute Deutsche, und sind darauf stolz, daß Sie Ihre Kinder und Kindeskinder in der kräftigen Muttersprache erziehen können.

Die Liebe für das alte, deutsche Vaterland sollte nie aussterben; es verhindert jedoch nicht, daß Sie auch die englische Sprache benützen, die doch so sehr mit der deutschen verwandt ist.

Die schönen Worte, die der Poet Arndt geschrieben hat, sind Ihnen wohl alle bekannt und wir können sie hier, wo Sie ein anderes Land zu Ihrem Land gemacht haben, wohl gebrauchen:

> „Was ist des Deutschen Vaterland?
> Ist's Preußenland? Ist's Schwabenland?
> Ist's wo am Rhein die Rebe blüht?
> Ist's wo am Belt die Möve zieht?
> Doch Nein! Nein! Nein!
> Sein Vaterland muß größer sein!"

Kann man nicht hier diesen Worten eine weitere Deutung geben?—Können Sie nicht als Mitbürger und Gründer einer neuen Nation dieselbe mit allem Edlen, was von dem alten Lande kommt, lenken und stärken?

Es ist uns eine wahre Freude, von allen Seiten zu hören, wie man die deutschen Ansiedler achtet und schätzt und sie als einen wichtigen Zusatz zu unseren Kräften betrachtet. Ihre Wissenschaft, ihre Liebe für die gute Erziehung der Jugend, sowohl in höheren Studien, als in den Studien, durch welche die gewerblichen Fort=bildungsschulen in Deutschland sich einen so ruhmhaften Namen ge=macht haben; ihre Sparsamkeit und ihr Fleiß, sind Canada viele Tausend Quadratmeilen Landes werth.—Die häuslichen Tugenden ihrer Frauen und Töchter sind ein schönes Beispiel für Alle.

Ich hoffe, daß die Zahl deutscher Einwanderer sich mehren wird und werde in meinen Erwartungen dadurch bestärkt, daß es bei Ihnen daheim gewiß Viele giebt, die überzeugt sind, daß das Vaterland nicht geschwächt wird, wenn deutsche Töchter jen=seits des atlantischen Meeres gute Männer finden. Es wird uns sehr angenehm sein, der deutschen kaiserlichen Familie sagen zu können, wie Sie in Canada glücklich leben, und als Män=ner, die dem Lande Glück bringen, angesehen werden.

In 1880, it was resolved that an Agricultural and Industrial Exhi-bition, supported by a Federal grant, should each year be held at some city of the Dominion. The first of these central and national meetings took place at Ottawa. It was largely attended, and opened by the Governor-General with these remarks:—

Mr. President and Gentlemen,—I thank you for the address which you have read to me, expressing that deep loyalty to the Queen which, not merely from hearsay, but from observation of the sentiments which animate the people of Canada, whether in the cities or in the country, I know to be real and universal. The Princess joins with me in asking you to accept our gratitude for your recognition of the interest we feel in the great efforts at present made, in various parts of Canada, to display to the best advantage the industrial achievements of our artisans. Some of the handiwork of our two largest Provinces can be seen in this building, while others are not unrepresented; and we have evidence of the skill which graces the strength of a new brother—the young giant of the west.* Everywhere proof is given that the Canadian can hold his own in the rivalry that brings Art to bear on the great natural products around us, and this is not surprising when we know that he comes from the races which in Europe have been the most renowned for the taste, the ingenuity, and the solidity of their workmanship. Where so many regions have but recently been peopled, there is, it need hardly be said, much to be done, and it is most satisfactory to see how each city and town is bending itself to the task to prove that there is no laggard in the patriotic competition. I have gladly attended several of these shows, and it is a feature peculiar to this country that the industrial exhibition so generally accompanies the agricultural show. Whether this shall always be the case as in the gathering inaugurated to-day, it will be of course for you to determine by experience of success in your venture in thus combining them. This is, perhaps, the first meeting to which more than a local character has been given. It will be a matter for your consideration, and for all in Canada interested in your endeavours, whether a novel practice be established here in moving to each Province in succession the

* Manitoba.

Central Exhibition, without injury to the local fairs, which will, in any case, be held. If you decide to move the agricultural show from Province to Province in successive years, no new practice would thereby be espoused, for such has been the custom of the national societies of England, Scotland, and Ireland. In the old countries the spaces to be traversed are much smaller, but the need of comparison between the various exhibits is also much less. The local shows are held there in almost every county, but the advantage derived from the annual moving of the national societies has been well expressed in the words of a former and justly beloved Viceroy of Ireland, who said that the experience the National Society had earned for itself had, by its annual movement, been carried through every part of the land, through each Province in turn ; and this had tended to ruse together the knowledge of the best specialties of each, whether in tillage or in pasture, in cereals or in green crops, or in the breeding and fattening of cattle. With us in Canada, if a similar practice were followed, we might perhaps add that comparison would benefit the proper employment of the best agricultural machinery, for the manufacture of which our Canadian artisans have won high commendation at the greatest international contests. If you discuss these questions, I am sure you will do so, not with the view of benefiting one city or Province only, but in the spirit which sees in all common efforts a means of uniting our Canadian people, and an instrument to make a national feeling create a national prosperity. We may congratulate our countrymen that in the live stock of all kinds shown to-day, we have a representation of those vast resources which yield so much in excess of our own requirements that we can relieve the wants of older lands ; and how great is the difference between the bygone traffic from the new world to enrich Europe and what we now witness! In other days the southern seas were covered with the towering galleons of Spain, bringing the ingots of gold and silver, wrought in the mines of America through the cruel labour of thousands of enslaved Indians. This was the wealth which poured into the treasuries of a nation whose riches reared the colossal palaces of the Escorial, and the wondrous Minster of Seville. The creation of such prosperity meant a short-lived reign of luxury and cruelty—the lifting up of an old country for a time— the abasement of a new land. How different the happy and more lasting wealth with which we are able to endow Europe from Canada, when the parent land and the Dominion alike reap equal fruits from a bounteous harvest. Our treasure fleets are now laden with golden grain, and flocks and herds; with riches wrung from no servitude, but derived from the free and noble toil of a liberty-loving, independent, and self-reliant people. It is to the men who have cleared the tangled forests, or have tilled the prairie lands, that we owe such great shows of agricultural wealth as those we have lately seen, and which prove how rich and inexhaustible are the veins of ore from which we can give enough and to spare.

May the endeavour of such a society as this, assisted

as it has been chiefly by individual efforts, but countenanced by the Dominion Government, be to extend for the general good of our country, the experience it earns and whatever success is secured by the co-operation of the citizens.

[During the delivery of the address the gates had been opened and the people allowed to come in so as to hear His Excellency's reply, and at its close they gave hearty cheering.]

The first Exhibition of the Royal Canadian Academy of Art took place at Ottawa in 1880. The experiment of collecting together the work of artists resident in the country, was a success from the commencement, and the annual meetings since held have fully warranted the formation of a National Society for the Promotion of Art. The Governor-General gave the opening address as follows :—

Ladies and Gentlemen,—It is now my duty to declare this first exhibition of the Canadian Academy to be open to what, I am sure, will be an appreciative public. That this ceremony should take place to-day is characteristic of the energy with which any project likely to benefit our community is pushed in this country, for it is only ten months ago, on the occasion of the opening of the Local Art Gallery at Montreal, that the proposal for the institution of the Canadian Academy of Arts was made. To-day the Academy is to be congratulated not only upon being able to show the pictures and the works of art which you see around you this evening, but upon the favourable reception which the appearance of such an association has received from all classes. I have indeed seen nothing but the kindest criticism. Although I believe some gentlemen have been good enough to propose we should postpone the initiation of this institution for the present, and should wait for the short and moderate space of exactly 100 years, and look forward to its incorporation in the year of grace 1980. It is difficult to meet such gentle criticism, but the Academy may be allowed to suggest that although in the words of the old saying, " art is long-lived," yet that " life is short." Art will, no doubt, be in vigorous life in Canada a century hence, but, on the other hand, we must remember that at that time these gentle critics may have disappeared from the scene, and they will themselves allow that it is for the benefit of the Academy that it should begin its existence while still subject to their own friendly supervision. It is impossible to agree with the remark, that we have no material in Canada for our present purposes, when we see many excellent works on these walls ; and if some do not come up to the standard we may set ourselves, what is this but an additional argument for the creation of some association which shall act as an educator in these matters ? Now, gentlemen, what are the objects of your present effort ? A glance at the constitution of the Society will show your objects are declared to be : the encouragement of industrial Art by the promotion of excellence of design, the support of Schools of Art throughout the country, and the formation of a National Gallery of Art at the seat of Government. The first of these objects, the encouragement of good design, receives an illustration in a room which I hope all present will make it a point to visit—a room on the second floor, where many tasteful and good designs have been exhibited in competition for prizes generously given by several gentlemen, who recognise the good effect such competitions are likely to have upon trade. Many of the best of these designs have been called forth by a prize offered by a member of the Legislature, and it is to be sincerely hoped that in future years his example, and the example of those who have acted in a similar manner, may be more widely and generally followed. English manufacture, as you know, has become famous for its durability; French manufacture for its beauty and workmanship; and here, where we have a people sprung from both races, we should be able to combine these excellences, so that Canadian manufacture may hold a high place in the markets of the world. The next object of the association is to be worked out on the same lines by the support afforded the local schools; and here I must emphatically impress on all who care for the encouragement of Art in Canada, that however popular the Academy exhibitions may become, however much you are able to strengthen its hands in assisting provincial efforts, the assistance it gives to any provincial schools can only supplement, and can never stand in the place of, provincial effort. It is true that the gentlemen belonging to the Academy give half of all they possess—one half of any surplus in all their revenues—in aid of local efforts, but it is by no means likely that that amount will be great. As the exhibitions are to be held each year in a different city, so that each Province may in turn be visited, it will pro-

bably be found best that any donation which can be
made shall be given to that town in which the yearly
exhibition is held.   I hope, for instance, that this year
it may be possible to give a grant in aid of a local
school to be formed at Ottawa.   With regard to the
third object I have mentioned, the gentlemen who
have been appointed academicians have patriotically
undertaken, as a guarantee of their interest in the welfare of Art in Canada, that it shall be a condition of
their acceptance of the office of academician that they
shall give, each of them, a picture which shall become
national property, and be placed here in an Art gallery.
These works, of which you already have several around
you, will be at the disposal of one of the ministers,
who may be charged with this trust, and it will be in
his option to decide whether they shall be exhibited
in other parts of the country, or lent for purposes of
Art instruction for a time to local schools.   If you are
not tired of these subjects, I would ask your attention
for one moment to the organisation by which it is
proposed to accomplish these purposes.   First, There
are a certain number of gentlemen who, after the
model of similar institutions in other countries, where
the plan has been found to work well, have been
chosen as academicians.   These comprise not only
painters, but architects also, and designers, engravers,
and sculptors.   There are others again, forming a
wider circle, and following the same professions, who
have been chosen as associates, from whose ranks the
academicians in the future will be annually elected.
These gentlemen, the academicians, will govern the

institution.   They have already been supported by very many men in the country who follow other professions, and who will have nothing to do with the governing of the society, but who have been requested to join and give their aid as entertaining a love for Art, and a desire that Art should be enabled to assist in the most practical manner the interests of the country.   It is probable that almost every gentleman of note in Canada will be upon this roll.   So much, then, for the purposes undertaken, and the machinery by which these are to be accomplished.   One word only as to the part which, at the request of several gentlemen, I have ventured temporarily to undertake. It seemed difficult, if not impossible, to get the body as at present constituted elected at the start, for scattered as the artists of the Dominion are, few knew the capabilities of others outside of his own neighbourhood.   Following, as we will have to do here therefore, an English precedent, it was thought best that the first list should be a nominated one.   However carefully this has been attempted, some omissions and faults have been made, and these will be corrected, for the plan followed at the commencement will not be pursued hereafter, but at a general meeting held during the time of the exhibitions, elections will form part of the business of the assembly.   Although it may be for the interests of the Academy that the Governor-General of the day should be the patron of the society, you will find that the more self-governed it is the more healthful will be its prospects.   At the outset the position of patron may be somewhat like the position of that useful but ugly instrument with which many of us are perhaps but too familiar, namely, the snow-plough.   At the first formation of an artist society he may be expected to charge boldly into mountains of cold opposition, and to get rid of any ice crusts in front of the train, but after the winter of trial and probation, and difficulties of beginning are over, and the summer of success has come, his position, in regard to the artists, must be more like that of a figure-head.   I have, however, great faith in the power of artists to make a figure-head useful as well as ornamental, although I do not know that they have shown a proof of this to-day by making their figure-head deliver a speech, which it is well known figure-heads never do, except on the strictest compulsion.   You may remember that in old days in Greece, an artist named Pygmalion, carved a figure so beautiful that he himself fell in love with his work and infused his own life into the statue, so that it found breath and movement.   I shall not expect the Academy always to be in love with its figure-head, but I believe that you will be able to instil into him so much of your energy and vitality, that if the vessel gets into difficulties you may enable him to come down from his place, and even to give her a shove astern.   Let me, at all events, express a hope, in which I believe all present will join, that the Canadian Academy, this fair vessel that we launch to-day, may never get into any trouble, but that from every city, and from every Province of the Dominion, she may receive a favouring breeze whenever and wherever she may show a canvas.

At Quebec, upon the festival of St. Jean Baptiste, on the 24th June
1880, there was a gathering of representatives of the French-
Canadian race from many cities of the United States as well
as of Canada, and the celebration in honour of their national
saint was exceptionally enthusiastic. An opportunity was thus
given to the Governor-General to show that appreciation of
French Canadians which has been so constantly exhibited by
his predecessors in office. He spoke in French and said :—

Gentlemen and Friends of the French-Canadian
race from abroad as well as from our own Province,—
I rise with the greatest pleasure to thank you for the
way in which you have received the toast which has
been proposed by the President in drinking the health
of the Princess and myself. The Princess has especially desired me to convey to you her gratitude, and
I regret that owing to the short duration of the stay of
Prince Leopold in this country, she has been unable
to remain with me for the imposing celebration which
we have witnessed to-day. She is at all times sorry to
quit Quebec—a place she loves as much for the moral
worth of its people as for the grandeur of its scenery.
As for myself, gentlemen, I have obeyed a pleasant
call in being amongst you to-day to testify my respect
for our French-Canadian fellow-citizens, and my appreciation of the value of the element furnished by its
noble and gallant race in influencing for good our
young and growing Canadian nationality. I am here
to show how much I prize the loyalty evinced by you
on all occasions towards Her Majesty the Queen,
whose representative I am. At the same time I do
not wonder at the devotion shown to so august an

embodiment of the principle of Constitutional Rule. The Queen sets the example of a Sovereign, who has at all times given constant proof, that with us the acts of power are the expressions of the will of the people. It is this that gives to her the highest rank amongst rulers in the eyes of the nations who acknowledge her sceptre.   It is among you especially that all men will expect that this should be recognised.   It was the Normans, who in France watched and guarded the cradle of that liberty at present enjoyed in England—it was the men of Normandy and Brittany who at a later age laid the foundations of the liberty-loving community of Canada.   The very usages in the Parliament of Britain survive from the days when they were planted there by our Norman ancestors.   I do not know that it has been observed before in Canada, but it has often occurred to me, that in the British Parliament we still use the old words, used by your fathers for the sanction of the Sovereign given to bills, of "la reine le veut," or "la reine remercie ses bons sujets, accepte leur benevolence et ainsi le veut,"—forms which I should like to see used at Ottawa as marking our common origin, instead of the practice which is followed, of translating into modern French and English.   In celebrating this fête, all can join in pride in the element predominant amongst us to-day, as it is to your race we owe the liberties of Runnymede and the practices that mark the free discussions of our Parliament.   I rejoice to see so many met together, and that we have representatives of our allies the French, as well as of those who have made a home—let us hope a temporary one only—among our friends in the United States. I rejoice to see these members of the race repatriated, if only for a time, and may assure them that our old and our new lands of the West are wide and fertile enough to justify us in detaining them here and in annexing any number who may be willing to be so treated. As they well know, they will always have with us the most perfect guarantees of liberty, the fullest rights of franchise, while they will not suffer so much as now from frequent waves of moral heat incurred by all who have to take part in constant electioneering; nor will they, on the other hand, have to endure the winter and moral cold which may be experienced by all who have to undergo the effects of a Gubernatorial or Presidential veto. Our visitors will see with us to-day the signs of a happy, a loyal, and contented people; they will see us sharing in that revival of trade which I am happy to say is marking the commencement of another decade; they will see us holding in highest esteem those traditions which associate us with the past; they will see you in the fullest enjoyment of your laws, your language, and your institutions; they will see, above all, that you use the strength you thus inherit from your ancestors for no selfish purposes, but as imparting vigour and unison with the powers of other races to our great confederation, and in cementing a patriotism which is willing to bear the burdens as it shares the glory of a great country, the greatest member of the mightiest Empire ever known among mankind.

Gentlemen of the Agricultural and Arts Association of Ontario,—Believe me that any service which I can render to your invaluable association will always be at your command, and you may be sure that it is the desire of the Princess always to join me in such endeavours. It must at the same time be remembered that ladies have not that iron constitution which it is necessary that an official should possess, and it is not always possible for them to be present as well in the body as in the spirit. I congratulate you on the great progress visible in the manufactures exhibited, and on having the Provincial Show held this year at Hamilton. In Ontario, where the science of agriculture is beginning to be so thoroughly understood, I fear I can say but little that may be of use to you, but I cannot too pointedly praise that most prudent of all speculations, which has made several of the gentlemen who lead the way in such matters purchase some of the best of British cattle. To be content with raising inferior stock is as unfortunate in economy as is an illiberal and unscientific treatment of the land. Great as are the advantages possessed in this country by the new soil, which has comparatively recently been broken up, yet the effects of unscientific farming are necessarily to be seen in many places, and it is quite as much an object of our agricultural exhibitions to point out defects of this nature, as it is to display the triumphs of those who, pursuing agriculture upon a wiser plan, can year after year show the superiority of a scientific and liberal culture of the land.   I have no doubt that much good will result in the advice given in the report which will be issued of the Agricultural Commission now sitting in this Province.   There is much upon which you may be congratulated.   The great increase in the numbers of horses raised here is meeting the demand for them—the growth of the cheese manufacture under the factory system—the increased attention given to root growing in connection with cattle feeding—the care bestowed on more general under-draining—the development of fruit and vine culture, and the excellence and cheapness of your agricultural implements, are all features upon which we may dwell with the utmost satisfaction.   Your pasture lands are so wide, and the facilities afforded by the country for the raising of stock are so great, that it will be your own fault if you allow any others, be they breeders in the old country or the United States, to take the wind too much out of your sails. It is to be desired that provision be made against bad usage of the meat sent to England, for sufficient care is not taken of it at present after debarkation, and it appears to disadvantage in consequence in the markets. It must be remembered that at the present moment you have advantages with regard to the protection afforded you in the permission given to land your cattle alive in the old country, when it is denied to the States, which cannot be expected to last.   It is impossible to urge too strongly the necessity of preparation against a time when American cattle will be again admitted alive into England.   Unless you get the very best stock, and produce high graded beasts, you cannot hold your own.   The necessary expense attending the purchase of high-bred cattle will now pay you, and if with their produce you can maintain your place in the European markets, you may be assured that the money so spent could never have been spent to better purpose.   I am informed that lately at Toronto—and I hope we may see the same feature here in two days—Galloways, Polled Angus, as well as good Shorthorns, were to be seen in the yards.   In sheep also, some of the gentlemen who with so much foresight lead the way amongst our agricultural communities, have made purchases this year of Shropshire and other high-class animals.   I trust that each year may see a marked improvement with respect to following such leaders, and I have the utmost confidence that with the spirit of enterprise which has made British North America proportionately equal to any area on this continent in population, and in all the arts which can lead to that population's prosperity and happiness, Canada will not be found to be one whit behindhand.

To an address presented at the opening of the Quebec Provincial Fair, held at Montreal, His Excellency, the Governor-General, replied, both in French and English, as follows :—

Gentlemen,—It is a happy augury for our country that the expressions of loyalty to the throne, and confidence in the institutions under which we live, should be emphasised by you, who represent the different races of which our nationality is composed, when we meet to-day under roofs which shelter the products of

the industrial and agricultural industry of a wide territory, now enjoying marked and unusual prosperity. It
is not only a personal sentiment of reverence toward the
august occupant of the throne, the faithful interpreter
of our constitutional law, but it is to the perfected
fabric of the experience of many centuries,—to the
freest form of government on earth, that you declare
your devotion. The love for such institutions can
therefore be no passing phase dependent upon any
single life ; but is a love that lives with the life of the
nation by whose decrees those institutions exist and
abide.

It is my happy duty to represent among you to-day
the countenance given yearly by the Federal Government to one of those great provincial fairs, by which
our people in each section of the country show the
high value they place upon the comparison and competition to be obtained by such exhibitions. Each
year Industrial Art is thus aided, and a stimulus is
given to the excellency of workmanship, which can
alone content a people with its manufactures, and
provide for their acceptance abroad. Each year at
such re-unions the prospects of fresh enterprise in
agriculture are discussed. For instance, we look forward with confidence to the new organisations for the
cultivation of the beet-root, to be undertaken under
favourable auspices, experiments having already proved
that the beet-root grown here possesses a far larger
percentage of sugar than can be shown by that of either
France or Germany. Again, in the exportation of
phosphates, which have proved themselves so excellent

as fertilisers that they have arrested the attention of
the Agricultural Chambers of Europe, fresh combina-
tions will ensure a large supply from the Valley of the
Ottawa. Lastly, the encouragement of the improvement in the breed of cattle, and the solution of the
problem how best to export them with profit, engage
your minds. It is almost certain that although in
some parts of our country the cattle must be fed during
winter for a longer period than in others, yet with
good management and proper co-operation, wherever
good crops can be produced, the winter will form no
obstacle to the profitable sale of cattle in the European
markets. By contributing last year at Ottawa, and
this year at Montreal, to a Provincial exhibition, the
government of our Union designates its desire in the
interest of the whole country to supplement each year,
at a different place, those provincial resources which
are so wisely lavished on many branches of education.
The grant given on the part of the Union by which
this meeting is constituted a Dominion Exhibition, is
the contribution made for a special branch of instruction. As by our constitution, education is a provincial
matter, such Federal grants, if made, must be given
where more than the interests of one Province only
are concerned. The object to be attained is to help
forward those who, owing to a less favoured fortune,
are behindhand, by enabling them to see the results
attained by their neighbours. The question must not
only be, "Will such an Exhibition pay its expenses?"
It must be asked, "Will such an Exhibition spread
useful knowledge over wider districts which require it?"

Let me, in concluding these remarks in answer to your address, express on the part of the Princess the gratitude she will feel at your mention of her name; and I shall now fulfil the duty, for the performance of which I have been invited here, in declaring this Exhibition open to the public.

At the laying of the foundation-stone of a new Museum at M'Gill University, Montreal, in 1880, His Excellency spoke as follows :—

Mr. Chancellor, Members of Convocation, Ladies and Gentlemen,—Now that my part in the physical exercises, which I cannot say I have graced, but have accomplished, is over, I have been asked to take also a part in the intellectual exercises of this day by saying a few words to you. When I first came to Canada, and afterwards at the time when Confederation was coming into being, the first political lesson that I learnt with regard to this country was that the Federal Government would have nothing whatever to do with education. The earliest lesson that I learnt, on arriving in Canada fourteen years afterwards, was that the head of the Federal Government was frequently expected to attend on such occasions as that on which we are assembled to-day, which has certainly a great deal to do with education. Perhaps, however, I may flatter myself by supposing that my presence here to-day has been desired more in the capacity of a friend than as an official—(applause) —and I hope that this may be the footing on which you will always allow me to meet you and see what you

are doing.   I can assure you I will never betray any
of your secrets to my Ministers, except under the
advice of my honourable friend on my right (the Lieu-
tenant-Governor Robitaille), who is the natural pro-
tector and guardian of this University, and of education
in this Province.   (Laughter.)   I share most heartily
with you in the joy you must experience at the prospect of possessing so fine a hall for the accommodation of the treasures which are rapidly accumulating
in your hands.   That the necessity for a large building should have been so promptly met by the sympathetic support and far-seeing generosity of Mr.
Redpath, proves that the race of benefactors, illustrated
by the names of Molson and M'Gill, has not died out
amongst us.   (Loud applause.)   The removal of the
geological collections belonging to the nation from
Montreal to Ottawa, which has been determined upon
as bringing more immediately under the eye of the
Legislature and the knowledge of the Government
the labours and results attained by our men of science,
necessarily deprives the residents of Montreal, who
are students, of the facilities hitherto afforded by the
presence in this city of those collections.   It is satisfactory to know that this loss will be palliated by such
noble gifts as those which have furnished you with
other collections, which are now to find at last a proper
place for their display.   (Applause.)   You who have
in your Chancellor and members of Convocation such
eminent and worthy representatives of judicial attainment, of classical learning, of medical and surgical
knowledge, and of scientific research, will well know

how to give full value to the last of these subjects, namely, to the culture of the natural sciences. (Applause.) Besides the direct utility of a knowledge of zoology, botany, geology, and chemistry, and of the kindred branches grouped under the designation of natural science, the pleasure to be derived from them is not amongst the least of the advantages of their study. (Hear, hear.) However forbidding the country in which he is placed, however uninteresting the other surroundings of a man's life may be, he need never miss the delights of an engrossing occupation, if the very earth on which he treads, each leaf and insect, and all the phenomena of nature around him, cause him to follow out new lines of study, and give his thought a wider range. This is enough to make a man feel as though in the enjoyment of a never-dying vitality, and I doubt if any one amongst you feels younger than your honoured Principal, although his studies have led him in fancy over every region, and must make him feel as if a perpetual youth had caused him to live through all geological time. (Laughter and applause.) To parallel a saying, spoken of another eminent man, he certainly has learnt all that rocks can teach, except to be hard-hearted. (Renewed laughter.) It seems to me peculiarly appropriate that he who first established the certainty of the "Dawn of Life" amongst the Laurentian rocks of Canada, should here, through his untiring zeal, officiate in launching into the dawn of public recognition the young manhood of his country. (Applause.) It is your great good fortune that in your Principal you have a leader who is an admirable guide, not alone in the fairy realms of science, but also through those sterner, and, to some, less attractive regions which own the harsher rule of the exigencies of the daily life around us. (Hear, hear.) He has traced in the rocks the writing of the Creator, and with the magic light, only to be borne by him who has earned the power through toil of reason and of induction, he has been able to see in the spirit and describe the processes of creation. His knowledge has pierced the dark ages, when through countless æons the earth was being prepared for man; he has shown how forests—vast as those we see to-day, but with vanished forms of vegetation and of life, grew, decayed, and were preserved in altered condition to give us in these days of colder skies the fuel we need. He has been for his beloved Acadia the historian of the cycles when God formed her under the primal waters, fashioned her in the marshes teeming in His fervent heat, caused His fire to fuse the metal in her rocks, and His ice to scourge the coasts, thereafter to be subjected to yet more stupendous changes, and raised and made fit for the last and highest of His works. (Loud applause.) But Dr. Dawson's great knowledge and wide learning have not led him, as they might lead many, to live apart in fastidious study and in selfish absorption, forgetful of the claims and contemptuous of the merits of others. (Hear, hear.) His wisdom in these difficult studies has not separated him from us; it has only been a fresh cause for us to hail that public spirit which makes him give all he has, whether of strength, of time, or of knowledge, for the benefit of his fellow-citizens. (Applause.) Just as it was not for Acadia alone, but in the interests of science, that his first labour was undertaken ; so now it is not for any especial locality, but for the good of the whole of our country, that he is head of this place of learning, whence depart so many to take their lot in the civil life of Canada. Even in his presence it is right that this should be said of him, here on this spot, where you are to raise a new temple of the practical sciences, and now that he, with you, has become the recipient of this gift, which is a tribute from one who has earned success in the hard battle of life, offered to men who, with so much devotion, are training other lives to win their way by knowledge through the difficulties that may lie before them. (Loud applause.)

A fine statue of Colonel de Salaberry, by Mr. Hébert of Montreal, was, in 1880, unveiled at Chambly. A large concourse of people, and representative men from all parts of the Province of Quebec, were present, and after eloquent speeches from Colonel Harwood and other gentlemen, His Excellency said :—

Accept my thanks for your address, which records your patriotic desire to honour in a befitting manner the memory of a patriot. I rejoice to be able to take part with you in this commemoration of a gallant soldier. We are here to unveil a monument dedicated to a man who worthily represented the loyal spirit of his age. That spirit exists to the full to-day. Should need arise, there are many among the Canadian nation who would emulate his example and endeavour to rival his achievements. This statue records a character typical of our countrymen. Content with little for himself, content only with greatness for his country—such was the character of De Salaberry; such is the character of the Canadian to-day. At Chambly, in the Province where he had the good fortune to have the occasion to manifest that valour which was the proud tradition of his race, we place his statue. It is raised in no spirit of idle boasting, but with a hope that the virtues shown of old may, unforgotten, light and guide future generations. These virtues were conspicuous in this distinguished man, whose military talents enabled him to perform his duty with signal advantage to our arms. In rearing this monument to him, let us not forget to pay a passing tribute to his brothers. They, with him, in the hour of danger, took to the profession of arms, we may almost say as a part of their nature. Three of them perished in upholding the honour of that flag which is to-day our symbol of unity and freedom. In this fair region, which was his home, a contrast between our times and those in which he lived comes forcibly before us. Where are now the wide tracts of fertile fields and a country traversed by railways or to be reached by the steamers on our rivers, De Salaberry and his voltigeurs, when they made their gallant defence, saw only scattered clearings among great forests. These, too, often concealed contending armies. While we cherish the recollection of gallant deeds performed, where English and French-speaking Canadians equally distinguished themselves, it is not necessary to dwell on the bitter associations of those times.   We are at peace, and live in what we hope will be an abiding friendship and alliance with the great and generous people of the south.   They then endeavoured to conquer us, but were in the end only enabled to entertain for the Canadians that respect which is the only true and lasting foundation of friend ship.   We must be thankful and rejoice that our rivalries with them are now only in the fruitful fields of commerce.   Our resources in these peaceful paths are daily supplying the sinews of strength and the power to us in resources and population which would make any war undertaken against Canada a war that would be a long and a difficult one.   They do not desire to invade us.   We trust that such a desire will never again arise, for nations do not now so often as of old interfere with their neighbours when no faction invites interference.   If in 1812 Canada was dear for her own sake to Canadians, how much more is she so now ?   Then possessed only of a small population, enjoying liberty under the ægis of a narrow constitution, now we see in her a great and growing people, self-governed at home, proud of the freest form of constitution, and able to use in association with her own representative the diplomatic strength of a great empire for the making of her commercial compacts with other nations.   With us there is no party which would invite incursions or change of government.   No man has a chance of success in Canadian public life, no one is countenanced by our people, who is not a lover of free institutions. In inviting here the Governor-General you have an officer present, who as the head of the Federal govern ment is nothing but the first and abiding representative of the people.   It is, however, not only as an official that I rejoice with you to-day.   Personal feelings make it a joyful hour for me when I can visit the cradle of so much worth and valour, surrounded as I am by the members of the family of Monsieur de Salaberry.   The Princess and I can never forget the intimate friendship which existed between Prince Edward, Duke of Kent, and Colonel de Salaberry—a friendship between families which, I may be allowed to hope, will not be confined to the grandfathers.   The Princess asked me to express the deep interest she takes in this celebration.   She wishes me to convey to you her sorrow that she is not here to-day with us.   She yet hopes to be able to see this monument, where for the first time Canadian art has so honourably recorded in sculpture Canadian loyalty, bravery, and genius.

In 1880, at St. Thomas in Ontario, over 6000 men of Highland descent were present at a meeting attended by the Governor-General, who spoke as follows in reply to an address delivered in Gaelic and English :—

Highlanders and Friends from the Land of the Gael,—You do not know how much pleasure you give me in coming forward, and in such a touching and eloquent address as that to which I have just listened, giving me the assurance of the unchangeable loyalty which animates your hearts, and of the pride with which you look back upon the country of your forefathers.   (Applause.)   It is not often that a man gets so many kindly words addressed to him from so great a meeting of his countrymen.   Although it is for Canada as a whole that I work in this country, and for her whole population of whatever race that my heart, as well as my duty, urges me to strive, yet it is a peculiar delight that such endeavours should be illustrated by meeting with those who are descended from men at whose side, in the dark ages of trial and of difficulty, my fathers fought and died. We have many ancient memories in common. You tell me that these are rehearsed among you. I know that among your cousins at home the tales of the deeds of the heroes of the Feinn of Ireland and of Scotland, and the achievements of the great men who have lived since their day, in successive centuries, are constantly repeated. I would give nothing for a man who could place little value upon the lives and times of his ancestors, not only because without them he himself would have no existence—(laughter)—but because in tracing the history of their lives, and in remembering the difficulties they encountered, he will be spurred to emulate, in as far as in him lies, the triumphs that have caused them to be remembered. (Cheers.) I would give nothing for a French-Canadian who could not look back with pride on the glorious discoveries and contests of the early pioneers of Canada. I would give nothing for a German who in Ontario could forget that he came from the race who under Hermann hurled back the tide of Roman invasion; nor for an Englishman who forgets the splendid virtues which have made the English character comparable to the native oak. (Applause.) Such reminiscences and such incentives to display in the present day the virtues

of our ancestors can have none but a good result.
Here our different races have, through God's providence, become the inheritors of a new country, where
the blood of all is mingling, and where a nation is
arising which we firmly believe will show through
future centuries the nerve, the energy, and intellectual
powers which characterised the people of northern
Europe. (Hear, hear.) And let our pride in this
country with reference to its sons not be so much seen
in pride of the original stock, as in the feeling of joy
which should arise when we can say, "Such an orator,
such a soldier, such a poet, or such a statesman is
a Canadian." (Cheers.) Keep up a knowledge of
your ancient language; for the exercise given to a
man's mind in the power given by the ability to express
his thoughts in two languages is no mean advantage.
I would gladly have given much of the time devoted
in boyhood to acquiring Greek to the acquisition of
Gaelic. My friends, let me now tell you how happy
it makes me to see that the valour, the skill, and the
bravery which used to make you chief among your
neighbours in the strife of swords, is here shown in
the mastery of the difficulties of nature. Your lives
are here cast in pleasant places. The aspect of the
fertility of your lands, of the success of their cultivation, and of your prosperity in their enjoyment, is
producing so powerful an effect upon your brethren at
home, that we have some difficulty in persuading the
most enterprising amongst them to remain in the old
country. (Laughter.) You know that economic
causes have forced much of the increasing population

of Scotland to seek the towns, and the change in the proprietorship of lands has united in a few unfortunate instances with the love for hunting in tempting men, in more modern times, to care more for their preserves of animals than for the preserves they could point to as being filled with men. My family has always loved, not for policy, but on account of their fellow-citizens, to place in the balance, against the temptation for gain among the people, the love of home; and have thus had many men on their lands. In a small country, of poor climate as compared with Canada, this must of course be regulated by the resources of the land. But I visit always with a peculiar pleasure those districts at home where a large population has been able to find a competent livelihood. One island known to many of you, namely, Tiree, has upon a surface of twelve miles long by about two in width over three thousand souls. At the present day I find that some of those who have visited Ontario, or who know from their friends what this land is like, now come to us and say, "We are tempted to go to Canada, for each of our friends there has for himself a farm as big as the whole island of Tiree." (Laughter.) This is only an instance of how much the western Highlander has thriven in these new and more spacious homes. (Cheers.) Some amongst you are of my name. I find that the Campbells get on as well as anybody else in this country. Lately a gentleman managed to praise himself, his wife, and me by making the following speech. He said, "I am glad to see you here as Governor-General. I always find that the Campbells in this country manage to get most excellent places." He then pointed to his wife, and proved his argument by the announcement, "My wife there is a Campbell." (Renewed laughter.) That you, your children, and children's children, may continue to prosper is the wish of my heart, and the desire of all in the Mother Country, who see that here you are one of the powers that constitute, in the new world, a community devoted to the great traditions, to the might and enduring grandeur of our united empire. (Loud cheers.) Had it not been so you would not have come to meet me here to-day. Some time ago I visited Killin, in Perthshire, a most interesting place. It is a rocky island covered with heather, grass, and pine trees, placed in the centre of the foaming waters of the river Dochart, which streams from Benmore. It was the ancient burial place of the gallant race of Macnab, a clan which with its chief came over to Canada and was illustrious in the history of this country. Its chief, Sir Allan, became, not by virtue of descent, but by ability and integrity, a leader in the public life of Canada. His son came to Killin to see this last resting-place of his fathers, and was there seen by a poet, who in some beautiful verses says :—

> " Would a son of the chieftain have dared to invade
> The isle where the heroes repose ; "

Were it not, that as—

> " A pilgrim he came to that place of the dead,
> For he knew that the tenant of each narrow bed,
> Would hail him as worthy of them."

He then asks how he and they had shown their metal, and in vindication of their fidelity to their ancient fame, he imagines that the very wind that waved the fir branches over the old tombs carries in rustling whisper, or in strong breath of storm, among the boughs :—

> " A voice as it flies,
> From the far distant forest that fringes the deeps
> Of the rushing St. Lawrence, replies :—
> That, however to Albyn their name
> Has become like a tale of past years that is told ;
> On the shores of Lake Erie that race is the same,
> And as true to the land of its birth and its fame,
> As their gallant forefathers of old."

May this be ever so with you, and may God prosper and bless you in all your undertakings. (Prolonged cheers.)

On his return to Winnipeg, after his tour through the North-Western Territories in 1881, His Excellency spoke as follows :—

Mr. Chairman and Gentlemen,—I beg to thank you most cordially for the pleasant reception you have given to me on my return to Winnipeg, and for the words in which you proposed my health and have expressed a hope for the complete recovery of the Princess from the effects of that most unfortunate accident which took place at Ottawa. I know that the Canadian people will always remember that it was in sharing the duties incurred in their service that the Princess received injuries which have, only temporarily, I trust, so much impaired her health. (Applause.)

Two years hence the journey I have undertaken will be an easy one for all to accomplish throughout its length, while at present the facilities of railway and steam accommodation only suffice for half of it.   For a Canadian, personal knowledge of the North-West is indispensable.   To be ignorant of the North-West is to be ignorant of the greater portion of our country. (Applause.)   Hitherto I have observed that those who have seen it justly look down upon those who have not, with a kind of pitying contempt which you may sometimes have observed that they who have got up earlier in the morning than others and seen some beautiful sunrise, assume towards the friends who have slept until the sun is high in the heavens.   (Laughter.) Our track, though it led us far, only enabled us to see a very small portion of your heritage now being made accessible.   Had time permitted we should have ex- plored the immense country which lies along the whole course of the wonderful Saskatchewan, which, with its two gigantic branches, opens to steam navigation settle- ments of rapidly growing importance.   As it was, we but touched the waters of the north and south branches, and striking southwestwards availed ourselves of the American railway lines in Montana for our return. It was most interesting to compare the southern moun- tains and prairies with our own, and not even the terrible events which have recently cast so deep a gloom upon our neighbours, as well as ourselves, could prevent our kinsmen from showing that hospitality and courtesy which makes a visit to their country so great a pleasure. (Loud applause.)   I am the more glad to bear witness to this courtesy in the presence of the distinguished consul of the United States, who is your guest this evening, and who, in this city, so honourably represents his country—(applause)—in nothing more than in this, that he has never misrepresented our own. (Loud applause.)   Like almost all his compatriots who occupy by the suffrage of their people official positions,, he has recognised that fact, which is happily acknowledged by all of standing amongst ourselves, that the interests of the British Empire and of the United States may be advanced side by side without jealousy or friction, and that the good of the one is interwoven with the welfare of the other.   (Cheers.)   Canada has recently shown that sympathy with her neighbour's grief which becomes her, and which has been so marked throughout all portions of our Empire.   She has sorrowed with the sorrow of the great commonwealth, whose chief has been struck down, in the fulness of his strength, in the height of his usefulness, in the day of universal recognition of his noble character, by the dastard hand of the assassin.   We have felt in this as though we ourselves had suffered, for General Garfield's position and personal worth made his own and his fellow citizens' misfortune a catastrophe for all English-speaking races.   The bulletins telling of his calm and courageous struggle against cruel and unmerited affliction, have been read and discussed by us with as strong an admiration for the man, and with as tender a sentiment for the anxiety and misery of his family, as they have been awaited and perused in the south.   It is fitting and good that this should be.   We have with the Americans, not only a common descent, but a similar position on this continent, and a like probable destiny. The community of feeling reaches beyond the fellowship arising from the personal interest attaching to the dignity of a high office sustained with honour, and to the reverence for the tender ties of hearth and home, sacred though these be, for Canadians and Americans have each a common aim and a common ideal. Though belonging to very different political schools, and preferring to advance by very different paths, we both desire to live only in a land of perfect liberty. (Loud cheers.) When the order which ensures freedom is desecrated by the cowardly rancour of the murderer, or by the tyranny of faction, the blow touches more than one life, and strikes over a wider circle than that where its nearer and immediate consequences are apparent. The people of the United States have been directed into one political organisation, and we are cherishing and developing another; but they will find no men with whom a closer and more living sympathy with their triumphs or with their trouble abides, than their Canadian cousins in the Dominion. (Cheers.) Let this be so in the days of unborn generations, and may we never have again to express our horror at such a deed of infamy as that which has lately called forth, in so striking a manner, the proofs of international respect and affection. (Hear, hear.) To pass to other themes awaking no unhappy recollections, you will expect me to mention a few of the impressions made upon us by what we have seen during the last few weeks. Beautiful as are

the numberless lakes and illimitable forests of Keewatin
—the land of the north wind, to the east of you—yet
it was pleasant to "get behind the north wind"—(laughter)—and to reach your open plains. The contrast is
great between the utterly silent and shadowy solitudes
of the pine and fir forests, and the sunlit and breezy
ocean of meadowland, voiceful with the music of birds,
which stretches onward from the neighbourhood of
your city. In Keewatin the lumber industry and mining enterprises can alone be looked for, but here it is
impossible to imagine any kind of work which shall not
produce results equal to those attained in any of the
great cities of the world. (Great cheering.) Unknown
a few years ago except for some differences which had
arisen amongst its people, we see Winnipeg now with
a population unanimously joined in happy concord,
and rapidly lifting it to the front rank amongst the
commercial centres of the continent. We may look
in vain elsewhere for a situation so favourable and
so commanding—many as are the fair regions of
which we can boast. (Loud cheers.) There may be
some among you before whose eyes the whole
wonderful panorama of our Provinces has passed—
the ocean-garden island of Prince Edward; the
magnificent valleys of the St. John and Sussex; the
marvellous country, the home of "Evangeline," where
Blomidon looks down on the tides of Fundy, and over
tracts of red soil richer than the weald of Kent. You
may have seen the fortified Paradise of Quebec; and
Montreal, whose prosperity and beauty is worthy of
her great St. Lawrence, and you may have admired

the well-wrought and splendid Province of Ontario, and rejoiced at the growth of her capital, Toronto, and yet nowhere will you find a situation whose natural advantages promise so great a future as that which seems ensured to Manitoba and to Winnipeg, the Heart city of our Dominion. (Tremendous cheering.) The measureless meadows which commence here stretch without interruption of their good soil westward to your boundary. The Province is a green sea over which the summer winds pass in waves of rich grasses and flowers, and on this vast extent it is only as yet here and there that a yellow patch shows some gigantic wheat field. (Loud cheering.) Like a great net cast over the whole are the bands and clumps of poplar wood which are everywhere to be met with, and which, no doubt, when the prairie fires are more carefully guarded against, will, wherever they are wanted, still further adorn the landscape. (Cheers.) The meshes of this wood-netting are never further than twenty or thirty miles apart. Little hay swamps and sparkling lakelets, teeming with wild fowl, are always close at hand, and if the surface water in some of these has alkali, excellent water can always be had in others, and by the simple process of digging for it a short distance beneath the sod with a spade, the soil being so devoid of stones that it is not even necessary to use a pick. No wonder that under these circumstances we hear no croaking. Croakers are very rare animals throughout Canada. It was remarked with surprise, by an Englishman accustomed to British grumbling, that even the frogs sing instead of croaking in Canada—(great cheering) —and the few letters that have appeared speaking of disappointment will be amongst the rarest autographs which the next generation will cherish in their museums. ' But with even the best troops of the best army in the world you will find a few malingerers—a few skulkers. However well an action has been fought, you will hear officers who have been engaged say that there were some men whose idea seemed to be that it was easier to conduct themselves as became them at the rear, rather than in the front. (Laughter and applause.) So there have been a few lonely and lazy voices raised in the stranger press dwelling upon your difficulties and ignoring your triumphs. These have appeared from the pens of men who have failed in their own countries and have failed here, who are born failures, and will fail, till life fails them. (Laughter and applause.) They are like the soldiers who run away from the best armies seeking to spread discomfiture, which exists only in those things they call their minds— (laughter)—and who returning to the cities say their comrades are defeated, or if they are not beaten, they should in their opinion be so. We have found, as we expected, that their tales are not worthy the credence even of the timid. (Applause.) There was not one person who had manfully faced the first difficulties— always far less than those to be encountered in the older Provinces—but said that he was getting on well and he was glad he had come, and he generally added that he believed his bit of the country must be the best, and that he only wished his friends could have the same good fortune, for his expectations were more than realised. (Cheers and laughter.) It is well to remember that the men who will succeed here, as in every young community, are usually the able-bodied, and that their entry on their new field of labour should be when the year is young. Men advanced in life and coming from the old country will find their comfort best consulted by the ready provided accommodation to be obtained by the purchase of a farm in the old Provinces. All that the settler in Manitoba would seem to require is, that he should look out for a locality where there is either good natural drainage, and ninety-nine hundredths of the country has this, and that he should be able readily to procure in Winnipeg, or elsewhere, some light pumps like those used in Abyssinia for the easy supply of water from a depth of a few feet below the surface. Alkali in the water will never hurt his cattle, and dykes of turf and the planting of trees would everywhere insure him and them the shelter that may be required. Five hundred dollars should be his own to spend on his arrival, if he wishes to farm. If he comes as an artisan he may, like the happy masons now to be found in Winnipeg, get the wages of a British Army Colonel,* by putting up houses as fast as brick, wood, and mortar can be got together. Favourable testimony as to the climate was everywhere given. The heavy

* Masons wages had risen to an extraordinary height in the Autumn of 1881. Excellent pay can now be obtained by brick-layers, carpenters, and blacksmiths.

night dews throughout the North-West keep the country green when everything is burned to the south, and the steady winter cold, although it sounds formidable when registered by the thermometer, is universally said to be far less trying than the cold to be encountered at the old English Puritan city of Boston, in Massachussets. It is the moisture in the atmosphere which makes cold tell, and the Englishman who, with the thermometer at zero, would, in his moist atmosphere, be shivering, would here find one flannel shirt sufficient clothing while working. I never like to make comparisons, and am always unwillingly driven to do so, although it seems to be the natural vice of the well-travelled Englishman. Over and over again in Canada have I been asked if such and such a bay was not wonderfully like the Bay of Naples, for the inhabitants had often been told so. I always professed to be unable to see the resemblance, of course entirely out of deference to the susceptibilities of the Italian nation. So one of our party, a Scotsman, whenever in the Rocky Mountains he saw some grand pyramid or gigantic rock, ten or eleven thousand feet in height, would exclaim that the one was the very image of Arthur's Seat and the other of Edinburgh Castle. With the fear of Ontario before my eyes I would therefore never venture to compare a winter here to those of our greatest Province, but I am bound to mention that when a friend of mine put the question to a party of sixteen Ontario men who had settled in the western portion of Manitoba, as to the comparative merits of the cold season in the two Provinces—fourteen of them voted for the Manitoba climate, and only two elderly men said that they preferred that of Toronto. You will therefore see how that which is sometimes called a very unequal criterion of right and justice, a large majority, determines this question. Now although we are at present in Manitoba, and Manitoba interests may dominate our thoughts, yet you may not object to listen for a few moments to our experience of the country which lies further to the west. To the present company the assertion may be a bold one, but they will be sufficiently tolerant to allow me to make it, if it goes no further, and I therefore say that we may seek for the main chance elsewhere than in Main street. The future fortunes of this country beyond this Province bear directly upon its prosperity. Although you may not be able to dig for four feet through the same character of black loam that you have here when you get to the country beyond Fort Ellice, yet in its main features it is the same right up to the forks of the Saskatchewan. I deeply regret that I was not able to visit Edmonton, which bids fair to rival any place in the North-West. Settlement is rapidly increasing there, and I met at Battleford one man who alone had commissions from ten Ontario farmers to buy for them at that place. Nothing can exceed the fertility and excellence of the land along almost the whole course of that great river, and to the north of it in the wide strip belting its banks and extending up to the Peace River, there will be room for a great population whose opportunities for profitable cultivation of the soil will be most enviable.

--

The netting of wood of which I have spoken as covering all the prairie between Winnipeg and Battleford,
is beyond that point drawn up upon the shores of the
prairie sea, and lies in masses of fine forest in the
gigantic half circle formed by the Saskatchewan and
the Rockies.   It is only in secluded valleys, on the
banks of large lakes, and in river bottoms, that much
wood is found in the Far West, probably owing to
the prevalence of fires.   These are easily preventible,
and there is no reason why plantations should not
flourish there in good situations as well as elsewhere.
Before I leave the Saskatchewan, let me advert to the
ease with which the steam navigation of that river can
be vastly improved.   At present there is only one
boat at all worthy of the name of a river steamer upon
it, and this steamer lies up during the night.   A new
company is, I am informed, now being organised,
and there is no reason why, if the new vessels are
properly equipped and furnished with electric lights,
which may now be cheaply provided, they should
not keep up a night and day service, so that the
settlers at Prince Albert, Edmonton, and elsewhere,
may not have, during another season, to suffer great
privations incident to the wants of transportation
which has loaded the banks of Grand Rapids during
the present year with freight, awaiting steam transport.
The great cretaceous coal seams at the headwaters of
the rivers which rise in the Rocky Mountains or in their
neighbourhood and flow towards your doors, should
not be forgotten.   Although you have some coal in districts nearer to you, we should remember that on the

headwaters of these streams there is plenty of the most
excellent kind which can be floated down to you before
you have a complete railway system.   Want of time
as well as a wish to see the less vaunted parts of the
country took me southwestward from Battleford, over
land which in many of the maps is variously marked
as consisting of arid plains or as a continuation of
the " American Desert."   The newer maps, especially
those containing the explorations of Professor Macoun,
have corrected this wholly erroneous idea.   For two
days' march—that is to say, for about 60 or 70 miles
south of Battleford—we passed over land whose excellence could not be surpassed for agricultural purposes.
Thence to the neighbourhood of the Red Deer Valley
the soil is lighter, but still in my opinion in most
places good for grain—in any case most admirable
for summer pasturage,—and it will certainly be good
also for stock in winter as soon as it shall pay to have
some hay stored in the valleys.   The whole of it has
been the favourite feeding ground of the buffalo.
Their tracks from watering place to watering place,
never too far apart from each other, were everywhere
to be seen, while in very many tracks their dung lay so
thickly that the appearance of the ground was only comparable to that of an English farmyard.   Let us hope
that the *entre-acte* will not be long before the disappearance of the buffalo on these scenes is followed by the
appearance of domestic herds.   The Red Deer Valley
is especially remarkable as traversing a country where,
according to the testimony of Indian chiefs travelling
with us, snow never lies for more than three months,

and the heavy growth of poplar in the bottoms, the quantity of the "bull" or high cranberry bushes, and the rich branches that hung from the choke-cherries showed us that we had come into that part of the Dominion which among the plainsmen is designated as "God's country." From this, onward to the Bow River and thence to the frontier line, the trail led through what will be one of the most valued of our Provinces, subject to those warm winds called the "chinooks." The settler will hardly ever use anything but wheeled vehicles during winter, and throughout a great portion of the land early sowing—or fall sow-ing—will be all that will be necessary to ensure him against early frosts. At Calgarry—a place interesting at the present time as likely to be upon that Pacific Railway line* which will connect you with the Pacific, and give you access to "that vast shore beyond the furthest sea," the shore of Asia—a good many small herds of cattle have been introduced within the last few years. During this year a magnificent herd of between six and seven thousand has been brought in, and the men who attended them and who came from Montana, Oregon and Texas, all averred that their opinion of their new ranche was higher than that of any with which they had been acquainted in the south. Excellent crops have been raised by men who had sown not only in the river bottoms, but also upon the so-called "bench" lands or plateaux above. This

* The Canadian Pacific Railway has now been completed to a valley in the Rocky Mountains beyond Calgarry, through which place it passes.

T

testimony was also given by others on the way to Fort Macleod and beyond it, thus closing most satisfactorily the song of praise we had heard from practical men throughout our whole journey of 1200 miles. Let me advert for one moment to some of the causes which have enabled settlers to enjoy in such peace the fruits of their industry. Chief amongst these must be reckoned the policy of kindness and justice which was inaugurated by the Hudson's Bay Company in their treatment of the Indians. Theirs is one of the cases in which a trader's association has upheld the maxim that "honesty is the best policy," even when you are dealing with savages. The wisdom and righteousness of their dealing on enlightened principles, which are fully followed out by their servants to-day, gave the cue to the Canadian Government. The Dominion through her Indian officers and her mounted constabulary is showing herself the inheritress of these traditions. She has been fortunate in organising the Mounted Police Force, a corps of whose services it would be impossible to speak too highly. A mere handful in that vast wilderness, they have at all times shown themselves ready to go anywhere and do anything. They have often had to act on occasions demanding the combined individual pluck and prudence rarely to be found amongst any soldiery, and there has not been a single occasion on which any member of the force has lost his temper under trying circumstances, or has not fulfilled his mission as a guardian of the peace. Severe journeys in winter and difficult arrests have had to be effected in the centre of savage tribes, and not once has the moral prestige which was in reality their only weapon, been found insufficient to cope with difficulties which, in America, have often baffled the efforts of whole columns of armed men. I am glad of this opportunity to name these men as well worthy of Canada's regard—as sons who have well maintained her name and fame. And now that you have had the patience to listen to me, and we have crossed the continent together, let me advise you as soon as possible to get up a branch Club-house, situated amongst our Rocky Mountains, where, during summer, your members may form themselves into an Alpine club and thoroughly enjoy the beautiful peaks and passes of our Alps. In the railway you will have a beautiful approach to the Pacific. The line, after traversing for days the plains, will come upon the rivers whose sheltering valleys have all much the same character. The river-beds are like great moats in a modern fortress—you do not see them till close upon them. As in the glacis and rampart of a fortress, the shot can search across the smoothed surfaces above the ditch, so any winds that may arise may sweep across the twin levels above the river fosses. The streams run coursing along the sunken levels in these vast ditches, which are sometimes miles in width. Sheltered by the undulating banks, knolls, or cliffs, which form the margin of their excavated bounds, are woods, generally of poplar, except in the northern and western fir fringe. On approaching the mountains their snow caps look like huge tents encamped along the rolling prairie.   Up to this great camp, of which a length of 200 miles is sometimes visible, the rivers wind in trenches, looking like the covered ways by which siege works zig-zag up to a besieged city.   On a nearer view the camp line changes to ruined marble palaces, and through their tremendous walls and giant woods you will soon be dashing on the train for a winter basking on the warm Pacific coast.   You have a country whose value it would be insanity to question, and which, to judge from the emigration taking place from the older Provinces, will be indissolubly linked with them.   It must support a vast population.   If we may calculate from the progress we have already made in comparison with our neighbours, we shall have no reason to fear comparison with them on the new areas now open to us.   We have now four million four hundred thousand people, and these, with the exception of the comparatively small numbers as yet in this Province, are restricted to the old area.   Yet for the last ten years our increase has been over 18 per cent., whereas during the same period all the New England States taken together have shown an increase only of 15 per cent.   In the last thirty years in Ohio the increase has been 61 per cent.—Ontario has seen during that space of time 101 per cent. of increase, while Quebec has increased 52 per cent.   Manitoba in ten years has increased 289 per cent., a greater rate than any hitherto attained, and to judge from this year's experience is likely to increase to an even more wonderful degree during the following decade.   Statistics are at all times wearisome, but are not these full of hope ?   Are they not facts giving just ground for that pride in our progress which is conspicuous among our people, and ample reason for our belief that the future may be allowed to take care of itself.   They who pour out prophecies of change, prescribing medicines for a sound body, are wasting their gifts and their time.   It is among strangers that we hear such theories propounded by destiny men. With you the word "annexation" has in the last years only been heard in connection with the annexation of more territory to Manitoba.   I must apologise to a Canadian audience for mentioning the word at all in any other connection.   In America the annexation of this country is disavowed by all responsible leaders. As it was well expressed to me lately, the best men in the States desire only to annex the friendship and good will of Canada.   (Loud cheers.)   To be sure it may be otherwise with the camp followers ; they often talk as if the swallowing and digestion of Canada by them were only a question of time, and of rising reason amongst us.   How far the power of the camp followers extends it is not for us to determine.   They have, however, shown that they are powerful enough to capture a few English writers, our modern minor prophets who, in little magazine articles, are fond of teaching the nations how to behave, whose words preach the superiority of other countries to their own, and the proximate dismemberment of that British Empire which has the honour to acknowledge them as citizens.   They have with our American friends of whom I speak at all events one virtue in common,

they are great speculators.   In the case of our southern friends this is not a matter to be deplored by us,
for American speculation has been of direct material
benefit to Canada, and we must regret that our
American citizens are not coming over to us so fast
as are the Scotch, the Irish, the Germans, and the
Scandinavians.   Morally, also, it is not to be deplored
that such speculations are made, for they show that
it is thought that Canadians would form a useful though
an unimportant wing for one of the great parties ; and,
moreover, such prophecies clothe with amusement
"the dry bones" of discussion.   But it is best always
to take men as we find them, and not to believe that
they will be different even if a kindly feeling, first for
ourselves and afterwards for them, should make us
desire to change them.   Let us rather judge from the
past and from the present than take flights, unguided
by experience, into the imaginary regions of the
future.   What do we find has been, and is, the ten-
dency of the peoples of this continent?   Does not
history show, and do not modern and existing tendencies declare, that the lines of cleavage among them
lie along the lines of latitude?   Men spread from east
to west, and from east to west the political lines,
which mean the lines of diversity, extend.   The
central spaces are, and will be yet more, the great
centres of population.   Can it be imagined that the
vast central hives of men will allow the eastern or
western seaboard people to come between them with
separate empire, and shut them out in any degree
from full and free intercourse with the markets of the

world beyond them? Along the lines of longitude no such tendencies of division exist. The markets of the North Pole are not as yet productive, and with South America commerce is comparatively small. The safest conclusion, if conclusions are to be drawn at all, is that what has hitherto been, will, in the nature of things, continue,—that whatever separations exist will be marked by zones of latitude. For other evidence we must search in vain. Our county councils, the municipal corporations, the local provincial chambers, the central Dominion Parliament, and last not least, a perfectly unfettered press, are all free channels for the expression of the feelings of our citizens. Why is it that in each and all of these reflectors of the thoughts of men, we see nothing but determination to keep and develop the precious heritage we have in our own constitution, so capable of any development which the people may desire. (Cheers.) Let us hear Canadians if we wish to speak for them. These public bodies and the public press are the mouthpieces of the people's mind. Let us not say for them what they never say for themselves. It is no intentional misrepresentation, I believe, which has produced these curious examples of the fact that individual prepossessions may distort public proof. It reminds me of an interpretation once said to have been given by a bad interpreter of a speech delivered by a savage warrior, who, in a very dignified and extremely lengthy discourse, expressed the contentment of his tribe with the order and with the good which had been introduced amongst them by the law of the white man.

His speech was long enough fully to impress with its meaning and its truth all who took pains to listen to him, and who could understand his language, but the interpreter had unfortunately different ideas of his own, and was displeased with his own individual treatment. When at last he was asked what the chief and his council had said in their eloquent orations, he turned round and only exclaimed,—"He dam displeased!" (Great laughter.)   And what did his councillors say? "They dam displeased!"   (Roars of laughter.)   No, gentlemen, let each man in public or literary life in both nations do all that in him lies to cement their friendship, so essential for their mutual welfare.   But this cannot be cemented by the publication of vain vaticinations.   This great part of our great Empire has a natural and warm feeling for our republican brethren, whose fathers parted from us a century ago in anger and bloodshed.   May this natural affection never die.   It is like the love which is borne by a younger brother to an elder, so long as the big brother behaves handsomely and kindly.   I may possibly know something of the nature of such affection, for as the eldest of a round dozen, I have had experience of the fraternal relation as exhibited by an unusual number of younger brothers.   Never have I known that fraternal tie to fail, but even its strength has its natural limit, so Canada's affection may be measured.   None of my younger brothers, however fond of me, would voluntarily ask that his prospects should be altogether overshadowed and swallowed up by mine.   So Canada, if I may express her feelings in words which our neighbours understand, wishes to be their friend, but does not desire to become their food.　She rejoices in the big brother's strength and status, but is not anxious to nourish it by offering up her own body in order that it may afford him, when over-hungry, that happy festival he is in the habit of calling a " square meal."　(Loud laughter.)　I must ask you now once more to allow me, gentlemen, to express my acknowledgments to you for this entertainment.　It affords another indication of the feelings with which the citizens of Winnipeg regard any person who has the honour, as the head of the Canadian Government, to represent the Queen—(cheers)—you recognise in the Governor-General the sign and symbol of the union which binds together in one the free and kindred peoples whom God has set over famous isles and over fertile spaces of mighty continents.　I have touched, in speaking to you, on certain vaticinations and certain advice given by a few good strangers to Canadians on the subject of the future of Canada. Gentlemen, I believe that Canadians are well able to take care themselves of their future, and the outside world had better listen to them instead of promulgating weak and wild theories of its own.　(Loud applause.) But however uncertain, and I may add, foolish may be such forecasts, of one thing we may be sure, which is this, that the country you call Canada, and which your sons and your children's children will be proud to know by that name, is a land which will be a land of power among the nations.　(Cheers.)　Mistress of a zone of territory favourable for the maintenance of a numerous and homogeneous white population,

Canada must, to judge from the increase in her strength during the past, and from the many and vast opportunities for the growth of that strength on her new Provinces in the future, be great and worthy her position on the earth. Affording the best and safest highway between Asia and Europe, she will see traffic from both directed to her coasts. With a hand upon either ocean she will gather from each for the benefit of her hardy millions a large share of the commerce of the world. To the east and to the west she will pour forth of her abundance, her treasures of food and the riches of her mines and of her forests, demanded of her by the less fortunate of mankind. I esteem those men favoured indeed, who, in however slight a degree, have had the honour, or may be yet called upon to take part in the councils of the statesmen who, in this early era of her history, are moulding this nation's laws in the forms approved by its representatives. For me, I feel that I can be ambitious of no higher title than to be known as one who administered its Government in thorough sympathy with the hopes and aspirations of its first founders, and in perfect consonance with the will of its free parliament. (Cheers.) I ask for no better lot than to be remembered by its people as rejoicing in the gladness born of their independence and of their loyalty. I desire no other reputation than that which may belong to him who sees his own dearest wishes in process of fulfilment, in their certain progress, in their undisturbed peace, and in their ripening grandeur. (Cheers.)

A Monsieur le Président et Messieurs les Membres de l'Association de St. Jean Baptiste de Manitoba.

Messieurs,—J'ai l'honneur de vous remercier au nom de sa majesté des sentiments de loyauté que vous venez d'exprimer.

C'est pour moi un plaisir d'entendre exprimer des sentiments de dévouement au trône, de quelque race qu'ils proviennent, soit de la bouche de Canadiens-français, d'Anglais, d'Ecossais, de Canadiens-irlandais ou de Canadiens d'origine quelconque.

Les gloires de chaque race aujourd'hui représentée au Manitoba se confondent dans la gloire commune de la nation Canadienne. Que chacune d'elles conserve précieusement ses associations historiques ! Elles sont en effet autant de motifs d'encouragement à travailler à augmenter la force et la valeur de la nation entière, une et indivisible. A l'avenir, votre rivalité ne consistera que dans la sainte rivalité de votre dévouement à Dieu et au grand pays qu'il vous a octroyé dans notre puissance du Canada.

C'est à un Canadien-français que revient la gloire d'avoir le premier exploré notre pays. Qu'il revienne aux descendants de cette race de cimenter leur union avec nos diverses races, et de leur donner ainsi de la force. Un Canadien-français me disait tout dernièrement à Québec : "Ma famille a souvent versé de son sang en combattant les Anglais." Je lui répondis : "Oui, monsieur, et ma propre famille en a versé encore bien plus en les combattant, car nous les avons combattus pendant plus de trois siècles." L'histoire de vos ancêtres est aussi glorieuse que celle de l'Ecosse ou de l'Angleterre.

L'accueil que vous me faites comme chef du gouvernement fédéral et comme représentant sa majesté la reine, me convainc que le jour de la St. Jean Baptiste est célèbré par vous comme le sont les fêtes de St. Georges, St. André et St. Patrice. Ce sera une fête qui célébrera en même temps les traditions de la race, de la foi, et l'inconquérable résolution d'affermir notre population dans une fraternité chrétienne et une nationalité animée de sentiments chrétiens.

In reply to the Archbishop of St. Boniface, Winnipeg.

Monseigneur et Messieurs,—J'ai l'honneur d'accuser réception de votre gracieuse adresse, renouvelant l'expression de vos sentiments de loyauté envers la couronne, et de vous assurer que j'en apprécie la sincérité du fond de mon cœur.

Son éloquence exprime, en termes qui prennent leur source dans le cœur, le devoir qui a été enseigné et pratiqué parmi vous, par des prédicateurs éloquents et des missionnaires héroïques.

Vos paroles remarquables seront transmises à la reine. Tout récemment encore, sa majesté me faisait part du plaisir qu'élle avait ressenti, en prenant connaissance des paroles prononcées par des hommes distingués de la province de Québec, lors de l'érection du monument à la mémoire du Colonel de Salaberry.

Ce monument, digne de l'art canadien, a été érigé en l'honneur d'un des enfants les plus illustres du

Canada. Doué d'une force physique qui aurait fait envi aux preux Paladins de Roncevaux, le Colonel de Salaberry mit toute son énergie et sa force au service de son pays, et contribua à repousser l'ennemi qui menaçait l'intégrité de l'Empire Britannique en attaquant le Canada.

Permettez-moi de vous remercier aussi de tout mon cœur de ce que vous avez dit à l'égard de la Princesse, qui espère être de retour au Canada à la fin d'octobre. J'aurais voulu qu'elle eût pu prendre part à la réception qui m'est faite à St. Boniface. Non seulement cette réception me cause une vive satisfaction, mais elle m'inspire le plus grand intérêt.

St. Boniface est le berceau de ce Canada plus grand que l'ancien. Sous les auspices de l'Eglise, les Canadiens-français sont venus ici et ont fondé une communauté heureuse et prospère. Leurs compatriotes des provinces de l'est peuvent être certains que, sous les mêmes auspices, leurs enfants trouveront ici les mêmes bienfaits de l'éducation qui les guidera dans la vie.

De nombreux Canadiens quittent la province de Québec pour se diriger vers le sud; ils abandonnent la vie saine des champs, et le bonheur de vivre avec leurs compatriotes pour la vie malsaine des manufactures sur la terre étrangère. Un certain nombre d'entre eux songent à rentrer au pays après des années d'absence, mais il leur serait incomparablement plus avantageux, à tous, de se diriger, de suite, vers les plaines du Nord-Ouest Canadien, où la fertilité du sol leur assurerait un avenir facile.

J'ai rencontré sur la ligne du chemin de fer, près du Portage du Rat, plusieurs de vos compatriotes qui sont occupés à l'achèvement de cette grande et importante œuvre nationale. Tous m'ont donné à entendre qu'ils avaient écrit à leurs amis, pour leur conseiller de venir s'établir à Manitoba. Ils ajoutaient que, quant à eux-mêmes, leur unique but était de se procurer des terrains dans cette nouvelle et fertile province.

Je remercie votre grandeur et vous messieurs du clergé de St. Boniface, de l'accueil si bienveillant que vous me faites; je me compte, volontiers, au premier rang de ceux qui se plaisent à reconnaître le prix du précieux élément fourni à notre population par la race Gauloise.

An address having been presented by the Board of Management of the Manitoba College, the following was His Excellency's reply:

To the Members of the Board of Management of the Manitoba College:—Gentlemen,—Let me thank you for your welcome. The wise experiment made in your confederation of colleges has been watched by all who take an interest in education. It has made Manitoba as famous among men of thought as its wheat and other produce have rendered it well known among men interested in agriculture.

Your example will probably be followed in the older Provinces, for where universities are not generally supported by the various denominations, and these separate themselves too definitely, it is difficult to secure that large number of students, which it is necessary to have, if a university is to attract the best men.

It was at a College in Ontario such as this that I first saw in practice that wise toleration and determination to unite for the common good which has guided you. I saw there the clergy of all denominations uniting in prayer, at a ceremony such as the present, celebrating the erection of new buildings for a college, free to all, but under Presbyterian direction. The same enlightened feeling has prevailed in the west, where, having a free course, you have instituted a university to which all colleges are affiliated.

Where States are ancient and the habits of men settled deep in old grooves, the efforts made by an individual and the movement of thought, may have but little apparent effect. Hearts may be broken over seemingly useless work, for the ways of the people are formed and custom precludes change. Here in a new land, with a people spreading everywhere over the country whose value has only so lately been realised, you enjoy the more fortunate lot of being able to trace for the communities the outlines of their future life. It is this which makes these first steps of such incalculable importance. Each touch you give will give shape and form and make a lasting impression, and your hands labour at no hard and inductile mass.

It is a real satisfaction to me that I am able to be present at a meeting which marks a fresh advance in the status of a college organised in connection with the University of Manitoba, and I thank you for the invitation you have given me.

Not even the constant exhibition of huge roots, tall heads of wheat, and gigantic potatoes and monster onions at the fairs in the eastern Provinces can do more to make Manitoba a temptation to settlers, than the proof you afford that their children shall be thoroughly educated by men belonging to the churches of which they are members, and in sympathy with their desires and hopes.

Where civil government is so perfect, where religious instruction and toleration are so well taught, and where education is prized even above the wonderful material prosperity guaranteed by the rich plains around you, men may be certain that they can choose no fairer land for themselves and for their children.

Before leaving Fort Shaw, Montana, September 1881, the members of the Mounted Police, who had accompanied the party for seven weeks, were paraded under command of Major Crozier, at His Excellency's request, who in bidding them farewell said:—

Officers, non-commissioned officers and men,—Our long march is over, and truly sorry we feel that it is so. I am glad that its last scene is to take place in this American fort where we have been so courteously and hospitably received. That good fellowship which exists between soldiers is always to the fullest extent shown between you and our kind friends. This perfect understanding is to be expected, for both our Empires, unlike some others, send out to their distant frontier posts not their worst, but some of their very best men.

I have asked for this parade this morning to take leave of you, and to express my entire satisfaction at the manner in which your duties have been performed. You have been subject to some searching criticism, for on my staff are officers who have served in the cavalry, artillery, and infantry. Their unanimous verdict is to the effect that they have never seen work better, more willingly, or more smartly done while under circumstances of some difficulty caused by bad weather or otherwise. Your appearance on parade was always as clean and bright and soldier-like as possible. Your force is often spoken of in Canada as one of which Canada is justly proud. It is well that this pride is so fully justified, for your duties are most important and varied. You must always act as guardians of the peace. There may be occasions also in which you may have to act as soldiers, and some-times in dealing with our Indian fellow-subjects you may have to show the mingled prudence, kindness, and firmness which constitute a diplomat. You have, with a force at present only 250* strong, to keep order in a country whose fertile, wheat-growing area is reckoned about 250 million of acres. The perfect confidence in the maintenance of the authority of the law prevailing over these vast territories, a confidence most necessary with the settlement now proceeding, show how thoroughly you have done your work. It will be with the greatest pleasure that I shall convey to the Prime Minister my appreciation of your services, and

* The number of the North West Mounted Police was raised in 1882 to 500 men.

the satisfaction we have all had in having you with us as our escort and companions throughout the journey.

A Society was founded by Lord Lorne, in 1882, for the encouragement of Science and Literature. Divided into sections, it was designed to furnish to Canada what the French Academy and the British Association give to Great Britain. At its first meeting, which took place in the Senate Chamber, he opened the proceedings with these remarks:—

Gentlemen,—These few words I do not address to you, presuming to call myself one of your brotherhood, either in science or literature, but I speak to you as one whose accidental official position may enable him to serve you, persuaded as I am that the furtherance of your interests is for the benefit and honour of Canada. Let me briefly state the object aimed at in the institution of this society. Whether it be possible that our hopes be fulfilled according to our expectation the near future will show. But from the success which has attended similar associations in other lands possessed of less spirit, energy, and opportunity than our own, there is no reason to augur ill of the attempt to have here a body of men whose achievements may entitle them to recognise and encourage the appearance of merit in literature, and to lead in science and the useful application of its discoveries. It is proposed, then, that this society shall consist of a certain number of members who have made their mark by their writings, whether these be of imagination or the study of nature. In one division our fellow - countrymen, descended from the stock of old France, will discuss with that grace of diction and appreciation of talent, which is so conspicuous amongst them, all that may affect their literature and the maintenance of the purity of that grand language from which the English is largely derived. They well know how to pay compliments to rising authors, and how with tact and courtesy to crown the aspirants to the honours they will bestow. Among Englishmen of letters the grant of such formal marks of recognition by their brethren has not as yet become popular or usual, and it may be that it never will become a custom. On the other hand, it surely will be a pleasure to a young author, if, after a perusal of his thoughts, they who are his co-workers and successful precursors in the wide domain of poetry, fiction, or of history, should see fit to award him an expression of thanks for his contribution to the intellectual delight or to the knowledge of his time. They only, whose labours have met with the best reward—the praise of their contemporaries—can take the initiative in such a welcome to younger men, and whatever number may hereafter be elected to this society, it is to be desired that no man be upon its lists who has not by some original and complete work justified his selection. The meeting together of our eminent men will contribute to unite on a common ground those best able to express the thoughts and illustrate the history of the time. It will serve to strengthen emulation among us, for the discussion of progress made in other lands, will breed the desire to push the intellectual development of our own. We may hope that this union will promote the completion of the national collections which, already fairly representative in geology, may hereafter include archives, paintings, and objects illustrating ethnology and all branches of Natural History.   In science we have men whose names are widely known, and the vast field for study and exploration afforded by this magnificent country may be expected to reward, by valuable discoveries, the labours of the geologist and mineralogist.   It would be out of place in these few sentences to detail the lines of research which have already engaged your attention.   They will be spoken of in the record of your proceedings.   Among those, the utility of which must be apparent to all, one may be particularly mentioned.   I refer to the meteorological observations, from which have been derived the storm warnings which during the last few years have saved many lives.   A comparatively new science has thus been productive of results known to all our population and especially to seamen.   Here I have only touched upon one or two subjects in the wide range of study which will occupy the time and thoughts of one half of your membership, devoted as two of your four sections will be to geological and biological sciences.   It will be your province to aid and encourage the workers in their acquisition of knowledge of that nature, each of whose secrets may become the prize of him who shall make one of her mysteries the special subject of thought. America already bids fair to rival France and Germany in the number of her experts.   Canada may certainly

have her share in producing those men whose achievements in science have more than equalled in fame the
triumphs of statesmen. These last labour only for
one country, while the benefits of the discoveries of
science are shared by the world. But widely different as are the qualities which develop patriotism and
promote science, yet I would call to the aid of our
young association the love of country, and ask Canadians to support and gradually to make as perfect as
possible this their national society. Imperfections
there must necessarily be at first in its constitution—
omissions in membership and organisation there may
be. Such faults may hereafter be avoided. Our
countrymen will recognise that in a body of gentlemen drawn from all our provinces and conspicuous
for their ability, there will be a centre around which
to rally. They will see that the welfare and strength
of growth of this association shall be impeded by no
small jealousies, no carping spirit of detraction, but
shall be nourished by a noble motive common to the
citizens of the republic of letters and to the student of
the free world of Nature, namely : the desire to prove
that their land is not insensible to the glory which
springs from numbering among its sons those whose
success becomes the heritage of mankind. I shall not
now further occupy your time, which will be more
worthily used in listening to the addresses of the pre-
sidents and of those gentlemen who for this year have
consented to take the chair at the meetings of the
several sections.

Gentlemen,—Our heartfelt thanks are due to you
for the welcome given to us, a welcome whose expression is embodied in this beautifully decorated address.
It echoes the loyal sentiments which remain predominant among those, who, wherever their business may
cause them to reside, remember that they have been
born under our British freedom. We shall gladly
keep our gift in recollection of a visit to one of
America's foremost cities, where the kindly feelings
of our cousins have been shown in the generous hospitality which they are ever ready to extend to the
stranger.   With you whose interests are bound up
with the greatness of California, and with the gigantic
trade of the United States, we can cordially sympathise.   Connected as we are for a time with the
fortunes of the sister land of Canada, we know how
much the welfare of the one country is affected by
the good of the other ; how the evil that falls on one
must affect the other also.   Our blood makes us
brothers, and our interests make us partners.   Our
governments are engaged in the same task, and from
experience there is no reason to think otherwise than
that they will be allowed to work in that perfect harmony which is essential for their peace and for the
peace of the world.   They are arching the continent
with two zones of civilisation ; with light, not of one
colour, but equally replacing the former darkness, and
the harmony between them is as natural as is the rela

tion in the rainbow of the separate hues of red and azure. Your presence here shows how our commerce is interwoven. In crossing the continent and marvelling at the wealth and power shown by every city of this mighty people, it is a pride to think how much of all they have is theirs by virtue of British and Irish blood; and when here and at New York, we reach the ports supplying this vast population, we find in the flags borne by the shipping, proof that it is still the old country that in the main ministers to and is benefited by the progress of her children.

At Victoria, in British Columbia, in 1882, at a public dinner in
his honour, the Governor-General said :—

Mr. Mayor and Council,—It is, I assure you, with more than common feelings of gratitude that I rise to ask you to accept my acknowledgments and thanks for this evening's entertainment. The reception the Princess and I have met with in Victoria, and throughout British Columbia, will long live in our memory as one of the brightest episodes of a time which has been made delightful to us by the heartfelt loyalty of the people of our Canadian provinces. Nowhere has the contentment insured by British institutions been more strongly expressed than on these beautiful shores of the Pacific. I am rejoiced to observe signs that the days are now passed when we had to look upon this community as one too remote and too sundered from the rest to share to the full the rapid increase of prosperity which has been so remarkable since the Union. Attracted at first by the capricious temptations of the gold mines, your valleys were inundated by a large population. It was not to be anticipated that this could last, and although population declined with the temporary decrease of mining, it is evident that the period of depression in this, as in every other matter, has been passed. (Applause.) I have everywhere seen signs that a more stable, and therefore more satisfactory, emigration has set in. Victoria has made of late a decided start. I visited with much pleasure many of the factories which witness to this, and I hope before I leave to have made a still more exhaustive examination of the establishments which are rapidly rising among you. That the wares produced by these are appreciated beyond the limits of the city is very evident throughout the Province, where cleanliness is insured by Victoria soap, and comfort, or at least contentment and consolation, by Kurtz's Victoria cigars. (Loud laughter and applause.) No words can be too strong to express the charm of this delightful land, where a climate softer and more constant than that of the south of England ensures at all times of the year a full enjoyment of the wonderful loveliness of nature around you. There is no doubt that any Canadian who visits this island and the mainland shores and sees the happiness of the people, the forest laden coast, the tranquil gulfs and glorious mountains, can but congratulate himself that his country possesses scenes of such perfect beauty. (Applause.) We who have been much touched by the warmth of your welcome will, I am sure, sympathise with the desire which will be felt by every travelled Canadian in the future, that every alternate year at least the Dominion Parliament should meet at New Westminster, Nanaimo, or in Victoria. (Laughter and applause.) Where men seem to live with such comfort, regret will inevitably arise that you have as yet so few to share your good fortune. Though your contribution to the revenue is at least a million dollars, there are only twenty thousand white men over the three hundred and fifty thousand square miles of Province. Various causes, the most formidable of these being physical, have hitherto contributed to this. The physical difficulties, tremendous as they are, are being rapidly conquered. There is no cause why any of a different character should not be surmounted with an equal success. What is wanted to effect this object is only cordial co-operation with the central Government. (Cheers.) There was perhaps a time when the Governor-General would not have been regarded, in his official capacity at all events, with as much favour as I flatter myself may now be the case. (Applause.) No wonder that the feeling is changed, now that the circumstances are better understood, for I challenge any one to mention any example in which a government, ruling over a comparatively small population of four and a half millions, has ever done as much as has the Canadian Government to insure for its furthest Provinces the railway communication which is an essential for the development of the resources of the land. (Cheering.) Mr. Francis* will back me, I am certain, when I say that the United States, with a population of fifteen or

* The United States Consul.

twenty millions, when California was first settled in
1849, did not push the railway through to the Pacific
Coast in the vigorous manner in which the Canadian
Government is now doing. (Loud cheers.) I have
full confidence that you will see that policy of enterprise and of justice nobly carried out. Early promises,
if made too hastily, showed that if there was profound
ignorance of the physical geography of your country,
there was at all events profound goodwill. Later
events have proved that in spite of all obstacles
"where there is a will there is a way." Pride in
national feeling has made the country strain every
nerve to bind still further with the sentiment of confidence the unity of the Confederation. (Applause.)
Where is now the old talk which we used to hear from
a few of the faint-hearted of a change in destiny or of
annexation? (Cheers.) It does not exist. To be
sure, here I have heard some vague terror expressed,
but it is a terror which I have heard expressed among
our friends on the American Pacific Slope also, and it
is to the effect that annexation must soon take place
to the Celestial Empire. (Great laughter.) Well,
gentlemen, I fully sympathise with this fear. None
of us like to die before our time, but I will suggest to
you, from the healthy signs and vitality I see around
me, that your time has not yet come. Your object
now is to live, and for that purpose to get your enterprises and your railways as part of your assets.
(Applause.) The rest will follow in time, but at the
present moment we must concern ourselves with
practical politics. Let us look beyond this Island

and beyond even those difficult mountains, and see what our neighbours and friends to the south of us are about. An army of workmen—exactly double that now employed in this Province—are driving with a speed that seems wonderful a railway through to the coast. In another year or two a large traffic, encouraged by the competition in freights between it, the Central and the Southern Pacific will have been acquired. You are, by the very nature of things, heavily handicapped here, and a trade, as you know, once established is not easily rivalled. Take care that you are in the market for this competition at as early a day as possible. When you are as rich as California, and have as many public works as Queensland, it may be time for you to reconsider your position. There is no reason ultimately to doubt that the population attracted to you as soon as you have a line through the mountains, will be the population which we most desire to have—a people like that of the old Imperial Islands, drawn from the strongest races of northern Europe,—one that with English, American, Irish, German, French and Scandinavian blood shall be a worthy son of the old Mother of Nations. (Loud applause.) Only last week, in seven days, no less than 900 people came to San Francisco by the overland route from the East. Your case will be the same if with "a strong pull and a pull altogether" you get your public works completed. I have spoken of your being pretty heavily handicapped. In saying this, I refer to the agricultural capabilities of the Province alone. Of course you have nothing like the available land that the central Provinces possess, yet it seems to me you have enough for all the men who are likely to come to you for the next few years as farmers or owners of small ranches. (Applause.) The climate of the interior for at least one hundred miles north of the boundary line has a far shorter winter than that of most of Alberta or Arthabaska. Losses of crops from early frosts or of cattle from severe weather are unknown to the settlers of your upper valleys. In these—and I wish there were more of these valleys—all garden produce and small fruits can be cultivated with the greatest success. For men possessing from £200 to £600 a year, I can conceive no more attractive occupation than the care of cattle or a cereal farm within your borders. (Loud applause.) Wherever there is open land, the wheat crops rival the best grown elsewhere, while there is nowhere any dearth of ample provision of fuel and lumber for the winter. (Renewed applause.) As you get your colonisation roads pushed and the dykes along the Fraser River built, you will have a larger available acreage, for there are quiet straths and valleys hidden away among the rich forests which would provide comfortable farms. As in the north-west last year, so this year I have taken down the evidence of settlers, and this has been wonderfully favourable. To say the truth, I was rather hunting for grumblers, and found only one! He was a young man of super-sensitiveness from one of our comfortable Ontario cities, and he said he could not bear this country. Anxious to come at the truth, and desiring to search to the bottom of things, we pressed him as to the reason. "Did he know of any cases of misery? Had he found starving settlers?" The reply was re-assuring, for he said, "No; but I don't like it. Nobody in this country walks; everybody rides!" (Laughter.) You will be happy to hear that he is going back to Ontario. Let me now allude, in a very few words, to those points which may be mentioned as giving you exceptional advantages. If you are handicapped in the matter of land in comparison with the Provinces of the Plains, you are certainly not so with regard to climate. (Cheering.) Agreeable as I think the steady and dry cold of an Eastern winter, yet there are very many who would undoubtedly prefer the temperature enjoyed by those who live west of the mountains. Even where it is coldest, spring comes in February, and the country is so divided into districts of greater dryness or greater moisture, that a man can always choose whether to have a rainfall small or great. I hope I am not wearying you in dwelling on these points, for my only excuse in making these observations is, that I have learnt that the interior is to many on the island as much a *terra incognita* as it was to me. I can partly understand this after seeing the beautifully engineered road which was constructed by Mr. Trutch, for although I am assured it is as safe as a church— (laughter)—I can very well understand that it is pleasanter for many of the ladies to remain in this beautiful island than to admire the grandeur of the scenery in the gorges. As you have adopted protection in your politics, perhaps it would not be presumptuous in me to suggest that you should adopt protection also in regard to your precipices—(great laughter)—and that should the waggon road be continued in use, a few Douglas firs might be sacrificed to make even more perfect that excellent road in providing protection at the sides. Besides the climate, which is so greatly in your favour, you have another great advantage in the tractability and good conduct of the Indian population. (Applause.) I believe I have seen the Indians of almost every tribe throughout the Dominion, and nowhere can you find any who are so trustworthy in regard to conduct—(hear, hear)—so willing to assist the white settlers by their labour, so independent and anxious to learn the secret of the white man's power. (Applause.) Where elsewhere constant demands are met for assistance; your Indians have never asked for any, for in the interviews given to the Chiefs their whole desire seemed to be for schools and schoolmasters, and in reply to questions as to whether they would assist themselves in securing such institutions, they invariably replied that they would be glad to pay for them. (Loud applause.) It is certainly much to be desired that some of the funds apportioned for Indian purposes, be given to provide them fully with schools in which Industrial Education may form an important item. (Hear, hear.) But we must not do injustice to the wilder tribes. Their case is totally different from that of your Indians. The buffalo was everything to the nomad. It gave him house, fuel, clothes, and thread. The disappearance of this animal left him starving. Here, on the contrary, the advent of the white men has never diminished the food supply of the native. He has game in abundance, for the deer are as numerous now as they ever have been. He has more fish than he knows what to do with, and the lessons in farming that you have taught him have given him a source of food supply of which he was previously ignorant. Throughout the interior it will probably pay well in the future to have flocks of sheep. The demand for wool and woollen goods will always be very large among the people now crowding in such numbers to those regions which our official world as yet calls the North-West, but which is the North-East and East to you. There is no reason why British Columbia should not be for this portion of our territory what California is to the States in the supply afforded of fruits. (Hear, hear.) The perfection attained by small fruits is unrivalled, and it is only with the Peninsula of Ontario that you would have to compete for the supplies of grapes, peaches, pears, apples, cherries, plums, apricots, and currants. Every stick in these wonderful forests which so amply and generously clothe the Sierras from the Cascade range to the distant Rocky mountains, will be of value as communication opens up. The great arch of timber lands beginning on the west of Lake Manitoba, circles round to Edmonton and comes down along the mountains so as to include the whole of your Province. Poplar alone for many years must be the staple wood of the lands to the south of the Saskatchewan, and your great opportunity lies in this, that you can give the settlers of the whole of that region as much of the finest timber in the world as they can desire, while cordwood cargoes will compete with the coal of Alberta. (Loud cheers.) Coming down in our survey to the coast we come upon ground familiar to you all, and you all know how large a trade already exists with China and Australia in wood, and how capable of almost indefinite expansion is this commerce. Your forests are hardly tapped, and there are plenty more logs, like one I saw cut the other day at Burrard Inlet, of forty inches square and ninety and one hundred feet in length, down to sticks which could be used as props for mines or as cordwood for fuel. The business which has assumed such large proportions along the Pacific shore of the canning of salmon, great as it is, is as yet almost in its infancy, for there is many a river swarming with fish from the time of the first run of salmon in spring to the last run of other varieties in the autumn, on which many a cannery is sure to be established. Last, but certainly not least in the list of your resources, comes your mineral and chiefly your coal treasure. (Applause.) The coal from the Nanaimo mines now leads the market at San Francisco. Nowhere else in these countries is such coal to be found, and it is now being worked with an energy which bids fair to make Nanaimo one of the chief mining stations on the continent. It is of incalculable importance not only to this Province of the Dominion, but also to the interests of the Empire, that our fleets and mercantile marine as well as the continental markets should be supplied from this source. (Hear, hear, and cheers.) Where you have so good a list of resources it may be almost superfluous to add another, but I would strongly advise you to cultivate the attractions held out to the travelling public by the magnificence of your scenery. (Cheers.) Let this country become what Switzerland is for Europe in the matter of good roads to places which may be famed for their beauty, and let good and clean hotels attract the tourist to visit your grand valleys and marvellous mountain ranges. Choose some district, and there are many from which you can choose, where trout and salmon abound, and where sport may be found among the deer and with the wild fowl. Select some portion of your territory where pines and firs shroud in their greatest richness the giant slopes, and swarm upwards to glacier, snow field, and craggy peak, and where in the autumn the maples seem as though they wished to mimic in hanging gardens the glowing tints of the lava that must have streamed down the precipices of these old volcanoes. (Loud cheering.) Wherever you find these beauties in greatest perfection, and where the river torrents urge their currents most impetuously through the Alpine gorges, there I would counsel you to set apart a region which shall be kept as a national park. In doing so you can follow the example of our southern friends,—an example which, I am sure Mr. Francis will agree with me, we cannot do better than imitate, and you would secure that they who make the round trip from New York or Montreal shall return from San Francisco, or come thence *via* the Canadian Pacific Railroad. (Loud and continued applause.) I thought it might interest you, gentlemen, this evening to hear the last news regarding that Railway, and therefore I should like to read to you a letter received only a day or two ago from the engineer in chief, Major Rogers. You will see he speaks hopefully and as-suringly :

" I have found the desired pass through the Selkirks, it lying about twenty miles east of the forks of the Ille-cille-want and about two miles north of the main east branch of the same. Its elevation above sea level is about 4500 feet, or about 1000 feet lower than the pass across the Rockies. The formation of the country, from the summits of the Selkirks to the Columbia river, has been much misrepresented. In-stead of the solid mass of mountain, as reported, there are two large valleys lying within these limits. The Beaver river, which empties into the Columbia river about twenty miles below the Black-berry (or Howse Pass route), rises south of the fifty-first parallel (I have not seen its source, but have seen its valley for that distance), and the Spellamacheen runs nearly parallel with the Beaver but in an opposite direction, and lies between the Beaver and the Columbia. I have great hope of being able to take with me this fall the results of a preliminary survey of this route. It necessarily involves heavy work, as must any short line across the mountains, a condition which will be readily accepted in consideration of the material shortening of the route."

This is the last news, and I hope we shall hear of its full corroboration before long. I beg, gentlemen, to thank you once more for your exceeding kindness, and for all the kindness shown us since our arrival. I have always been a firm friend of British Columbia, and I hope before I leave the country to see still greater progress made towards meeting your wishes.

At a meeting of the National Rifle Association, held at Ottawa, 8th March 1883, His Excellency, spoke as follows :—

I believe all who value those qualities which lead to good rifle-shooting—steadiness and sobriety—and this means every family in the country, the father and mother, as well as the young men belonging to it, should give their ten cents or twenty-five cents, as they can afford it, to swell the funds of the association. As this association thus encourages personal, as well as a military training, it merits the support of all classes. We know that the amount of personal training that is required produces a love of temperance among those who attend the meetings of the association, and we know that by the military training given, a military sentiment is developed, which makes men at least not averse to discipline in moderation. It has been said by my predecessor, and I agree with the remark, that Canada is certainly the most democratic country upon the North American continent, but we know that although everybody may have been born equal, yet that equality suddenly and mysteriously disappears as soon as the schoolboy goes upon the school bench, or the rifleman goes upon the rifle ground. The militiamen of Canada show that a democratic people do not tolerate unearned superiority, but recognise the superiority given by training. I cannot let this opportunity pass without saying a last word as to the point of view from which I regard the importance of militia training in Canada. It is more perhaps from the point of view of an Imperial officer than from that of a man temporarily holding a Canadian civil appointment. There is a certain amount of feeling in this country that our whole militia force is a mere matter of fuss and feathers, of "playing at soldiers" in fact. I think that is always a most unfortunate feeling, because I cannot say how anxiously in the old country those steps are watched by which Canadians perfect themselves for purposes of self-defence. Englishmen know that in case of any trouble arising, which I hope not to see, and do not believe we shall see, they are bound and pledged to come to your assistance. The question must necessarily be asked, With what army are they to operate? with one that will be of real assistance, or with one that will have no more cohesion than that which fell under the organised blows of the Prussian army before Orleans? I can always point to the efforts made in Canada before my time to have an organised system of military training. I can point to the grants given by the Government for the encouragement of individual and regimental proficiency in rifle shooting. I can point also to the military schools for the militia which are being founded, and to the steps which are to be taken that officers shall always have some training received from those schools before they undertake the responsibility of leading their fellow-citizens in the ranks. I can point also to that splendid institution, the Military College at Kingston, and I can certainly say to the old country people, that should any misfortune arise that should compel us to operate together, they will in time find in Canada officers who will be perfectly able and ready to lead men, who from their physical powers and from their military sentiments and from their hardihood are likely, under proper training and guidance, to form some of the best troops in the world. (Loud cheers.)

At the Second Meeting of the Royal Society, at Ottawa, May 1883, the Governor General said :—

Mr. President, Mr. Vice-President, and Members of the Royal Society of Canada,—When we met last year, and formally inaugurated a society for the encouragement of literature and science in Canada, an experiment was tried. As with all experiments, its possible success was questioned by some who feared that the elements necessary for such an organisation were lacking. Our meeting of this year assumes a character which an inaugural assembly could not possess. The position we took in asserting that the time had come for the institution of such a union of the scientific and literary men of this country has been established as good, not only by the honourable name accorded to us by Her Majesty, a designation never lightly granted, but also by that without which we could not stand, namely, the public favour extended to our efforts. Parliament has recognised the earnest

purpose and happy co-operation with which you have
met and worked in unison, knowing that the talents
exhibited are not those of gold and silver only, and
has stamped with its approbation your designs by
voting a sum of money, which in part will defray the
expense of printing your transactions. And here, in
speaking of this as a business meeting, I would venture
to remind you, and all friends of this society throughout the country, that the $5000 annually voted by
the House of Commons will go but a very short way
in preparing a publication which shall fully represent
Canada to the foreign scientific bodies of the world.
We have only to look to the Federal and State Legis-
latures of America to see what vast sums are annually
expended in the States for scientific research. We
see there also how the proceeds of noble endowments
are annually utilised for the free dissemination of
knowledge. It is, therefore, not to be supposed that
he comparatively small parallel assistance provided
by any Government can absolve wealthy individuals
from the patriotic duty of bequeathing or of giving to
such a national society the funds, without which it
cannot usefully exist. You will forgive me, as one
who may be supposed to have a certain amount of
the traditional economical prudence of his countrymen, for mentioning one other matter on which, at
all events, in the meantime, a saving can be effected.
While it is necessary to have accurate and finely
executed engravings of beautiful drawings for the
illustration of scientific papers, it is necessary that the
printing of the transactions should occasion as little

cost as possible; and I believe you will find it advis-
able for the present that each paper shall be printed
only in that language in which its author has communicated it to the society. Your position is rather
a peculiar one, for although you work for the benefit
of the public, it is not to be expected that the public
can understand all you say when your speech is of
science in consultation with each other. The public
will therefore, I trust, be in the position of those who
are willing to pay their physicians when they meet in
consultation, without insisting that every word the
doctors say to each other shall be repeated in the
hearing of all men. When funds increase, it seems
to me that the economy it will probably now be necessary to exercise in regard to this may be discarded.

In the sections dealing with literature it is proposed
to establish a reading committee, whose duty it shall
be to report on the publications of the year, that our
thanks may be given to the authors who advance the
cause of literature among us. To assist in that most
necessary enterprise, the formation of a national
museum, circulars have been addressed by the society
to men likely to have opportunities for the collection
of objects of interest, and the Hudson Bay Company's
officers have been foremost in promoting our wishes.
The Government is now prepared to house all objects
sent to the secretary of the Royal Society at Ottawa,
and contributions for collections of archives, of anti-
quities, of zoology, and of all things of interest are
requested. I rejoice, gentlemen, that I have been
able to be with you now; that a year has elapsed

since our incorporation, as this period allows us in some measure to judge of our future prospects. These are most encouraging, and the only possible difficulty that I can see ahead of you is this : that men may be apt to take exception to your membership because it is not geographically representative. I would earnestly counsel you to hold to your course in this matter. A scientific and literary society must remain one representing individual eminence, and that individual eminence must be recognised if, as it may happen accidentally, personal distinction in authorship may at any particular moment be the happy possession of only one part of the country. A complete work, and one recognised for its merit, should remain the essential qualification for election to the literary sections, and the same test should be applied as far as possible to the scientific branches. If men be elected simply because they came from such and such a college, or if they be elected simply because they came from the east, from the west, from the north, or from the south, you will get a heterogeneous body together quite unworthy to be compared with the foreign societies on whose intellectual level Canada, as represented by her scientific men and authors, must in the future endeavour to stand. One word more on the kindly recognition already given to you. In America, in France, and in Britain, the birth of the new institution has been hailed with joy, and our distinguished president is at this moment also a nominated delegate of Britain. An illness we deplore has alone prevented the presence of an illustrious member of the Academy of France, and the French Government, with an enlightened generosity which does it honour, had expressed its wish to defray the expenses of the most welcome of ambassadors. We have the satisfaction of cordially greeting an eminent representative of the United States, and I express the desire which is shared by all in this hall, that our meeting may never want the presence of delegates of the great people who are dear as they are near to us.

It is, gentlemen, greatly owing to your organisation that the British Association for the advancement of science will next year meet at Montreal, following in this a precedent happily established by the visit last year of the American Association. These meetings at Montreal are not without their significance. They show that it is not only among statesmen and politicians abroad that Canada is valued and respected; but that throughout all classes, and wherever intellect, culture, and scientific attainment are revered, her position is acknowledged, and her aspiration to take her place among the nations is seen and welcomed.

I am sure that your British brethren have chosen wisely in selecting Montreal, for I know the hearty greeting which awaits them from its hospitable citizens. The facilities placed at the disposal of our British guests will enable them to visit a large portion of our immense territory, where in every part new and interesting matters will arrest their attention, and give delight to men who, in many cases, have but lately realised our resources. Their words, biassed by no interests other than the desire for knowledge, and founded on personal observation, will find no contradiction when they assert that in the lifetime of the babes now born, the vast fertile regions of Canada will be the home of a people more numerous than that which at the present time inhabits the United Kingdom.

I must not now further occupy your time, but would once more ask you to accept my heartfelt thanks for the determination shown by all to make the Royal Society a worthy embodiment of the literary activity and the scientific labour of our widely-scattered countrymen throughout this great land.

The Governor-General's reply to addresses from the Royal Academy and the Ontario Society of Artists, Toronto, June 1883 :—

Mr. O'Brien, Mr. Allan, and Ladies and Gentlemen, —I beg to thank you most cordially for the most kind and courteous addresses which you have been so good as to present to us. We shall keep them as mementos of the part we have been able to take in promoting Art in the Dominion. That part has necessarily been a very small one. I have been able to do very little more than make suggestions, and those suggestions have been patriotically and energetically acted upon by the gentlemen who have taken in hand the interests of Art. But what we have done we have done with our whole hearts. The Princess has taken the deepest interest from its inception in the project of establishing a Royal Academy. When, owing to

the unfortunate accident at Ottawa, she was unable to
visit the first exhibition of the Academy held in that
city, I remember she insisted that I should bring up
to her room nearly every one of the pictures exhibited,
in order that she might judge of the position of Canadian Art at that time. (Applause.) It is very fitting
that your first meeting in Toronto should be held in
a building devoted to education, such as this Normal
School. I have not yet had the pleasure of seeing
the Exhibition, but I am given to understand that it
is an excellent one, and shows marked progress. That
the Exhibition should be held in this building shows
the appreciation of your efforts on the part of the Government of Ontario. It symbolises the wish of your
association to promote education by extending Art-
training, and training in design. It is therefore most
fitting that the Normal School in Toronto, the great
centre from which come the masters of education for
Ontario, should be chosen as the place in which to hold
this Exhibition. Perhaps when the Exhibition is next
held in this city, you will be privileged to meet in a
Hall belonging to the local Art Society—a gallery of
paintings. A proper gallery is yet wanting. I have
seen a good many such in other places, notably in
Boston, New York, and Montreal. I am accustomed
to think that Toronto is quite in the front rank, if not
ahead of any other city upon this continent. It
should not be behindhand in this respect. I know,
at all events, one eminent Toronto man who lives not
far from here, whose features and form are as well
known as those of the Colossus were to the inhabi-

tants of Rhodes in ancient days, who is not satisfied
with himself, nor is the world quite satisfied, unless
he is at least twenty lengths ahead of everybody else.*
The position he has earned for himself is such that
the Provincial Government and the Dominion Government, with my full consent, are prepared to spend
$117,000 this year in securing his habitation, so that
it shall not be swept away by the waves of Lake Ontario. (Applause and laughter.) I am sure—though I
speak in the presence of much better authority—that if
the association here shows itself as much ahead of the
world as the gentleman to whom I have referred, the
Provincial and Dominion Government will, in the
same manner, back up your position by money grants
if necessary. (Renewed laughter.) It has been a
great satisfaction to me that when the Royal Academy
was founded, I had the great assistance and support
of the gentleman who was then President of your
local association, Mr. O'Brien. As this may be the
last time I shall have an opportunity to speak on Art
matters in Canada, I should like to acknowledge the
debt of gratitude which all those who had to do with
founding the Academy owe to him. With untiring
zeal, good temper, and tact, he worked in a manner
which deserves, I think, the highest recognition. As
a result of the labour bestowed upon the project, we
see here to-night the Academy and the old Society in
one unbroken line. With regard to the work done
by the Academy, you are aware we have held three
or four annual meetings, and marked progress has been

* Mr Hanlan, Champion Sculler of the World.

seen. The patriotic determination not only to hold meetings in towns where good commercial results could be obtained, but in others, is shown by the holding of a meeting in Halifax and other towns where it was not expected that a very large number of pictures could at once be sold. The good results of this course are shown by the fact that as a result of the meeting in Halifax, a local Art society is to be established there. A local association has been started at Ottawa, and is making good progress. In Montreal a great impetus has been given to the local society, and throughout the Dominion the cause of Art has been promoted by a central body bearing a high standard and encouraging contributions from all parts of the country. We have also to pride ourselves upon the enterprise of our artists in seeking instruction abroad. Several names might be mentioned of those who have gone and have diligently studied at Paris and elsewhere. At the Paris Salon this year, two of our lady members, Miss Jones and Miss Richards, have been very successful in having every picture they sent admitted to the Exhibition. (Applause.) A subscription was made in Montreal, some years ago, for an excellent statue which was erected at Chambly, the subject being Colonel de Salaberry, and the artist, Mr. Hébert of Montreal, one of your members. I am happy to say that Mr. Hébert was successful in the face of strong competition from Italy, France, England, and America, in carrying off the prize for the best model for a statue to be erected in honour of Sir George Cartier by the Dominion Government.

Another of our members, Mr. Harris, has received a commission from the Federal Government to paint a picture commemorative of the Confederation of the Canadian Dominion. These are marked proofs that the position attained by our academicians is now recognised; and it shows also, if I may be allowed to say so, the influence a society like this may virtuously exercise upon the Government and the treasury. (Laughter and applause.) There is only one other subject I would like to mention, though it has no direct connection with Art. But it is one mooted by Lord Dufferin, I think, in this very place, at all events in Toronto, some years ago. He asked me when I came not to lose sight of it, but to push it upon all possible occasions. I allude to the formation of a national park at Niagara. I believe I am correct in saying that on the American side the suggestion originated with a mutual friend of Lord Dufferin's and mine, Mr. Bierstadt. Lord Dufferin took the most energetic steps in promoting the project. He wrote to the gentleman who was then governor of New York. Some difficulties arose at the time, still steps were taken by which the project might have been successfully carried out before now. However, a change came, and a less sympathetic *regime* followed that of the governor with whom Lord Dufferin had communicated. I believe that now our neighbours are perfectly ready, and have nearly, if not quite, carried a measure for the scheme so far as it affects them. Their part of the work is of course a much more serious undertaking than ours. I request the influence of the Canadian Academy, and of the Society of Artists, in asking both the Dominion and Provincial Governments to take measures to meet the Americans in this movement, if they have made or are about to make it. We should secure the land necessary to make this park, so that the vexatious little exactions made of visitors may cease. I am sure it will be an immense boon to the public at large, as well as to the inhabitants of this Province and of the State of New York, if this scheme, so well initiated, shall ultimately prove successful.

Ottawa, May 1883.—Address to His Excellency.—Mr. Speaker announced the receipt of an informal intimation from the Senate that they were awaiting the arrival of the Commons to present the farewell address to His Excellency the Governor-General, in view of his early departure from the country.

On the arrival of Mr. Speaker and the members of the Commons in the Senate Chamber, the following address was read to His Excellency and H.R.H. the Princess Louise by Sir John Macdonald.

To His Excellency the Governor-General of Canada, etc., etc.,—May it please your Excellency, We, Her Majesty's dutiful subjects, the Senate and House of Commons of Canada in Parliament assembled, desire on behalf of those we represent, as well as on our own, to give expression to the general feeling of regret with which the country has learned that your Excellency's official connection with Canada is soon about to cease. We are happy, however, to believe that in the councils of the Empire in the future, and whenever opportunity enables you to render Her

Majesty service, Canada will ever find in your Excellency a steadfast friend, with knowledge of her wants and aspirations, and an earnest desire to forward her interests.

Your Excellency's zealous endeavours to inform yourself by personal observation of the character, capabilities, and requirements of every section of the Dominion have been highly appreciated by its people, and we feel that the country is under deep obligations to you for your untiring efforts to make its resources widely and favourably known.

The warm personal interest which your Excellency has taken in everything calculated to stimulate and encourage intellectual energy amongst us, and to advance science and art, will long be gratefully remembered. The success of your Excellency's efforts has fortified us in the belief that a full development of our national life is perfectly consistent with the closest and most loyal connection with the Empire.

The presence of your illustrious consort in Canada seems to have drawn us closer to our beloved Sovereign, and in saying farewell to your Excellency and to her Royal Highness, whose kindly and gracious sympathies, manifested upon so many occasions, have endeared her to all hearts, we humbly beg that you will personally convey to Her Majesty the declaration of our loyal attachment, and of our determination to maintain firm and abiding our connection with the great Empire over which she rules.

His Excellency the Governor-General made the following reply :—

Honourable Gentlemen, — No higher personal honour can be received by a public man than that which, by this address, you have been pleased to accord to me. In asking you to accept my gratitude, I thank you also for your words regarding the Princess, whose affection for Canada fully equals mine. It will be my pride and duty to aid you in the future to the utmost of my power. Now that the pre-arranged term of our residence among you draws to its end, and the happiest five years I have ever known are nearly spent, it is my fortune to look back on a time during which all domestic discord has been avoided, our friendship with the great neighbouring Republic has been sustained, and an uninterrupted prosperity has marked the advance of the Dominion. In no other land have the last seventeen years, the space of time which has elapsed since your Federation, witnessed such progress. Other countries have seen their territories enlarged and their destinies determined by trouble and war, but no blood has stained the bonds which have knit together your free and order-loving populations, and yet in this period, so brief in the life of a nation, you have attained to a union whose characteristics from sea to sea are the same. A judicature above suspicion, self-governing communities entrusting to a strong central Government all national interests, the toleration of all faiths with favour to none, a franchise recognising the rights of labour by the exclusion only of the idler, the maintenance of a Government not privileged to exist for any fixed term, but ever susceptible to the change of public opinion and ever open, through a responsible Ministry, to the scrutiny of the people—these are the features of your rising power. Finally, you present the spectacle of a nation already possessing the means to make its position respected by its resources in men available at sea or on land. May these never be required except to gather the harvests the bounty of God has so lavishly bestowed upon you. The spirit, however, which made your fathers resist encroachment on your soil and liberties is with you now, and it is as certain to-day, as it was formerly, that you are ready to take on yourselves the necessary burden to ensure the permanence of your laws and institutions. You have the power to make treaties on your own responsibility with foreign nations, and your high commissioner is associated, for purposes of negotiation, with the Foreign Office. You are not the subjects but the free allies of the great country which gave you birth, and is ready with all its energy to be the champion of your interests. Standing side by side, Canada and Great Britain work together for the commercial advancement of each other. It is the recognition of this which makes such an occasion as the present significant. Personal ties, however dear to individuals, are of no public moment. These may be happy or unhappy accidents, but the satisfaction experienced from the conditions of the connection now subsisting between the old and the new lands can be affected by no personal accident. I therefore rejoice that again it has been your determination to show that Canada remains as firmly rooted as ever in love to that free union which ensures to you and to Great Britain equal advantage. Without it your institutions and national autonomy would not be allowed to endure for twelve months, while the loss of the alliance of the communities which were once the dependencies of England would be a heavy blow to her commerce and renown. I thank you once more for your words, which shall be dear treasures to me for ever, and may the end of the term of each public servant who fills with you the office which constitutes him at once your chief magistrate and the representative of a united empire, be a day for pronouncing in favour of a free national Government defended by such Imperial alliance.

At the conclusion of His Excellency's reply, Mr. Speaker returned to the Commons Chamber, followed by the members. The last paragraph of the speech from the Throne was as follows:—

Honourable Gentlemen of the Senate: Gentlemen of the House of Commons,—I desire to thank you for the great honour conferred on me by the presentation of a joint address. The Princess and I have both been profoundly touched by your words, and the message of which you make us the bearers, comes, as we personally know, from a people determined to maintain the Empire. The severance of my official connection with Canada does not loosen the tie of affection which will ever make me desire to serve this country. I pray that the prosperity I have seen you enjoy may continue, and that the blessing of God may at all times be yours, to strengthen you in unity and peace.

APPENDIX.

APPENDIX.

The Annual Exhibition of Arts and Manufactures of the Province of Ontario for 1883 was held at Toronto. The formal opening was on Sept. 15th, and His Excellency, who was invited to open it, and who was received with the greatest enthusiasm, spoke as follows.

Ladies and Gentlemen,—I only wish my voice were strong enough to carry to each of you the thanks we owe to every citizen of Toronto, for nowhere have we received more kindness, and nowhere have we had occasion to feel greater gratitude for receptions accorded us, than in your city. These farewells I feel to be very sad occasions. I know that if the matter had rested with the Princess she would have wished to postpone them for another year—(cheers)—for we have spent many happy days in Canada, and would have wished to prolong them. That, however, could not be. The time for departing, I am sorry to say, has very nearly come. For my part, I feel as if the sands of the last days of happiness had nearly run out. (Cheers.) I beg to thank you, sir, for the reference which you have made in your address to the visit of Prince George of Wales. (Loud cheers.) It is now nearly twenty-four years, I think, since his Royal Highness the Prince of Wales (loud cheers) came here, he being at that time, nearly of the age which Prince George has now attained. ' I have often heard from him of the kindness and loyalty with which he was greeted in Canada,, (Cheers.) I know it has been a matter of regret to him that he has been unable in recent years to repeat his visit. I know how he watches with the greatest interest and sympathy the progress of this country, and how he hopes at some future day he may possibly revisit it. (Loud cheers.) In the address you desire me to convey to Her Majesty the assurance of your loyalty—an assurance which we shall deliver, not that any such assurance is needed—(Cheers)—the reverence and loyalty with which Her Majesty is regarded is well known to me, but we will faithfully carry out your commission. It is a message of devotion to the Throne and Empire coming from a great community. (Loud cheers.) I do not know anything more remarkable in the recent history of this great continent than the story of this populous and extensive Province, whose shores are washed by the beautiful waters of Erie, Huron, and Ontario. Within the lifetime of a man, indeed only sixty years ago, nothing but an untouched growth of wood was visible throughout this wide region, where there are now myriads of happy homesteads—(cheers,) and, while this remarkable result has been accomplished in so short a time, we see no diminution in the progress and prosperity of the Province. During the last few years Ontario may be said to have become a Mother Country, for she has sent out colonies to the West by tens of thousands, and yet, owing to the rapid and natural increase of her people, and to the manner in which the void occasioned by the departure of these has been filled up from across the seas, we still see the population constantly increasing—(cheers)—and I believe the next census will show as great an increase as the last, and that, I believe was 18 per cent. (Loud cheers.) I was very much struck some time ago by the manner in which some men, comfortably situated here, wished, nevertheless, to see the West. I had occasion to ask for the services of two men for a friend of mine who had taken a farm in Manitoba. One was got immediately, and an Ontario gentleman, to whom I applied, came to me and said : " You will be surprised to hear who the second man is whom I have obtained for your friend ; he is a man having a large farm and a very comfortable homestead, and, while he does not wish to leave the Province permanently, he desires to go to the North-West to see the country, and has volunteered to go as a hired man for a year to Manitoba " He left for that year his wife and child at home. I hope by this time he has been able to rejoin them. I do not think the desire prevailing amongst you in Ontario to go westward need cause the men of Ontario one moment's anxiety. Your ranks will be quickly refilled. Numbers are now coming in from the Old Country— and I beg to congratulate the Government of Ontario on the successful way in which they have put forward the attractions, I may say the great attractions, of this

Province as compared with those of the West, with the view of arresting some of those who were on their passage farther west. (Cheers.) I had a conversation only yesterday with a gentleman who is at the head of the Agricultural Science Department of South Kensington, in London ; and to show you there is a wide field open for the surplus population of a class you wish to attract, I would like to quote that gentleman's words. He is a great authority, a Government official, and I am sure his name is known to many of you—Professor Tanner. (Cheers.) He told me that over 7,000 men are studying agriculture in Great Britain at the present time ; that over 6,000 had passed last year the examination provided by Government ; that of those 6,000 there certainly would not be an opportunity in Great Britain for the employment of more than one-tenth ; that is to say that nine-tenths will assuredly, if they wish to follow out the course which their studies would indicate as the career they seek to pursue, have to find a place outside the limits of the old country. I would certainly recommend them to come here. (Cheers.) I have made such recommendations often at home. Sometimes I have been told that I incur a great responsibility for doing so. (Cheers.) I shall be very glad to assume the responsibility for the rest of my days. (Renewed cheering.) I shall only ask of Ontario societies when they invite women to come here, to back me in advising the old country people not to send too many instructresses of youth—(hear, hear)—for wherever I have made a speech in England advising women to emigrate, I have always received about 500 letters on the succeeding day from people who said they were perfectly confident that there was an opening for a good governess in Canada. (Laughter and cheers.) I wish to emphasize the fact that there is hardly any opening, for we grow our own stock in that respect—(Loud cheers),—and I believe in the Exhibition of which we shall soon be making an examination strangers will see that among the objects placed in the most honourable position is the school desk, the school bench, and the school book. (Renewed cheers.) They will find these exhibited along with the best products of the factory, the forest, the field and the mine. I say, I shall continue to recommend this Province, for you have inspired me with additional confidence—(Cheers)—perhaps because the community have confidence in themselves. (Renewed cheers.) I will say nothing more, for I feel I might expatiate at too great a length upon your prospects. (Continued cheers.) I beg now formally to declare the Toronto Exhibition of 1883 to be open to the public. (Loud and continued cheering.)

The following is the Governor-General's reply to an address presented in the Queen's Park, Toronto. Several thousand persons had assembled although the rain had descended in torrents for some hours.

Mr. Mayor and citizens of the city of Toronto,—Ladies and Gentlemen of this great Province of Ontario, —I have again to thank you for a loyal and affectionate address, conveying your reverence and love to the

Queen. Already several of the Queen's children have visited Canada. On this occasion you have been welcoming, kindly and cordially, a grandson of her Majesty. (Cheers.) On all occasions on which members of the Queen's family have visited this country they have met with a welcome which evinces your determination to sustain the Empire in which Canada occupies so large a place. I thank you, sir, for what you have stated with regard to my term of office. You have had the good fortune to enjoy five years of prosperity and progress. I would, if you will allow me, take the words you have addressed to me as not in any sense conveying a personal compliment, but as expressing your appreciation of the value of the office which I have had the honour to hold for five years, and your wish to maintain its dignity. I confess that I am not so desirous of any personal popularity, but I am jealous for the position of the Governor-General. I need not tell you, who know it already, the value of the constitutional rules under which its functions are exercised. They who disparage the office by telling you that it is one of no influence would be the first to cry out against its powers, and they would be right to do so, should those powers be used in excess of constitutional privilege. It is sufficient that the ministers, both of the last Government and the present, regard the office as valuable, and desire its continuance. There is, however, one point in connection with it which I should wish to impress upon you. In some quarters, although not, I am satisfied, by the people at large, the presence of a Governor-General is held to imply something called " etiquette " — (Laughter), — and implies also the establishment of a " court." I wish to say from my experience in Canada I am sure that this is by no means the case. Etiquette may perhaps be defined as some rule of social conduct. I have found that no such rule is necessary in Canada, for the self-respect of the people guarantees good manners. (Cheers.) We have had no etiquette and no court. Our only etiquette has been the prohibition of any single word spoken by strangers at the Government House in disparagement of Canada. (Cheers.) Our only court has been the courting of her fair name and fame. (Cheers.) Now, ladies and gentlemen, you ask me why it is I am so enthusiastic a Canadian. I believe I am perhaps even more of a Canadian than some of the Canadians themselves. I ascribe it to the very simple cause that I have seen perhaps more of your country than have very many amongst you. I know what your great possessions are, and to what a magnificent heritage you have fallen heirs. I know that wide forest world out of which the older Provinces have been carved. I know that great central region of glorious prairie-land from which shall be carved out future Provinces as splendid or yet more splendid than those of which we now proudly boast. I know also that vast country beyond the Rocky Mountains, that wondrous region sometimes clothed in gloomy forest, sometimes smiling beneath the sun in pastoral beauty of valley and upland, or sometimes shadowed by Alpine gorges and mighty mountain peaks—the territory of British Columbia. And in each and all of these three immense sections of your great country I know that you have possessions which must make you in time one of the foremost among the nations, not only of this continent, but of the world. (Cheers.) It is because I have seen so much of you and of your territories that I am enthusiastic in your behalf, and that the wish of my life shall be the desire to further your interests ; and I pray the God who has granted to you this great country that he may in his own good time make you a great people. (Loud cheers.)

On leaving Ottawa, an address was presented by the Corporation of the city. The Governor-General replied as follows : —

Mr. Mayor, members of the Corporation, and citizens of Ottawa—We both thank you most cordially for your words, which are so full of kindness.

It is indeed a sorrowful thought to us that the present must be our last meeting for all time, as far as any official connection between us is concerned ; but we shall hope that it will not be the last occasion on which we shall again be brought together, for it would be indeed a melancholy prospect to us were we not able to look forward to some future day on which we might revisit the scenes which have been so much endeared to us, and witness the continuance of that progress which has been so marked in the Dominion during the last five years.

You kindly wish us God-speed, and hope that our future career may be happy ; but we can never again have a happier or more fortunate time than that spent amongst you ; indeed, whenever, in the future, life's path is darker, we can take comfort and refreshment from the recollection of the bright days passed under the beautiful clear sunshine of the Canadian seasons.

If in any way we have been able to please you in the personal intercourse which it has been our happiness to have experienced on civic occasions, and in social meetings at Government House, we shall certainly leave with the feeling that there is no community more easy to please. The interest and affection we have for you will always endure, and I hope that when any of you visit the Old Country (should I happen to be there) you will let me again see you.

But, gentlemen, however pleasant may have been the friendships begun during the last few years, or the official relations at my office, it is important that we should not over-value individual likings. So long as the Governor-General follows the example set by our beloved monarch as a constitutional sovereign, so long should the favour he finds with the people endure, and any personal popularity is a thing of no account. You have been pleased to endorse afresh the system under which we live and which you think infinitely preferable to that which obtains among our neighbours to the south of us. But my constitutional governorship is nearly over, and now that I am practically out of harness, I mean to assume autocratic airs, and confess to you that I have sometimes wished for the benefit and adornment of your city to become its dictator with plenary power of raising federal and local taxes for any object which may have seemed best to my despotic will. But I have faith in popular rule, and believe that when I next visit Ottawa I shall see the city not only embellished by the completion of some of the good buildings which are now rising, or about to be erected, within its limits, but that I shall see every street, and especially those which are widest, planted with flourishing shade trees. I shall probably see a new Government House, from whose windows the beautiful extent of your river shall be visible, as well as the noble outlines of your Parliament Buildings. Leading from this to the city I shall mark how the long, fine avenue planted in 1884, an avenue which will stretch all the way along Sussex street past New Edinburgh to Government House, has sent forth beautiful branches of the foliage of the maple, which perhaps at intervals may mingle with a group or two of dark fir-trees. I am sure I shall see any boulders now lying by the wayside broken up to form the metal for excellent roads, and of course no vestiges of that burnt wooden house at the corner of Pooley's Bridge will remain. Indeed, I shall see few tenements which are not of brick or stone both in Ottawa and Hull, and last, but not least, I am sure we shall find the Ministry and Supreme Court properly housed in official residences such as are provided for those functionaries by most of the civilized nations of the world.

But do not think that I say anything of this prophetic vision in any spirit of detraction of what we possess here at present. I know well that without Federal help, such as is given at Washington, and with the limited area from which assessments can be drawn, it must take time to build up an ideal city, and I have always found the Ottawa of to-day a very pleasant place as a residence. You have a society of singular interest and variety, because so many men of ability are brought together at the seat of government, and I believe that a gayer and brighter season than the Ottawa winter is hardly to be met with. By the increase of good accommodation afforded by the hotels, an improvement, which has been most notable within the last few years, has been effected for the comfort of visitors, and its results are apparent in the great number of strangers who throng your city during the time of the sitting of Parliament. Ottawa should become during these months more and more the social centre for the Dominion, and in contributing towards this, and in working for this end, you will not only be benefitting yourselves, but aiding in strengthening the national spirit and the unity of sentiment between the provinces which may be greatly fostered in convening together, not only the leading men of the Dominion, but those ladies belonging to other centres of social life in Canada, without whose patriotic feeling it would be vain even for the ablest statesman to do much towards national unity and purpose.

For our part we shall always look back upon many of the months spent in this city as being among the brightest and pleasantest, and in bidding you farewell we wish to express a hope that it may only be farewell for the present.

Z

Let me now thank you once more, and may all good remain with you and yours.

LORNE.

Government House, Ottawa, 9th October, 1883.

At Montreal, on his departure, the St. Jean Baptiste Society and the Caledonian Society presented addresses. Lord Lorne thanked them for the personal good wishes expressed, but referring to the presentation to the Governor-General of addresses from societies representing some race or old national sentiment among Canadians, he said that he would suggest that, for the future, Canadians should approach the Head of the Government only as Canadians, the Mayor or Warden representing all. Although among themselves they might and would always cherish recollections of the nationality from which they sprang, a Governor-General must recognize them only as that which they now are, namely, component parts of the Canadian people.

His Excellency then replied as follows to the address presented by the Mayor on behalf of the city : —

To the Mayor and Corporation of the City of Montreal.

Gentlemen,—Your kind words remind us rather of what we would have wished to have done than of any accomplishment of those desires. It is but little that an individual placed at the head of your Government as its impartial chief magistrate can or may do, and it is perhaps as well that this is so, for it would be a matter of regret, and one to be deplored, if the esteem in which that high office is held should depend on any

individual's capacity for capturing popular sympathy. The position is one capable of much good in moderating counsel, and even in the suggestion of methods of procedure in government ; but any action the head of the state may take must be unknown, except at rare intervals, to the public, and must always be of such a nature that no party may claim him as their especial friend. As a sign of the union of your country with the rest of the Empire, he has other functions more important than that of making Canada well known abroad, which it may be in his power greatly to use for your benefit. Steam communication has made the advent of emigrants easy, and the emigrant is a better advertiser for you than any official can be. In short, so far as the public activity of a Governor-General is concerned, he should rely rather on the approbation of posterity than on any personal recognition, taking care only that his name be associated with constitutional rule, and his impartial recognition of whatever Ministry the country, through the House of Commons, elects for his advice. It is a source of much satisfaction to me to know that my successor is certain to follow in this respect the example of the Queen, whose representative he is.

It would be impertinence in me to speak of his private character, for they who desire to know of this have only to go and hear what is said by his loving tenantry and friends on his estates in County Kerry, Ireland, where an emphatic tribute to his personal worth has been lately paid him at Dereen. In a few days þe will land upon your shores, and I am certain he will receive that warm welcome which a generous and loyal people are ever ready to accord to the temporary representative of constitutional government.

You have alluded, sir, to that happy day in November, five years ago, when Montreal gave us so splendid a welcome. I remember when the horses became unmanageable it was the good will of the citizens to honour us by detaching them, and by drawing the carriage for a long distance until we reached the great Windsor Hotel. I told them at the time that I considered it an omen of how a Governor might always trust to them for support. That impression was strengthened during my stay in Canada, together with this other, namely, that if anything goes wrong, it is easy for the people to take matters into their own hands, and to change the programme, substituting another where order and active purpose may be clearly discerned.

My residence amongst you has led me greatly to honour your people, and in honouring them it has been my privilege to honour also its men of both sides of politics in the State, who have been chosen by the constituencies to lead their political life. Almost the only pain I have experienced during my term here has been caused by the personal attacks which are too frequently made on both sides against party men. Believe me, gentlemen, such personal attacks do no good in advancing any cause, but belittle the nation in the eyes of strangers. They are also, as a rule, as unwarrantable as they are repulsive, useless and mischievous. I have seen a good deal of the public life and of the politicians of many countries, and I unhesitatingly affirm that you have in general in Canada as pure and noble-minded statesmen as may be found anywhere the wide world over. Where in other lands you see those who have had political power and patronage occupying palaces and raising themselves to be amongst the richest of the people, we here see perhaps too much of the other extreme, and men who have led parties to battle and been the victorious leaders in honest political strife are too often left to live in houses which an English squire would not consider good enough for his bailiff. This leads me to speak to you of a wish which I have often cherished, but which, to reveal a Cabinet secret, I have never succeeded in persuading any Canadian statesman to support by a speech in the chambers of the Legislature. They fear, I suppose, that selfishness would be assigned as their motive. I therefore come to you, the people, to propose it, and to ask you—the representatives and citizens of the wealthiest community in Canada—to take it up. It is this: that we should have at Ottawa official residences not only for the Judges of the Supreme Court, but for the Dominion Ministers of the day. This is, of course, a matter which would indifferently benefit whatever party may be in power. Should you encourage the idea through your representatives you will be only following in the footsteps of many other peoples. Every little state in Germany provides good residences for its Ministers. At Berlin and at Paris the nations of France and of Germany look upon it as a matter of course that the

Ministry should possess fit residences. Why should we not follow an example so obviously good, and, because we rightly ask the Judges of the Supreme Court and federal Ministry to reside at the Capital, furnish them with the means of doing so in a manner suited to the dignity of this nation ?

Forgive me for detaining you at length, but in speaking to you it is impossible not to remember that I am addressing the wealthiest and greatest community in the country. Montreal must always keep her pre-eminent position on the St. Lawrence, situated as she is at the end of the ocean waterways, which form so imperial an avenue to the artificial navigation connecting the great lakes that lie at the limits of the vast grain region of the prairies. But while our thoughts naturally turn westward to the vast interior with gratitude to the Giver for so wondrous a wealth in the new soils of the central continent, let us be thankful also for the Providence which has enabled our thrifty and hardy people to turn to good account the banks on both sides of the great stream flowing from hence seawards. Let us be thankful that this great arterial channel has tempted people not only up its own current, but up the channels of its tributaries, and that under the guidance of men like Labelle and others, we are gradually having the great country to the north opened up by settlements which have spread along the Ottawa, the River Rouge, the Lievre and the Saguenay, until the long silent shores of Lake St. John have become the busy scenes of agricultural life. Let us be grateful also that we have this country garrisoned by men who are as true to the Constitution and the Throne as they are faithful to their Church, and while we direct our own young men and the youthful emigrant from Europe to the North and to the West, let us take care to point out to the stranger the advantages which are so manifest here for those who either desire a city life or who wish to reside upon the fruitful and long cleared farms of the ancient provinces of Old Canada.

Now, *Monsieur le Maire*, accept our thanks and our farewell, but let me express our wish that our parting may be only for a time, and *au revoir*.

On the 20th October the Corporation of the City of Quebec presented a farewell address. The Governor-General in the course of his reply, made the following remarks : —

Where the laws, the language, and the institutions of each of the Provinces forming our great Confederation are guarded by a constitution which sees its own strength in the happy continuance of local privileges, what wonder is it that success and progress are everywhere to be seen. The Englishman, Scotchman or Irishman here finds the traditions of his country continued ; the French-Canadian enjoys the most absolute liberty and safety under the flag which secures to him in common with all citizens of every Province a national life, the natural and legitimate desire of the growing communities of this great country. From East to West the spreading colonies are now able to give each other the hand. They are beginning to find out what vast possessions they have. They value national coherence and the maintenance of local laws. They glory in that glorious name which you first assumed— a Canadian.

You know me well enough by this time to make it superfluous for me to render any long *éloge* upon your characteristics. Although we leave you we shall always be with you in spirit, and cherish a desire to assist you.

The words of affectionate regret come easily, and I have but little advice to give you. If there be any, it would be that no part of the Dominion should exclude itself from the influence of the rest. They who know only themselves and avoid contact with others go backwards; they who welcome new impressions and compare the ideas of other men with their own, make progress. Open your arms to the immigrants who come, while you endeavour to repatriate your own people; there is room enough here for all; continue to make the country to the north of you a second line of wealth-giving lands for the first line formed by the valley of the St. Lawrence. Remember to direct some of your young men to the West. I feel that you throughout Canada are on the right track. You have only to keep it. With the motto—" Our Rights and our Union " you will, with the blessing of God, become a people whose sons will be ever proud of the country of their birth.

May your triumphs continue to be the triumphs of Peace, your rewards the rewards of Industry, Loyalty, and Faith !

THE END.